MAGNIFICUS PRIME

CAGE & MARS #1

TOBY NEIGHBORS

MYTHIC ADVENTURE PUBLISHING, LLC

Magnificus Prime – Cage & Mars #1

© 2020, Toby Neighbors

Published by Mythic Adventure Publishing, LLC

Idaho, USA

ISBN: 978-1-952260-16-2

Copy Editing by Julie Duke

ALSO BY TOBY NEIGHBORS

Toby Neighbors Online
www.TobyNeighbors.com
Facebook
www.Facebook.com/TobyNeighborsAuthor
Instagram
Instagram @TobyTheWriter

Recon Platoon Bravo

Captain Walter Sullivan
Second Lieutenant Blake Cage
Staff Sergeant Wyatt Dole
Corporal Felicity Dole - Scout
Private Porter Bailey - Scout
Corporal Devon Al'Farrah - Sniper
Private Amber Case - Radio Operator
Corporal Samantha Jones - Trooper
Private Lucinda Fuego - Trooper
Private Joelle Cotumba - Trooper
Private Albert Malone - Trooper
Private Junior Knoxx - Trooper
Private Lori Cunningham - Trooper
Private Grant Laubin - HeWE
Private Jean Pierre Seinne - HeWE
Private Miranda Dux - HeWE
Private Billy Oberton - HeWE
Private Ted Ficklestine - HeWE

CHAPTER 1

BLAKE CAGE

"Another riot," Cage said.

"Close?" Felicity asked.

"Not especially. But we should keep our eyes open."

"I always have my eyes open."

"Not always," Cage said with a wink.

"Just because you're my husband doesn't mean you know everything about me, Blake Cage."

"I know enough," he replied with a grin. "And I'm looking forward to learning the rest."

They were walking down a crowded street between towering buildings of glass and steel. Cage liked to think the buildings were beautiful once, but the glass was stained, and the steel had been blackened from toxic air and the patina of age. The once great city was just another section of the continental sprawl. There weren't many natural places left on Earth. Cage had only seen them in documentaries or historic films.

Earth had become a tightly controlled world as health care

improved and diplomacy brought an end to most conflicts. The population boom, as it was noted in history books, had necessitated a strict distribution of food, water, medicines, and most of all, personal freedom. Cage and Felicity had waited a year for approval to get married, and they were both still waiting on jobs. When Cage wasn't studying history via the free online university courses, he and Felicity walked the streets. Their government-appointed housing was just a single room, barely large enough for a bed and a tiny table. Getting out wasn't just an option; it was the only thing keeping them sane.

But getting out of the house wasn't always safe. There were constant protests, which often turned violent. The one thing the government couldn't seem to control was crime. Street gangs ruled the streets. They moved in small groups, always looking for someone to hassle, rob, or beat to death. Cage had learned long ago how to move through the city without drawing attention. Felicity was a different story. Nearly six feet tall with an athletic figure and dark brown skin, she was impossible to miss—which was why her father had taught her martial arts from the time she was a toddler. Citizens weren't allowed to carry weapons, but Felicity Mars *was* a weapon. Most of the local tough guys had learned that the hard way. And the only thing they respected was strength, which Felicity had in spades. While the gangs ignored Cage, they stepped aside for Felicity.

Cage had his phone out. It kept a running check on reports of rioting. There was a "hot zone" app that was designed to alert citizens nearing parts of the city with reports of civil unrest, but Cage wasn't checking on their safety. Felicity had a keen sense of what was happening around her at all times, and he trusted her instincts more than any government-funded app on his phone. Instead of looking at the hot zones, he looked at the potential job postings. There was nothing new that matched their qualifications.

"Any news?" Felicity asked.

"Nothing on the job front," Cage said.

"Want to go to the library or the museum?"

The library was his favorite place in the city. The museum was hers. Both were free, had decent air filtration systems, and got them off the streets for a little while.

"Museum," Cage said.

They set out to traverse the eight city blocks to reach the Metropolitan Museum System. The best thing about the museum, in Cage's opinion, was the sheer size of it. There were different wings that housed everything from fine art to antiquities. A person could spend hours wandering through any one of the different exhibits.

Unfortunately, they didn't make it to the museum before city restriction alarms went off, signaling an immediate curfew. The sirens were loud, and people began cursing them. A row of police vehicles flew past, just above the heads of the pedestrians. Cage and Felicity saw several officers in riot gear, their faces covered by dark helmets, hanging onto the armored exterior of their emergency response vehicles.

"Looks like a bad one," Cage said.

"I guess so," Felicity said. "Time to go home."

It didn't seem fair, but they didn't have a choice. Neighborhood supervisors would soon be handing out citations for anyone still out during the emergency curfew. Breaking the law would go on a person's permanent record and make getting a job even more difficult.

"Do you think things will ever change?" Felicity asked after they turned back toward the block of government housing buildings where their tiny apartment was just one of thousands.

"Sure," Cage said. "We'll get jobs eventually."

"And then what?" she asked. "Wage controls are set. Even with both of us working, we'll be lucky to earn enough to ever move out of government housing."

"Maybe we'll get transferred," Cage said. "It's always a possibility."

"Things aren't different anywhere else," Felicity complained. "We're stuck."

Cage knew that what she was saying was true. Even if they got decent jobs, which certainly wasn't likely given the fact that there were dozens of applicants for every job opening —many with more experience than Cage—they were stuck. He would have to take anything he was offered, and there was no guarantee he would have the opportunity for promotion. Cage and Felicity were still young, newly married, and full of hope in a system that was slowly crushing their dreams.

"If you could have whatever you wanted," Cage asked, "what would it be?"

"I don't know," Felicity said. "Some space to move around, I guess. Something out of the city. And something that matters, you know? I want to make a difference."

Making a difference was something they talked of often. It seemed to them that people had become cogs in a giant, plane-tary machine. Free enterprise was a thing of the past. The only way to escape government job placements was on the colony ships, but the cost was too high. They could work their entire lives and still not earn enough for passage to a new world—and neither of them had the types of skills that were needed on a colony world. Perhaps if Cage had studied engi-neering or some branch of science, he would have had a better chance to qualify for a colony job. But his passion was history. He could have taught at the university level if higher education wasn't completely automated.

"Maybe things will change," Cage said, knowing that neither of them believed that it would.

They were riding the elevator to the forty-second floor of building 21GACD when the news came. The elevator was packed with people and stopped at every floor. Cage felt his phone vibrate in his pocket, but he didn't check it. Instead, he waited until it was their turn to leave the crowded compartment. The long, poorly lit hallway that led to their apartment was one of the most dangerous places in the city; there were forty apartments lining the long corridor and no surveillance or security. If a person was desperate, crazy, or just in a rage, catching some hapless person trying to get to their apartment made for an easy target. Fortunately, the hallway was clear.

Cage hurried to their door and unlocked the series of security devices meant to keep them safe. Felicity stood back, watching for anyone who might come out and try to give them trouble.

"Got it!" Cage said.

"Good," Felicity said.

Inside their tiny studio apartment, the wailing sirens could still be heard. The air was stale, and the refrigerator was mostly empty. The entire home was a stark reminder of their poverty. Cage pulled out his phone and looked at the screen.

"Look at this," he said, tapping a button that cast the news story to the media wall. The wall opposite their bed was one big monitor. The news story appeared, and they both sat on the end of their bed and read it.

"A new world," Felicity said.

A video popped up before they could finish. Cage swiped it away.

"Interesting," Cage said.

"I guess," Felicity said. "It's not like we can afford passage."

"It's eighteen light years away, in the Fortuna system."

"Well we can't even get jobs in the city. They aren't going to send us to a colony world."

"But it's being developed by Magellan Corporation," Cage said as he began typing into his phone's internet browser.

"Why does that matter" Felicity said.

"Magellan is a privately owned corporation," Cage said. "They don't use the government staffing protocols."

"So what?" Felicity said.

"Look!" Cage said, streaming a new web page onto the wall. "They're hiring!"

"For the militia?"

"Yes, it's military," Cage said. "But in addition to standard pay, a five-year enlistment gains a person the right to settle on the colony."

"Are you serious?" Felicity asked, suddenly much more interested.

"I read about it months ago," Cage explained. "But they only organize and hire for the militia when they're colonizing a new world. There haven't been any habitable worlds discovered in years. We have to go for it."

"Wait," Felicity said. She was looking at her own phone, scrolling through the information about the Magellan Corporation. "It says they don't hire married couples for the militia."

Cage could hear the anguish in her voice. A colony world was a dream come true. The chance to start something, to grow with it from inception, was the only way a young couple really had to build a better life, but the opportunities were so rare and the requirements so strict that they had almost no chance of getting selected.

"So we don't tell them," Cage said, his heart thumping in his chest as he suggested it.

"They'll know, Cage," Felicity insisted.

"Will they?" he replied. "Look, they want fit, able-bodied people. We go down there, apply, let them run a few tests and see if we're good candidates. They aren't using government records, babe. They're a private corp. Government records are so backed up that they haven't even gotten around to changing your last name. Your ID still shows that you're Felicity Mars. They won't know if we don't tell them."

"You're serious?" Felicity said. "You want to join a militia and pretend we're not married?"

"For a chance to join a colony on a new world," Cage said, nodding his head. "Yeah, I want to do it."

"It's eighteen light years from Earth," she pointed out.

"That won't matter to us. We'll be in cryogenic sleep almost that whole time. And what's five years if we get to be together for the rest of our lives on a world where we can have space and really make a difference?"

"You've thought about this," she said.

"Sure, but it wasn't a possibility until now. There weren't any new planets being colonized."

"If we stay here, we'll get jobs," Felicity said.

"But there's no guarantee that we'll like them. And there's no way we'll ever get ahead. You said it yourself—we're stuck. This is a chance to get out of the city and out from under government control. Just imagine it—a new world to explore, more food, more opportunities for us. And if we have kids, I mean, come on. They would be way better off on a colony world."

"I can handle it," Felicity said. "Can you? You're not exactly the soldierly type, babe. I love you, and I'm not trying to rain on your parade, but I just want to make sure that if we do this, we both do it. I don't want to get shipped off to a colony world only to discover that you were left behind."

"That won't happen," Cage said. "I promise."

"Okay," Felicity said with a smile. "I'm game."

"We'll go tomorrow," Cage said. "I'll get all our paperwork filled out electronically tonight."

He was so excited that his eyes were shining, and he could see the same thing in his wife's brown eyes. He stood up and pulled her to her feet.

"We can do this," he said, wrapping his arms around her.

"You make me feel like anything is possible," Felicity said.

"As long as we're together," Cage said, "anything *is* possible."

CHAPTER 2

FELICITY MARS

"We're really doing this?" Felicity asked.

"Absolutely," Blake replied.

She loved his confidence, but she couldn't help but feel nervous. They were taking a big chance. Lying on an application to a private business wasn't really against the law—she thought the worst that could happen was that they wouldn't get the jobs—but she couldn't help but feel like she was breaking a rule. Her father had raised her on rules. Right and wrong weren't nebulous concepts to her, and lying was definitely on the wrong side—but she couldn't turn her back on an opportunity. She and Blake had married young, but there were benefits to being married. The government gave married couples a bump over single individuals in their job placement program, and it had entitled them to a government-subsidized apartment, which allowed them to move out of the tiny homes their parents had raised them in. It had seemed like a win-win situation at the time, but she couldn't help but worry that perhaps it would keep them from being able to join the Magellan Corp Militia, which from her point of view was the only chance they had to get ahead in life.

"We already have appointments," Blake said. "You're at two fifteen, I'm at three twenty."

"Where?" Felicity asked.

"The Magellan complex—it's north of here about two hours away by train," Blake said. "If we get the job, we'll lose our housing here, but that shouldn't matter. I'm betting the training will be on their property and we'd be launching for the Fortuna system soon."

"Won't it take them months to prepare?" Felicity asked as she pulled on a jacket.

"Probably not," Blake said. He had sat up half the night reading about the Magellan Corporation's other colonies. "They've had five years to prepare for this. My guess is once they get us trained, they'll send us out."

"But we'll get to see our parents again, right?"

"I would think so," Blake said, heading for the door. "Come on. We can't be late."

She followed him out the door, her mind full of possibilities—which all vanished as soon as they stepped out of their tiny apartment. Only ten paces down the hallway, between their apartment and the elevators, two desperate-looking men were assaulting their neighbor, a middle-aged man named Mr. Cervanté. One of the men had long, greasy hair tied into a bun at the back of his head. The other was shorter with a scar over one eye and a knife in one hand. It looked like an old kitchen knife, the blade worn down from years of sharpening. There were rust spots on it, as well. The shorter man was holding it up where Mr. Cervanté could see it.

"That's all I have, I swear," Cervanté said.

"Hey!" Felicity shouted. She sensed Blake tense beside her. "Let him go!"

She pushed Blake back a little—not that she was trying to protect him. He could give as good as he got in a fight, and he was no coward. She didn't worry about him holding his own, but she needed the room to maneuver.

"What have we here?" the knifeman said, turning his attention to Felicity. "Ain't you a sweet young thing?"

"You better shut your mouth if you know what's good for you," Blake growled behind her.

"I tell you what," the knifeman said to Blake. "You go back inside, and we'll forget all about you."

"Your funeral," Blake said, standing his ground.

"I told you to let him go," Felicity said. "I won't say it again."

The knifeman and his greasy-haired companion both laughed. It was the moment that Felicity had been waiting for. Their guard was down, and she charged at them. Three steps into her run she jumped, angling her body back and driving her right foot straight into the knifeman's chest. The impact slowed her momentum a little; the man wasn't very big and didn't weigh much. She turned her body—just as she had trained for years with her father—and landed on her feet while the knifeman flew backwards, hit the floor, and flopped completely over. The knife went clattering across the floor away from the assailant.

Blake was hurrying forward just as the greasy-haired man let go of Mr. Cervanté and turned toward Felicity. She lashed out, her striking hand rigid, the fingers bent at the middle knuckle. She drove her hand, fingers first, straight into the greasy-haired man's throat. His eyes went wide and he staggered backward, his hands clutching his throat. She hadn't hit him at full strength, but the shock to his windpipe was more than just painful. He was coughing and gasping for breath until Blake plowed into him from behind. The greasy-haired man's head whipped back as his body suddenly fell forward. He hit the floor hard and didn't move.

When Felicity turned back to the knifeman, he was crawling toward the rusty old blade.

"Leave it," she said, "or I'll break every bone in your hand."

It was a bit of a bluff. She knew there were dozens of little bones in the human hand—breaking them all would take time and expert knowledge of anatomy—but she was confident she'd break enough to make him wish he'd listened. Fortunately, he had enough sense to know when he was defeated and began crawling away.

"What'd they take?" Blake asked.

"My key," Mr. Cervanté said, "and a couple hundred credits. That one."

He pointed to the greasy-haired man who was unconscious at their feet. Blake reached down, rummaged through the man's filthy pockets, and pulled out the key.

"They followed me up here," Mr. Cervanté said. "I didn't know who they were on the elevator. But when they got off on my floor and followed me, I knew they were trouble."

"Here's your key and your money," Blake said, handing the older man his meager possessions.

At that moment, Felicity knew that one way or another, they had to get out of the city—not because of the danger, but because she didn't want to be a middle-aged woman with nothing to show for her life other than a government-issued apartment and a few hundred banking credits.

"Let's go," Felicity told Blake. "We can't be late."

"Wish us luck, Mr. Cervanté," Blake said.

"Good luck," the older man said. "Thank you both so much."

He was safely locked inside his apartment before they reached the elevator. The man who had threatened them with the knife was gone. He had chosen the stairwell. His companion, the man with the greasy hair, still lay unconscious between doorways in the long, dirty corridor. Felicity watched him while Blake picked up the knife.

"What are you going to do with that?" she asked.

"I'm not leaving it here," Blake said. "We'll toss it in the trash. Are you okay?"

"Fine. You?"

"Sure," Blake said. "You did the hard work."

"I'd hardly call that hard work," she said. "They were thugs, not fighters."

"Still, it makes a guy feel safe to know his wife can kick butt and take names."

"You better stop calling me that. You wouldn't want to blow our chances at getting hired because you called me your wife."

"Good point," Blake said.

"How friendly should we be?" she asked. "I don't want to pretend like we don't know each other."

"Friends, then," Blake said. "Nothing needs to change about our past, how we met, or anything like that. Just omit the romantic parts, and we'll be fine."

"I can do that if it gets us out of here," Felicity said. "I don't want to be pushing fifty and still barely getting by."

"That's not going to happen," Blake said. "One way or another, we're getting out of this place and crafting ourselves a better life."

The elevator doors opened and they stepped inside. Felicity didn't mind public displays of affection, but she knew that as a woman, being seen as a sexual being carried certain risks, and not just to her, but to Blake as well. And it was a distraction; even holding hands might keep her from reacting as quickly to a threat. Her father had taught her to always have situational awareness, and that practice had come in handy more than once. She didn't see people as a threat, but she didn't let down her guard, either. Maybe things would be different on a colony world. She certainly hoped so. But she knew one thing was certain: things couldn't get much worse.

CHAPTER 3

BLAKE CAGE

Cage trusted his wife. She was a capable, fearless person with a powerful sense of right and wrong, but the attack just down the hall from their own apartment made him nervous just the same. Perhaps he could have taken out the two thugs on his own, but it was just as possible that they could have gotten the jump on him. And if they'd managed to take Felicity by surprise...he didn't want to think about it.

The knife made him even more nervous. Weapons were strictly prohibited. He had already made sure his fingerprints weren't on the old kitchen knife, but he didn't relax until they dropped the rusty blade down the trash chute. Possession of a weapon was a felony, and it would have been impossible to convince anyone that the knife was just a cooking implement.

After getting rid of the knife they left their building, made their way to the nearest transit station, and boarded the D train headed north. After discussing their situation on the way to the train depot, they decided not to sit together. The odds of being seen or the story being questioned was minimal, but their desperation to get accepted into the Magellan Corporation colony program was at an all-time high.

The train was actually an elevated monorail that used magnetics to create a friction-free transport. The ride was smooth, but the train cars were not. There were many continuous riders, people who got on board in the morning and rode all day long. Some were homeless, others were desperate individuals who had been out of work so long they didn't know what else to do with their time. The train cars smelled musty, and many of the riders smelled worse. There was graffiti on the walls, and most of the hard, plastic seats had names or lewd messages scrawled on or carved into them.

Cage spent the hour-long ride reading and trying to ignore the passengers around him. Some followed suit. It was the unwritten code of public transportation: keep to oneself, don't speak unless absolutely necessary, and don't stare. But there was always someone looking to chat him up. Usually it was a hustler, someone playing on his good nature for money or food. Sometimes it was one of the crazies; conspiracy fanatics were the worst. As luck would have it, one boarded Cage's car at the second stop and made a bee line for him.

"You heard the news?" the man asked.

Cage could smell the whisky on his breath and the sour smell of body odor. It wafted off the man in waves.

"I'm reading," Cage said.

He could have moved, but experience told him the man would move with him. And if he got nasty, there was no telling what a crazy might do. Cage couldn't risk it.

"Yeah, but did you hear?"

"About what?" Cage asked, using a tone he hoped would convey his boredom with the man and whatever he was talking about. He didn't look up from his phone or do anything that might be interpreted as showing interest.

"The new planet," the crazy said, shaking his head. "Oh, man, you know it's only a matter of time, right? People can't leave well enough alone. We've got to spread out to every conceivable planet. It's madness."

"Why?" asked a teenager sitting across from Cage.

"Why?" the crazy asked, leaning even closer to Cage as if he'd asked the question. "*Why?* Are you insane? It's a mathematical impossibility that we're alone in the universe. The earth is four billion years old, but man has only been around for about thirteen thousand years."

"What does that have to do with other planets?" the kid asked.

"Ha, are you pulling my leg?" the crazy man asked Cage. "You've got to be pulling my leg. Nobody's that dumb. Think about it. Just think about it!"

He was getting worked up. Cage was wondering how long he should endure this. He gave the teenager across from him a glare, but the kid just grinned. It was obvious the teenager knew exactly what he was doing. Revving the crazies up just for kicks was a common enough prank, and there was no way out for Cage. He would just have to sit tight and endure his misfortune until the train reached his stop.

"Billions of years. Billions! The odds that another species didn't get to the stars before we did is astronomical. And cosmologically speaking, they wouldn't need a major head start—even as little as a few hundred years, and we would be so technologically inferior that there would be no hope for survival."

"You think the aliens are coming for us?" the kid across the aisle suggested.

"Do I think it? Do I think it! It doesn't matter what I think," the crazy said. "It's what I *know*. We're pushing our luck, and I mean really pushing it. We're walking on the thinnest of ice, and there is no turning back. I mean, all we have to do is cross paths one time and it's game over, man. Game over!"

Cage got to his feet and looked down at the crazy, who was starting to get up too.

"I wouldn't," Cage said. "I'm not here for you, but that doesn't mean I won't make an exception."

"I ain't doin' nothin!" the crazy said loudly.

Cage walked to the far end of the train car and sat down in an empty seat. The plan worked for about five minutes. At the next stop, the man moved back beside him and kept up a steady dialogue for the rest of the trip. When Cage's stop finally came up, he left the train quickly.

Every part of the city was the same; old buildings towered everywhere, and the streets were laid out like a grid. Cage and Felicity had memorized two different paths from the train to the Magellan Corporation headquarters. Cage wandered slowly. He had time to kill and wanted to arrive at a different time from his wife. He couldn't help but wonder what she was doing and how her interview was going. Just to ensure that they didn't get seen together, they decided not to meet up until they were back in their own section of the city.

At three o'clock in the afternoon, Cage walked up to the security booth at the main entrance to the Magellan Corporation's office complex.

"Hi, I'm Blake Cage. I have an appointment at three twenty."

The security guard looked bored, and Cage wasn't the only person trying to get in. The man checked his digital display and nodded. "Here's a visitor pass," the guard said as he handed Cage a laminated card with an alligator clip on one end. "Keep it visible at all times. Go straight to the waiting room in building C. That's inside the gate, and follow the sidewalk to your right. Check in at the display and wait to be called."

He waved Cage through like he had given the same speech a thousand times. Cage clipped the visitor's pass to his shirt and followed the sidewalk to building C. He went inside and stood in line for his turn to check in. Ten minutes later, he was sitting in the waiting area when his name was called.

"Cage, Blake T., please report to interview room eight."

He moved quickly to the door with a big "8" painted on the surface. He opened it and found a man in his fifties taking notes on his display pad.

"Have a seat," the man said.

Cage sat down and waited as the man made a few notations. When he finally looked up, Cage saw dark bags under his eyes, and there were crumbs on the front of his shirt.

"You're applying for the militia?" the man asked.

"Yes, sir," Cage said.

"Have you been in the military previously?"

"No, sir."

"Do you have a criminal record?"

"No, sir."

"Are you married?"

There it was. The dreaded question he'd been hoping they wouldn't ask him. All the questions they were asking had been on the electronic form he had filled out the night before. Cage tried his best to sound confident, but he could feel his conscience squirming as he told the lie.

"No, sir," Cage said.

"Mmmmm," the man said.

He was flipping through pages on his display pad. Cage couldn't see what he was looking at. His heart began to speed up, and sweat began to pop out on his back. They had caught him in the lie, and there was no way to know what they might do to him.

"It says here you've achieved a degree?" the man said. "A master's level in history. Is that true?"

"Oh," Cage said, a feeling of relief so strong his eyes stung with unshed tears. "Yes, sir. Online courses. I like to keep busy."

"Interesting. What's your plan with that degree?"

"I don't really have one," Cage confessed. "I like history. I've been waiting for work and the classes are free, so I took them."

"I'll have to confirm that you've earned this degree, Mr. Cage. But everything looks in order. I believe you'll be an asset to our program. Sign here," the man said, spinning the display around, "and put your palm on the screen for an initial scan. At the beep, please give verbal consent to join the Magellan Corporation Militia. This is a voluntary agreement to serve a term of no less than five standard years, not counting cryogenic stasis. Furthermore, you release the Magellan Corporation from all responsibility if you are injured, wounded, maimed, or killed."

Cage signed the form using his fingertip. A square appeared on the screen as the man recited his speech. Cage put his hand on the scanner and let it record his finger and palm prints. When the device beeped, words appeared on the screen. Cage read them out loud.

"I, Blake T. Cage, voluntarily agree to join the Magellan Corporation Militia."

"Very good," the man said, spinning the display back around. "We'll send formal instructions to your email account. You'll report back here in two days for physicals. If you are cleared, you'll officially be enlisted in the MCM. Congratulations, and welcome to the colony program."

The man stuck out a hand, and Cage shook it.

"Is that all?" Cage asked.

"That's it. You're free to go."

Cage left and couldn't wipe the smile from his face. It seemed too easy. Of course, he still had to pass the physical, but he couldn't imagine that he wouldn't. He might not be as in shape as Felicity, but he was healthy enough. And then they could kiss their sorry little apartment goodbye. Earth was overcrowded, insanely expensive, and depressing. Cage looked up; the sun was just starting to go down, and the stars wouldn't be out for at least another hour—but soon enough, he would be among them.

CHAPTER 4

FELICITY MARS

Felicity looked for Blake on her way back to the train station, but she didn't see him. It wasn't that she wanted to talk to him—they had made their plans to keep their distance, and she wouldn't have broken them—but she would have given him a signal. The interview was a formality. It didn't seem like anyone was being turned away. Anyone willing to serve in the militia was being accepted; it made sense, but it also seemed wrong, somehow. Felicity had been to several interviews. She was officially a minority, which meant that she got more opportunities for work, but in every instance the people interviewing her had looked down their noses at her. It was obvious that they considered anyone without a job to be a second-class citizen. Those job interviews had been long, and it always seemed like they were testing her, trying to trick her into saying the wrong thing.

In contrast, the interview for the Magellan Corporation Militia had been a simple affair. The interviewer didn't look down at Felicity but rather seemed intent on moving as many people through the process as possible. She was asked a handful of simple yes or no questions and then admitted to their program. One part of her felt anxious—the fact that it had been so easy made her fear that she was getting her hopes up and that somewhere along the way the rug would be pulled out from under her—but the other part of her wanted to jump up and down and squeal with excitement.

She boarded the train back to her section of the city and decided that since she was at least an hour ahead of Blake, she would stop in at her parents and tell them their plan to join the militia. It would be a tough conversation. Going to a colony world was good for Felicity and Blake, but it meant that she would never see her family again. With the Fortuna system being eighteen light years away from Earth, it would be thirty-six years before she could return, if not longer. And Felicity had no plans to return. By the time word got back to them, her parents would be too old to make the trip even if she could get them accepted into the colony once her term of enlistment was complete.

She left the train and went directly to Bleaker street. Her parents lived in an ancient building in a small, two-bedroom apartment. She had shared a bedroom with her two brothers until she married Blake, but that wasn't the sole reason for marrying young. Her father worked at the public maintenance department, and her mother was a secretary in the food logistics department. They both worked ten hours a day, six days a week and still barely made enough money to live on. Having three children was a stretch, but they sacrificed and made do. Felicity respected them for their love and support, but she wanted a better life. Fortunately, her parents wanted a better life for her too. They would be thrilled at the prospect of her joining a colony planet—but not as part of a militia. Her father had trained her to fight, but that didn't mean he wanted her putting herself in danger voluntarily.

She still had a key to the apartment and let herself in just a few minutes before her parents got home for the day. Her mother came home first and was happy to see her until she realized that Blake wasn't there as well.

"What's wrong?" her mother asked. "Don't tell me you two are fighting already."

"No, ma'am," Felicity said. "Blake's at an interview."

"Oh, really? I hope he gets it. I want to see the two of you get out of that shoebox apartment. Government housing isn't safe."

"I know."

"Did something happen?"

"Something is always happening," Felicity said. "But nothing to be worried about."

"Well, I'll always worry. That's a mother's prerogative. Something you'll understan— Wait, you're not pregnant, are you?"

"No, mom."

Her mother dropped into a chair. "Oh, well, that's good, that's good. Don't get me wrong, children are a blessing, but I don't want you being forced into an abortion. I see too many people forced to get procedures done against their will."

A moment later, her father came in the door with her younger brother. They both hugged Felicity, then her father sent her younger brother to get ready for training. Felicity felt tears in her eyes. She couldn't remember a day in her life when her father didn't come home after working ten hours and immediately spend at least an hour training her.

"Why's my baby girl home?" her father asked. "And where's my new son-in-law?"

"Blake's in an interview," Felicity said, trying to hold herself together. She had no idea how hard telling her parents goodbye would be.

"Good, I hope he gets it," her father said.

"Simon, sit down," Felicity's mother told her father. "She's got something to tell us."

"Something good, I hope," her father said.

"It is good, but bittersweet," Felicity said, unable to stop the tears. "I was accepted into the Magellan Corporation Militia today."

"The what?" her father asked.

"Colony guard," her mother said. "Honey, why are you crying?"

"I've still got to pass the physical," Felicity said, wiping the tears from her eyes.

"That's a piece of cake," her father said.

"And when we leave..."

Her parents fell silent, letting the announcement sink in.

"How far away?" her father asked.

"Eighteen light-years," Felicity said.

"Oh," her father replied.

"That new planet," her mother said, nodding. "Are you sure about this?"

"Yeah," Felicity said. "We both are."

"That's where Cage is interviewing?" her father asked.

Felicity nodded. "They don't take married couples."

"You lied?" her mother asked.

"Why the hell not?" her father said. "Being married shouldn't make a difference."

"I want to make a difference," Felicity said. "I can do that on a new world."

"You get to stay when your enlistment period is up?" her father asked.

"Yes."

"How long is it?" her mother asked.

"Five years," Felicity said.

"How much time do we have with you?" her father said.

"I don't know yet. Physicals are in two days. Training starts after that."

"Well, keep us in the loop," her father said. "We both have some vacation accumulated. We'll make the most of the time we have left."

"And send you off in style," her mother said.

"We couldn't be prouder of you," her father added. "I always said you'd change the world. I just didn't know it wouldn't be this one."

CHAPTER 5

BLAKE CAGE

Physicals were a standard affair. Each person was given medical scans, blood was drawn, and they all were put through basic physical fitness routines. Cage had hoped that he would be in a group with Felicity, but the men and women were separated into different buildings.

After the physicals, they were herded into an auditorium and shown an orientation video. A full term of service was five years with basic pay. At the end of their enlistment, each person would be given land, a bonus, and the option of reenlisting if they so desired, and the colony needs accommodated extended service.

At the end of the presentation, the candidates were told that information regarding their status would be mailed to them, including the date and location for basic training. Cage was excited to catch up with Felicity, but before he could leave the building, an officer approached.

"Are you Blake T. Cage?" the officer asked.

"Yes, sir," Cage replied, feeling a lump forming in his stomach.

His fear all along would be that he and Felicity would be caught, their marriage exposed, and both of them expelled from the program.

"Would you come with me, please?" the officer said.

The officer turned and headed back through the throng of people exiting the auditorium. Cage followed. They went through a doorway, down a short hallway, and into a room. On the wall beside the door, a name plate read "General Phillip Haley." Cage took a deep breath and stepped inside.

"Candidate Cage," the officer who had escorted him said.

An older man, who had just a tiny bit of gray hair along the crown of his head above his ears, looked up. "Very good, Lieutenant."

The officer left and closed the door. General Haley waved at the empty chairs facing his desk. Cage sat down, trying not to let his nerves get the best of him. He had no reason to believe that the MCM had discovered that Cage and Felicity were married, but he couldn't help but worry about it.

"We've verified your academic record," the general said. "Would you be interested in an officer's position?"

"I'm sorry?" Cage asked, trying to understand what he was being offered.

"We have a lot of people enlisting in the militia," the general explained. "But most aren't leadership material. We need smart, talented people to go through officer training and lead platoons. Normally, depending on the unit, we try to pair new officers with more experienced leaders. Once you complete basic, you would go through OT school while the enlisted personnel have unit-specific training. Once you complete that, you'll be assigned a platoon, which will be made up of enlisted personnel and a few veteran NCOs."

"But I'd be part of the militia going to the new colony?" Cage asked.

"Yes, absolutely. You'll conduct your initial five-year commitment on the new colony, and then you'll have an opportunity to decide if you want to stay or join a new colony program."

Cage nodded, trying not to show his surprise. It had never crossed his mind that he might be picked to be an officer. But it seemed like there was no reason not to accept the offer.

"You'll get a pay bump, of course, and a larger parcel of land when your initial enlistment is complete. I've got officers who choose to stay in the service and sell their land allotment. But you'll have plenty of time to sort through those types of decisions. As an officer, you'll be an official employee of the Magellan Corporation. I've checked your physical, and the offer is yours if you want it."

Cage didn't want to jump at the offer, even though saying yes seemed like an easy decision. His instincts told him to wait. Of course he wanted to discuss it with Felicity, but he couldn't really ask for that. He was about to say yes when the general leaned back in his chair and put his hands across his stomach.

"I can also authorize a signing bonus, if you accept right now," the general said. "You'll have to pass OT training, but I've never had a college grad who didn't."

Cage nodded. "Yes, sir," he said, trying not to grin like a child. "I accept."

"Outstanding. Let's do the paperwork," the general said, extending a hand. "Welcome to the company, Cage. You'll be a good addition to this colony program."

It took a while to fill out all the forms, but he left the building with an official Magellan Corporation name badge and a check for ten thousand credits. Felicity had gone home, which they had discussed. Two people from the same section of the city wasn't strange, but any indication that they had a prior relationship might cause suspicion. Once he was away from the Magellan facility, he checked his phone and found a number of messages from Felicity.

He sent her a text to let her know he was okay and on his way home. An hour and a half later, he walked into their little apartment and Felicity jumped off the bed.

"What happened?" she said, throwing her arms around him. "What's with all the mystery?"

In response, Cage held up the check. Felicity looked at it, and her eyes opened so wide he could see the white all around her dark brown irises.

"What is this?" she said, snatching the check out of his hands and looking at it more closely.

"Well...it looks like my history degree isn't being wasted."

"I don't understand," Felicity said.

"You're looking at an officer in the Magellan Corporation Militia," Cage said. "I go to basic just like you, but then I attend Officer Training school."

"Really?" Felicity said, still looking at the check.

"Really. And that, my love, is a signing bonus. As an officer, I'm an official employee of Magellan Corp." He pulled the check from her hands and wrapped his arms around her. They were eye to eye. "I thought we could split the money and give it to our parents."

"Really?"

"We won't need it," Cage said. "The company will supply

everything we need, and I don't think banking credits from Earth will be worth much on a colony world."

"I think it's an incredibly generous thing to do," Felicity said.

Cage gave her a little kiss. He loved making her happy. And while five thousand credits weren't riches, he knew that both of their families could use the money. And leaving them with something would help alleviate the guilt of leaving them behind.

"We have good things ahead of us," Cage said. "I can feel it."

"Me too," she whispered.

She grabbed him suddenly, pulled him in for a kiss, and then gave him a push. He landed on the bed, and she landed beside him. It was time to celebrate.

CHAPTER 6

BLAKE CAGE

Their orders to report for training came the next day: they had three days to pack up their things and prepare for their new life. Once their basic training started, they would move into the Magellan facilities and have very little leave before the projected date to depart for the new planet. All the information sent to them was classified. They weren't allowed to share dates, times, or destinations. In fact, most of the salient details were withheld.

Cage and Felicity spent time with their families. There were tears and promises to write, but mostly, there was excitement. They had found a way to a new and better life. Their parents were supportive. The money was accepted after some convincing, and what little belongings the young couple had were packed up. They didn't lose their apartment right away, although Cage filled out the appropriate online forms. Nothing about the government moved swiftly. Still, when they left the little apartment before dawn on reporting day, they felt the nostalgia already.

"A lot of memories," Cage said.

"Our first home," Felicity said, shaking her head. "What a dump."

"It wasn't the walls or the building that made it home," Cage pointed out. "It was love."

"And we'll have to remember that," she pointed out. "This isn't going to be easy, you know. I like having you around."

"The feeling's mutual," Cage said. "We'll find a way to make it work. We always have."

They left the building before the day had really begun. The only time the city seemed quiet was in the hour before dawn. They saw a few diehard party people making their way home, but the throngs of people who usually filled the streets were gone. The train station had a few commuters, but it still felt empty. Cage wrapped an arm around his wife while they waited for the train that would take them north to the Magellan facility.

"You'll have to make decisions without me," he said quietly.

"I know," she said.

"It's possible that we get split up, perhaps even put on different ships."

"I'm afraid of that," she replied.

"Well, don't be. We're heading to the same place. It's a new world, so almost all the work will be done at one central location for most of our enlistment."

"But we could go for weeks without seeing each other," she said.

"I know, but it's worth it. We get through basic, then through training school, then make the trip. One day at a time."

The train pulled into the station, and they stood up.

"You better be thinking about me, Blake Cage," Felicity said.

"Every day, baby," Cage replied.

They kissed. It was a tender kiss goodbye, and then they boarded different cars on the train. The ride out through the dark city seemed to take forever. The sun was coming up, casting long, red streaks across the sky as they disembarked. Cage couldn't help but wonder how many more sunrises or sunsets he was likely to see before leaving Earth and the Sol system forever.

At the facility, Cage was sent to a smaller briefing room rather than the large auditorium where the other recruits were gathering. There were only eight people in the room, and they were greeted by General Haley.

"All right, this is just a little informal briefing," the general said. "You are all selected for OT school once you've completed basic, but you will not receive any special treatment until you've completed basic. Keep in mind that the point of basic training is to get you into top physical conditioning and prepare you for military service. A big part of that is military discipline. When an officer—which will be you at some point—orders troops into harm's way, there can't be hesitation. So prepare yourself for an intense introduction to the militia. We don't coddle anyone in basic."

Cage hadn't expected any special treatment, and he knew that the training would be grueling, but he didn't like thinking about it. The anticipation was often worse than the experience itself, and he didn't want to worry too much in advance.

"Please understand that you are not officers yet. You are all candidates," General Haley went on explaining. "You don't have the right to order anyone to do anything. Military structure is intended to bring about efficiency, not to give one person power over another. The very best leaders set an example for those that follow them. I don't want you pushing from behind. We lead from the front. Are you all clear on that?"

"Yes, sir," the candidates all said.

"If I get reports of misconduct, you will not be accepted into OTS. This is not a game. Lives are on the line—not just your troopers', but the lives of our colonists. The company only makes a profit if the colony is successful, and it's our job to make sure they have whatever they need to be successful. So learn, soak in every bit of knowledge that is shared with you. Learn from your experiences. Listen to the veteran officers and NCO's. You never know when the most insignificant fact might just save your life. You are all part of Zebra platoon. Now head out and join the enlisted men and women in the auditorium—but keep in mind, I'm watching you. I expect only the best from our officers. Dismissed!"

The general left the room, and Cage stood up along with the other officer candidates. As he was leaving, a woman next to him said, "Time for the fun to begin."

Cage looked over and saw the name on her Magellan employee card that was clipped to the collar of her shirt. It read "Drucker, Lyla." She was shorter than Cage and thin, but there was a hardness to her eyes. It was clear that she wasn't as young as she first appeared and had seen some difficult times.

"I guess so," Cage said.

"I'm Lyla."

"Blake Cage. It's nice to meet you."

"Pleasure's all mine, Cage. All mine."

She winked at him, and Cage realized that she was flirting. It took him by surprise; it had been a long time since anyone had flirted with him. He was so used to being with

Felicity and giving her all his attention that even if someone else had flirted, he doubt he would have noticed. It made him realize that there would be men flirting with his wife—men who had no idea she was married. He suddenly began to wonder if they had made an enormous mistake.

CHAPTER 7

FELICITY MARS

The introduction to basic training was done by holographic projection. The auditorium had a stage, and hidden by a curtain liner at the top was a holoprojector that cast the image of a man in uniform. Felicity got the feeling that he was an actor and not actually a member of the militia.

"Welcome to the Magellan Corporation Militia, or as we like to call it, the MCM. That's right, go ahead and give yourselves a round of applause. You've earned it."

The hologram actor was smiling and clapping slowly. No one else in the auditorium was clapping. There were a few chuckles, but otherwise the crowd was quiet.

"Getting approved for the MCM isn't easy; we only take the best of the best. That's you. And your service will be pivotal in the days ahead. Mankind is expanding our territory among the stars, and you're part of that. It's something to be proud of."

The hologram continued the introductory speech. Felicity

was only half-listening as she scanned the crowd around her. From where she sat, she didn't think the actor was right; if she was seeing the "best of the best" here, humanity was in serious trouble. It looked to her like the MCM took any warm body that wasn't riddled with disease. Most of her fellow classmates looked homeless. There was a wide range of ages, from kids just out of high school to middle-aged people that Felicity was surprised could pass the physical.

"Today," the hologram went on in a cheerful, inspiring voice, "you'll be assigned to a platoon for basic training. Once we're done here in the auditorium, you'll join your platoon mates and be issued everything you'll need for the next eight weeks. I can't promise that basic training will be easy, but I have the utmost confidence that each and every one of you is capable of rising to the challenge."

When the lecture was finally over, the auditorium was emptied row by row. Felicity gave her name to a woman standing just outside the room, and she joined thirty-nine other enlistees in platoon Lima. They walked from the administration building out to a row of warehouses. In the first, they were put on benches while their heads were shaved down to stubble. Some of the women were crying over their lost hair, but not Felicity. She made a habit of keeping her hair short and manageable. The last thing she wanted was for her hair to get in her eyes if she had to defend herself. She caught a glance of herself in a mirror and thought the haircut looked decent on her. She had strong cheekbones and a narrow chin. It made her wonder what Blake looked like with his thick, wavy hair shaved off. Would they even recognize each other?

After getting their haircuts, they were given a series of shots. Felicity didn't normally like having things injected into her body that she didn't ask for, but the shots weren't optional;

living in close quarters with complete strangers made health an important issue. After the shots, they walked to a section of the warehouse where rows of metal shelves were filled with bins. Administrators were busy moving among them, gathering goods to hand out to the enlistees. Felicity was issued three sets of loose-fitting workout clothes, underwear, socks, boots, and toiletries. Her T-shirts were light green with the word "Lima" printed on the front.

With their stack of clothes and toiletries, they were ushered out of the warehouse to an even larger building. Felicity guessed it was sometimes used as a hangar. The floor was concrete, and there were four sections surrounded by curtains that hung from the ceiling by long chains. Inside the curtains were bunkbeds, each with lockers at the foot. They were assigned to their bunks. Felicity's bunkmate was a frail-looking kid with acne named Jonas.

In the middle of the warehouse were two makeshift bathroom facilities—one for men, one for women. They all showered. Their civilian clothes were bagged up, labeled, and sent off to be added to the cargo being loaded onto the ships prepping for the trip to the Fortuna system.

Once they were settled, a gruff man who Felicity guessed was in his sixties began shouting at them.

"Lima platoon, your basic training has begun!" The old man shouted, pronouncing lima like *lee-mah*. "Line up at the foot of your bunks in front of your locker. Move!"

Felicity had taken the bottom bunk. She stood up quickly and moved in front of the locker where the rest of her clothes were stored. Jonas was on the top bunk; he struggled to get down and tripped in the process. He fell down and took his time getting up. The old man spotted him and hurried over, but not out of concern.

"Are you kidding me?" The old man bent down and screamed right in Jonas's face. "You're the sorriest sack of worm shit I've ever seen. Can you not even get down off your bunk without falling on your ass? Get in line before I break you in half!"

Jonas was breathing hard by the time he got to his locker. Felicity could sense him trembling with fear or rage, she didn't know which. The old man walked up and down the line of enlistees. Whenever he spoke, it was a gruff shout.

"My name is Master Sergeant Eugene Davies. You will call me 'Master Sergeant.' Is that clear?"

Felicity and a few others replied, "Yes, Master Sergeant." But others said "Yes, sir," and there were even a few "Yeah"s.

"Do not call me sir! I'm not an officer, and I never will be. And if any of you worthless, sorry-ass recruits replies with anything other than 'yes, Master Sergeant' when I ask you a question, you will have my boot planted on your throat while I rip out your entrails with my bare hands. Is that clear?"

"Yes, Master Sergeant," the entire platoon shouted.

"From this point on, you know nothing. You are to do nothing without permission. You don't eat without my say so. You don't sleep without my say so. You don't use the bathroom, brush your teeth, or change your damn clothes without my say so. Is that clear?"

"Yes, Master Sergeant."

"Very good. At least you're not so stupid that you can't take basic instructions. Here is what you need to know while in this barracks. First, when I or any of your instructors tell you to fall out, this is what that means: You, standing in front of your locker, eyes front, mouth shut. I will teach you how to stand at attention soon enough. Secondly, as you have undoubtedly noticed, this is a platoon of mixed genders. For those of you too stupid to know what I'm saying, gender means male and female or somewhere in between. That being said, for the next eight weeks you will all be completely asexual. Anyone caught getting physical with another recruit will rue that day for the rest of his or her life. And if anyone forces themselves on another recruit—or anyone for that matter—they will deal with me one on one, and when we're done, only one of us will be breathing and walking around among the living. I will not tolerate any fraternizing of any kind during basic. Is that absolutely clear?"

"Yes, Master Sergeant."

"Very good. Let's get acquainted with your instructors. Staff Sergeant Kiev and Staff Sergeant Banning will be your instructors along with myself. Our job is to get you combat-ready. First we train the body, then the mind. With that said, let's begin with a short run. Staff Sergeant Banning, get these sloppy, lard-eating slugs out of my barracks and in formation for a run."

"Yes, Master Sergeant," Banning replied. "Everyone, fall out! That means move, people. Let's go!"

They all jogged to the door in the corner of the building.

"Oh man, I hate running," Jonas whined.

"Then why are you here?" Felicity asked.

"My dad signed me up," the young man said. "He said it would build character."

"It will," Felicity said, "if you survive."

CHAPTER 8

BLAKE CAGE

Cage was used to running; Felicity kept him in shape. Twice a week they ran the stairs of their building. It was one of the few places they could exercise in peace. Running outside was only for people trying to get away from danger. The streets were too busy, and the parks had long since been built over. There were gyms for people with jobs and excess money, but most people couldn't afford the pricy memberships.

But Cage had never run in boots. They fit well—the foam padding formed to the contours of his feet and gave him plenty of support—but they were heavy. Zebra Platoon was jogging up and down an old airstrip. Aerial vehicles had stopped using runways with the advent of the repulsorlift engine, but it took another half century for the older aircraft to wear out beyond repair. Most of the old airports had been repurposed, but the landing strip on the Magellan property was still in use, only not for takeoffs and landings.

Zebra platoon wasn't the only group running. Each group

had their own unique color; Cage saw Bravo in bright red, and Foxtrot in white. His own T-shirt was black with "Zebra" printed in white letters across the chest. His bunkmate was none other than Lyla Drucker, who had latched onto Cage like that crazy person on the train—only he couldn't get off to escape her. Being bunkmates meant they were side by side when they fell into formation for run. She was breathing heavily as they jogged, and Cage could only imagine how she felt. His own legs were burning from the effort, and sweat was dripping down his recently shaved head straight into his eyes.

Cage studied every platoon they passed, searching desperately for a sign of his wife. He finally spotted her in a green shirt. His heart flipped at how good she looked. Her dark skin was covered in a slight sheen of sweat, and her shaved head brought out the fine features of her face. When she spotted him, she winked. Despite his fatigue, Cage couldn't stop smiling. She was in Lima platoon: the green shirts. He made a mental note ensuring that he wouldn't forget.

"How can you be smiling?" Lyla asked. "I'm dying over here."

"Yeah, me too," Cage said. "But we're better off than some people. We don't have to run the longest—just long enough."

"And that makes you happy?"

"It makes me happy to know I can do it," Cage said.

It was true. He felt good knowing he was capable. There were others really struggling. Some, he knew, wouldn't survive basic training. Their bodies simply wouldn't hold up. He was lucky that he was young and healthy. But that wasn't why he was smiling; seeing his wife, thinking of their future, knowing they were going to make it off an overcrowded world to a new planet where they could carve out their own destinies—that's what made him smile. But he couldn't reveal that to Lyla.

Cage had expected a good exercise, but instead he was hit with a grueling run that seemed to go on and on. One by one, four members of Zebra platoon went down, unable to continue. They were pulled off the airstrip but otherwise left where they fell. People were struggling in every platoon. More groups joined the slog, forcing everyone to slow down. Cage couldn't feel his legs, but he was doing better than most. Several members of his platoon got sick, but to their credit, they kept running.

Lyla, who hadn't stopped chatting Cage up every chance she got, had finally fallen silent. Cage could hear her wheezing beside him. His own mouth was painfully dry, his throat burning, and there was a stitch in his side.

"Don't give...up," Cage gasped. "You...got this."

Lyla didn't even look up at him. Her face was pinched in determination, every breath precious. People in other platoons looked desperate. Staff sergeants followed along, screaming at anyone who struggled. Even Felicity, when Cage could see her, looked particularly focused and determined.

Cage began to wonder what the grueling run was for. There had to be a purpose; the officers wouldn't subject their new recruits to such a devastating introduction to the MCM without a good reason. The only purpose that Cage could fathom was to identify the strongest candidates, but that would require some type of oversight, and Cage couldn't tell if anyone was even watching them. Hundreds of recruits were running. Most were barely staying on their feet, but a few—like Felicity—still had energy left. Zebra platoon reached the end of the runway, and Cage couldn't help but hope that they stop. He was disappointed again. They made the turn and kept running, and as they turned back, Cage spotted it: There were all kinds of buildings around the runway—some were new, others old—but one of the most striking was the old control tower. The room at the top was enclosed with glass; in the bright sunlight of midday it looked dark and empty, but it was the perfect place to observe the runners.

Cage was studying the tower as he ran. It helped to be able to focus on something other than the pain he was in or his dwindling energy. He was so focused on the tower and trying to see if there were people inside that he didn't notice Staff Sergeant Goreski jog up beside him. The staff sergeant slapped him hard on the back of the shoulder before screaming at him.

"Stay focused, recruit!" Goreski bellowed. "Eyes straight ahead! Head down."

"Yes...Staff Sergeant," Cage said, his voice harsh.

He put his head down, feeling like he'd done something wrong, but he didn't miss Goreski glance up at the tower and give a subtle nod. It wasn't much, but it confirmed what Cage thought—not that it helped. They still had to run. Lyla dropped to the ground a few minutes later. Cage started to help her, but Staff Sergeant Holms took his place.

"Let her go," Holms said. "Stay on task."

"Yes...Staff...Sergeant," Cage said.

He was close to dropping himself, and it bothered him to leave a comrade behind, even though he didn't really like Lyla. She was nice enough but clearly had her eyes on more than just friendship. Even if Master Sergeant Preston hadn't warned them that fraternization would get them kicked out of the MCM, Cage wouldn't have been interested in her. He was loyal to his wife, and the grueling run was only making him more appreciative of what Felicity Mars was capable of.

A moment later, a horn sounded: One long blast, and the staff sergeants began calling their platoons to a halt. Cage kept running, waiting for the call from Holms, and didn't slow down or look around. He could tell Holms was watching him to see what he would do. He kept his eyes straight ahead and pretended he couldn't feel the staff sergeant's eyes on him. After nearly a minute, Holms called for a halt.

Cage could barely believe it was real. He knew he had to keep moving or his entire body would cramp up. He put his hands on his head the way that Felicity had shown him to keep his lungs open. Breathing deeply, he slowed to a walk. It was such a relief to have endured the marathon that he felt like crying. He finally came to a stop when he spotted Felicity. She was over a hundred yards away from him, the sun shining on her dark skin. Cage thought she looked like a vision, the embodiment of a legendary warrior from long ago, unfazed by the carnage around her.

In a casual manner, he reached up and touched the back of his shoulder where Staff Sergeant Goreski had slapped him. He could just feel the small, fingernail-size patch on his T-shirt. Cage didn't know what it was, but he recognized that he'd been marked, probably for whomever was in the tower watching them.

Magellan employees arrived a few seconds later on hover carts with large coolers and disposable cups. Cage was desperately thirsty, but he made sure the rest of his platoon was in line ahead of him. When he finally reached the cart, he was handed a cup of flavored water.

"What is it?" he asked, his voice husky. The words seemed to tear their way through his parched throat.

"Electrolytes and amino acids," the worker said. "It'll keep you from cramping too bad."

Cage nodded, then stepped to the side to let the next person get their drink. He sniffed the drink; it had a pleasant fruit flavor. He took a long drink, sucking eagerly at the liquid. It felt like magic flowing over his swollen tongue and down his raw throat. Cage knew better than to drink too much too fast. After his initial, greedy pull, he forced himself to sip and keep moving. He felt completely spent but didn't want to show it. Some recruits were bent over, others had dropped onto the hot concrete. Cage kept walking, making small circles. He finished his drink just before the line opened up. He got a refill and kept moving.

After a few more minutes of rest, Staff Sergeant Goreski called Zebra platoon into formation. For the first time, the platoon leaders were actually patient. They waited as several members slowly got to their feet. Once they formed up, Cage saw that they were down by nearly half. He counted only twenty-four members of his platoon. His body was exhausted, but his mind was buzzing with questions. What had become of their platoon mates? Were they in the infirmary or discharged from the militia? Who was in the old control towering watching them, and what were they looking for? Most of all, Cage wondered about the patch on his shoulder. What did it mean? He would have to wait for answers, but waiting wasn't his strong suit.

CHAPTER 9

FELICITY MARS

The run had been grueling, but she had endured worse. Her father wasn't cruel, but he'd had no qualms about pushing his children to the limits. *You'll never know what you're capable of if you don't push yourself,* he used to say to her.

After the run, they returned to their barracks—at least those who were still able to walk on their own. In the cool interior of the large hangar, they were led in stretching exercises. After an hour of post-run care, they were taken to lunch. Food for the recruits was simple fare: a nutrient-dense wafer loaf smothered in a rich sauce and served with roasted red potatoes and cups of fruit cocktail. Felicity couldn't say how it actually tasted; she was so hungry that the highly engineered food tasted gourmet.

The rest of the day was spent in the classroom. She dropped into her bunk shortly after the evening meal, and despite the fact that it was the first night she was spending away from her husband since they were married, she fell fast asleep.

Basic training shifted into a daily routine. Up before dawn, the platoon completed two hours of cardio and functional strength training that included various forms of sit-ups, pull-ups, push-ups, and squats. Most of those who fell in the first day's marathon rejoined the platoon after some basic medical attention. Jonas told her that he'd been given IV fluids and allowed to rest for two days before being cleared to come back.

After breakfast, the platoon spent hours marching. They learned to walk in formation and make various maneuvers according to verbal commands. They practiced marching through different types of terrain but mostly on rugged, uneven ground. A huge dirt track had been constructed deep inside the Magellan Corporation property. They used big earth-movers to change the track, even sometimes adding water so that the recruits were forced to march through thick, clinging mud.

An hour before lunch was spent cleaning their gear. At first that meant changing clothes, looking after their boots, and doctoring the blisters and bruises on their feet. It didn't take long before they were given heavy vests, the pockets and ammunition loops filled with weights to simulate battle armor. After the vests came backpacks. Felicity could feel her strength growing. She had always been fit and strong for her size, but lean. Now, with the super food—as she'd come to think of it— she was putting on pounds of muscle. She was certain that it was laced with growth hormones and quick recovery stimulants, but it was all part of the program. No one was checking them for performance-enhancing drugs, and she didn't object.

In those brief moments when she had a spare minute to look at herself in the bathroom mirror, she couldn't help but admire the changes. Her shoulders and arms were rounding out, and she could see the muscles in her abdomen without even trying. She wondered what Cage would think of her. There were times when she wanted so desperately to be with him. They had only seen each other a handful of times since basic training had begun. They had spoken like two people who were mere acquaintances, and she had certainly noticed the differences in him. He walked differently. His chest and back had grown thick with muscles. Most of all, he seemed happy.

After lunches came training periods. They started with classroom work, learning the ranks and divisions of the MCM, but after the first few days, their training time became more hands-on. First came medical training, followed by weapons. Felicity had trained in martial arts from a very young age, but weapons were illegal. She'd never held a gun or even dreamed of firing one before joining the militia. They spent days learning the components of a weapon and how to disassemble, clean, and reassemble it. Only when they could properly care for each weapon were they taken to the range and allowed to shoot.

The range was inside another huge building. It consisted of multiple firing lanes with automated targets. They learned to shoot from prone positions on the ground, then on their knees, then standing. They worked with a variety of weapons, starting with simple laser pistols and moving up to standard assault rifles, then more specialized weapons.

Training lasted through most of the afternoon. They were given protein drinks after their weapons training and then spent two hours every day in hand-to-hand combat training. It was Felicity's favorite part of the day, and her instructors quickly realized that she was a highly competent fighter. She was a master of hand-to-hand fighting, and they gave her special instructions on simple weapons such as knives and clubs. If a rifle malfunctioned, it could still be deadly in the hands of a trained fighter. Felicity even got to help train the rest of her platoon. They ate dinner late and spent the last hour of the day washing and caring for the minor injuries they inevitably suffered during training.

The first half of their eight-week basic training went by quickly, but the second half was more difficult. She had little trouble adapting to the grueling physical demands, but by the fifth week, most of her platoon mates had, as well. It was no surprise that once they weren't in constant survival mode that some of them began seeing her as more than just a competent peer; there were flirtations, offers, and even a few propositions. She rebuffed them all. A few of the men had to be convinced that no meant no. One man—a large, older man named Virgil—had put his hand on her arm and pulled her toward him. She used the sudden shift in momentum to drive her knee into his groin. He bent over in pain, releasing her arm, and she followed up with a double ear slap, clapping his head with her hands. He dropped to the ground, groaning in pain, just before Staff Sergeant Kiev discovered the scene.

"What's happened here?" she demanded.

"My platoon mate is having some sort of episode, Staff Sergeant," Felicity said. "I have no idea what brought it on."

She left Virgil on the floor, and as the story spread, so did the reality that Felicity wasn't an easy target. Unfortunately, some of the other people in the platoon were more willing to break the rules. Felicity didn't actually see anything, but she wasn't fooled by the games she saw others playing. It was easy to divide the platoon into two groups: one was serious and determined to do well, and the other, larger group of recruits had no discipline and was obviously only interested in getting to a colony world.

Jonas was in the latter group. As his physical fitness improved, so did his disdain for authority. He never rebelled openly, but when their instructors weren't around, he let his opinions fly without regard for how foolish he looked or sounded.

Surprisingly enough, it was Staff Sergeant Anna Kiev who bonded the most with Felicity. There was a distance to be maintained between the instructors and the recruits, but Kiev was the combat coordinator. Her job was to teach the recruits hand-to-hand combat, and Felicity's high level of skill in various martial art forms gave them a common ground. Many of the more serious recruits bonded with the staff sergeants, both of whom were veterans from previous colony deployments.

By the sixth week, Felicity was nearing her breaking point. They'd had one rest day each week, but her platoon's day off never matched up with Blake's. She missed him and her family so much that she was even having thoughts of quitting.

"You look upset," Staff Sergeant Kiev said. "What's wrong?"

"Nothing," Felicity said. "I'm just tired."

"I didn't think you ever got tired," the older woman teased. "What's really bothering you?"

Felicity didn't answer right away. She had to be careful what she said and to whom. She trusted the staff sergeant, but she couldn't tell her everything.

"I suppose I'm feeling homesick," Felicity finally replied.

"Let me guess: you broke up with a boyfriend to join the MCM."

That wasn't Felicity's issue, but the dynamics were the same, and she decided it would be okay to let her friend assume her guess was correct.

"Maybe," Felicity said.

"It happens more often than you might think," the older woman said. "In your mind the relationship is right where you left it, but you have to realize the odds are that your boyfriend has probably moved on."

"That's encouraging," Felicity said sarcastically. "What's next? Are you going to tell me I've only got a few weeks left to live?"

"No, nothing like that," Kiev said. "It's just—you need to start thinking about the future. You're a beautiful woman. I'm sure there are plenty of people who would bend over backward to make you happy."

"I would never break the rules."

"That's just it," Kiev said. "In two weeks, you'll graduate from basic training and get assigned to a specialist school. After basic, the rules lighten up. Officially, fraternization is frowned upon, but as long as you're discrete...well..."

"Are you serious?"

"I'm not telling you to go crazy, but if there's someone you have your eye on..." Kiev said. "Hold things together for a couple more weeks and you can start living again."

The very thought of reconnecting with Blake made Felicity feel like she might start crying. She had earned a reputation for toughness, but she was still a person, and her feelings ran deep—especially where Blake was concerned.

"I can do it," Felicity said.

"I never doubted it," Kiev said.

Dinner that night was the same boring fare. It was high quality food, but the lack of variety was frustrating. Felicity had long since seen the food as fuel, and nothing more. The final meal of the day was a signal to her body and mind that she could begin to relax. The social interactions were more animated and fun. And for the first time in weeks, she felt hopeful that things were going to get better soon.

CHAPTER 10

BLAKE CAGE

Six weeks of basic training had crawled by, and Cage was finally starting to enjoy it. He didn't mind the physical exercise or learning to fight in hand-to-hand combat. In fact, most of what he was taught he already knew from working out with Felicity. But the repetitive nature of things had worn him down initially. The afternoon training sessions were the worst. He enjoyed shooting, but his instructors drilled them constantly on things that Cage picked up right away. He understood the need to do things over and over until it was all muscle memory, but the boredom drove him crazy.

Worst of all, he missed Felicity so intensely that he struggled to hold himself together, especially during the afternoons. Lyla had returned to the platoon, and her flirtations ensued. After a while, once she realized she couldn't convince him to fool around with her, she found someone else to break the rules with. It galled Cage to see someone who would eventually be an officer breaking the fraternization rules, but Lyla didn't seem to mind—and she wasn't satisfied with just one suitor. It was as if she reveled in the idea that she was isolated with a group of available men.

As the training became more advanced, so did his instruction. Master Sergeant Billy Preston was regularly sharing strategy with Cage. Each weapon they trained on had different uses in a variety of combat situations. The recruits had all turned over their personal items when their basic training began, but seeing Cage's hunger to do more than just learn to use the weapons, the master sergeant had given him a reader with combat tactics on it. They were nearing the end of basic, which would mean officer training school. He hadn't realized it, but Cage discovered that being an officer was the only way he would survive in the MCM. His mind was too active to be content just waiting for orders. He needed the mental as well as the physical challenge.

The best thing about the sixth week was Zebra's day off. Cage had seen the schedule when he was visiting Master Sergeant Preston in his small room beside the barracks. During week six, Zebra platoon would share their day off with Foxtrot, Charlie, and Lima platoons. Their days off were usually filled with naps, mending clothes, playing cards, and sneaking food from the mess hall. Occasionally groups of recruits gathered, but rarely from different platoons. They didn't even eat at the same times. Cage had barely seen his wife for six weeks, and he was determined not to miss this chance to reconnect.

When their day off finally rolled around, Cage didn't sleep in. He was up early and went by himself to the mess hall. The dining area was made up of long tables with bench seats. People came and went on their own when they had time off. Cage waited until the platoons on duty finished their hasty morning meal, then loitered in the mess hall. Most of his platoon mates wandered in. Cage moved the food around on his tray, pretending to eat but complaining that his stomach wasn't feeling great.

Eventually Felicity came to the mess hall. She was with three of her platoon mates, two other women and a young man with acne on his face. Cage couldn't help but notice his broad chest and wide shoulders. His face looked young, but his physique was imposing. Still, he did his best not to pay attention to his wife, who got her breakfast and sat down near the center aisle of the dining room. All Cage needed was a break. He got it when Staff Sergeant Holms appeared. Cage hopped up and carried his tray toward the staff sergeant. He had to time his approach carefully. He met Holms right at the spot in the aisle that was closest to where Felicity was seated. She didn't look at him except for a quick glance as he approached. Cage rubbed his stomach.

"Staff sergeant," Cage said, just a bit louder than he needed to. "My stomach isn't feeling well. I think I'll head over to the infirmary and get it checked out."

"Fine," Holms said. "It's your day off. I don't care what you do."

The staff sergeant pushed past Cage, who glanced down at Felicity. She was staring straight ahead, but her hand closest to Cage was on her thigh. He could just barely see that she was making the okay sign. It was enough for him. He returned his tray of half-eaten breakfast and left the mess hall. Cage took his time strolling over to the infirmary. His stomach wasn't bothering him—in fact, he felt great. Instead of going inside and getting checked out, he sat on a bench just outside. No one questioned him, and after half an hour, to his great relief, he saw Felicity approaching. She went straight to the bench and sat down.

"I can't believe how great you look," Cage said.

"Don't start that," Felicity said. "I'm too weak to say no to you if you go there."

"Sorry," Cage said. He looked down, unable to control the grin on his face.

"Two more weeks," Felicity went on. "Can you make it?"

"I can do anything if it means spending more time with you," Cage said.

"My staff sergeant said the rules are loosened up after basic."

"Oh, really?" Cage said. "That's the best news I've heard in weeks."

"Me too. I had no idea it would be this hard."

"You still think it's worth it?"

"Nothing is worth being apart from you."

"But you still want to go?"

"Yes," Felicity said. "We've put in too much work to throw it all away now. Besides, the worst is nearly over."

"Any idea what school you'll be in?"

"None," she replied. "They haven't even talked with us about it."

"Are you doing okay?"

"Yeah, I'm holding up. What about you? Are you really sick?"

"No, but I had to see you. I've missed everything about you."

"I miss you too, Blake."

They wanted more of everything—more time, more conversation, more privacy—but they couldn't get it. Cage had to leave or risk arousing suspicion. The general's warning about watching them was ringing in the back of his mind like a warning klaxon. If Lyla Drucker was any indication, no one was paying them any attention at all, but Cage couldn't take that chance.

"I should go," Cage said.

"Thanks for working this out," Felicity said.

"I'll meet you after we finish basic. They have to give us a little time off."

"Maybe, but we have to be careful."

"I will be. You look great."

"You're looking fine yourself. Now get out of here before I lose all self-control."

He stood up and brushed her leg with his hand. It wasn't as casual as he had intended, and it sent a vibration all through his body. He felt every muscle tighten to fight the urge to pull her to her feet and kiss her. Part of him wanted to hold her so badly, he would have started basic training all over again just to smell her skin and feel her breath on his cheek. But he fought his desire and walked stiffly away from her.

Two more weeks felt like an eternity.

CHAPTER 11

FELICITY MARS

Seeing Blake was the catalyst that got her through the final two weeks of training. She wasn't the only person to struggle with the routine, and it didn't help much when word came out about their graduation day with its subsequent leave: It wasn't much. They were graduating early in the morning and would then have twenty-four hours of liberty, from noon to noon. When they got back to the Magellan Corporation complex after that, they would immediately start their four weeks of specialized training.

With only a few days left of basic training, Felicity was summoned to the auditorium in the admin building. She was the only recruit in Lima platoon to be called, but there were recruits from other units there as well, thirty-six all together. They filled the two rows near the stage.

There was no hologram at the meeting. A tall woman with a muscular build entered, followed by two men. They were all officers. The men were both captains, but the woman was a major. She stepped to the front while her companions waited by the stage.

"Good afternoon," she said, giving the recruits a moment to quiet down. "I am Major Hera Tarantino, recon commander of Project Fortuna. With me are captains Sullivan and Choi. You've been summoned here because you have special skills that would be of use to us. We're forming two recon platoons, and we'd like you to volunteer."

A hand went up a few seats down from where Felicity was sitting. Major Tarantino nodded to the recruit.

"May I ask what recon is, Major?"

"That's an excellent question," Tarantino said. "Recon is short for reconnaissance, which is essentially a preliminary survey to gather intelligence. In a military setting, and for our purposes, the recon platoons will be the first humans on the newly discovered planet in the Fortuna system. We will scout locations for the colony. Orbital scans and imagery can only tell us so much—we need boots on the ground. Once the colony location is selected, recon will continue to make exploratory ventures.

"If you're looking to stand guard or patrol the colony, recon is not for you. We are the tip of the spear, the vanguard of any combat operations. We go in first and we take the most risks, but it's never boring. I've been leading recon platoons for a decade. Trust me when I tell you that recon is where you want to be. We have the best weapons and the finest personnel in the MCM. We're inviting you to join us."

Felicity was impressed. She liked the idea of being in an elite unit where her skills would be appreciated. Most of her platoon were just killing time, doing whatever they had to in order to get to a colony. She had learned from basic training that doing the same thing day after day wasn't in her nature.

She needed variety, and it seemed as if the recon platoon would allow her that.

"Let me be clear," Major Tarantino continued. "Recon training is the hardest. We aren't preparing you to stand watch over a shipment of food or to help distribute supplies. You won't be patrolling the colony on Friday nights. We will be escorting scientific teams that will be studying the colony world or protecting engineers working to bring vital resources to the colony. You will have to be in the best shape of your life —not just at graduation, but for the entire enlistment period. We carry heavy weapons and survival gear. We carry out rescue operations and investigate reports of close encounters with native animal life. I expect the very best from you on every mission, with absolutely no excuses."

Her warnings may have been discouraging to some people, but the major was speaking Felicity's language. She didn't know how Blake would feel about her joining recon, but she had no doubts about herself.

"You will all go through recon training together," Tarantino said, "and then split into recon platoons Alpha and Bravo. Are there any questions?"

There were a few questions, but they weren't consequential. Someone asked if the recon units paid more. They didn't. Someone else asked if they got better food. Felicity was only half-listening. She didn't care about the pay, the food, if they got preferential treatment for taking more risk, or if they would be of greater rank than the other recruits. She was ready to move on from training and actually do something.

When the meeting ended, all thirty-six recruits agreed to join the recon program. Felicity wanted to tell Blake that she had been selected. Not being able to share her excitement with him was one of the hardest aspects of their time apart, but she reassured herself that soon it would change. They were only a couple days from graduation, and then things would be better. At the very least, she and Blake would have twenty-four hours to be together, and she knew just how she wanted to spend it.

"Recon?" Staff Sergeant Kiev asked. "That's elite. Congratulations!"

"Thanks," Felicity said as they rolled from one position to another on the grappling mat.

Staff Sergeant Anna Kiev had paired everyone up and ordered them to practice their jiu-jitsu grappling. Felicity was the only recruit who could give the staff sergeant a challenge.

"Don't let it go to your head," Kiev said, pushing down on Felicity's thigh in the hope of getting her one leg free and moving into side control.

Felicity was on the bottom and had both of her legs wrapped around the staff sergeant's left leg. She waited, holding her superior tight until Kiev tried to jerk her leg free. When she did, Felicity released her and bucked her hips upward. The move sent Kiev off-balance and too far toward Felicity's head. The younger woman slipped out from beneath the staff sergeant and flung herself onto Kiev's back. She wrapped one arm around Kiev's neck, but the staff sergeant tucked her chin down to avoid being choked.

Felicity was firmly on Kiev's back, who was on her hands and knees. Felicity wrapped her legs around the staff sergeant and hooked her feet under the older woman's thighs. Kiev tried to throw Felicity off her back. She bucked and simultaneously dropped her head toward the mat. The momentum was enough to make Felicity slip forward a little, but not enough to get Kiev free. Felicity slipped her free arm under Kiev's armpit, giving her an anchor but not progressing the chokehold. The staff sergeant made a sudden change of tactics; she flopped to the side and rolled onto her back, putting all her weight on Felicity and freeing both of her arms to fight off the younger woman's attack. She focused on Felicity's right arm that was wrapped around the staff sergeant's neck. She pulled it straight and tried to use her shoulder as a fulcrum to bend the arm backwards at the elbow. But Felicity was ready for the move. Whenever Kiev tried to pull her arm straight, Felicity rotated her arm to keep from getting her elbow in a bind.

Slipping her legs up and over the staff sergeant's hips, Felicity hooked her left foot under her right knee, so that her legs were completely encircling her superior's midsection. Then she tightened her legs, using the muscles built from years of running stairwells. She could hear Kiev struggling to draw in a breath. At that moment, she pulled her arms free and arched her back, tightening her legs even further. Kiev did the most natural thing in the world: she put her hands on Felicity's legs and pushed down, trying to relieve the pressure that was making it hard for her to breathe. She pushed down hard, and as she did her head lifted up. Felicity's arms shot forward like a deadly serpent. One arm hooked under Kiev's chin and grabbed hold of the bicep of her other arm, which she folded behind the staff sergeant's head. As one arm pulled up into Kiev's throat, the other pressed down on the back of her head, cutting off her air supply completely.

Staff Sergeant Kiev fought desperately to break free for a moment—and then tapped Felicity's arm. Instantly the younger woman released her. Kiev rolled to the side, untangling from the young recruit.

"You get me...every time," Kiev said.

"I've had lots of practice," Felicity admitted.

"You'll make a good recon soldier. Just be careful. If there's any trouble out there, recon always finds it."

The staff sergeant's words were supposed to be a warning, but to Felicity they were an invitation to excitement. She was ready to begin the recon training and couldn't wait to share the news with her husband.

CHAPTER 12

BLAKE CAGE

Graduation was held in the auditorium. Cage guessed that a quarter of the initial group was gone. No one in his platoon had failed basic, but a few had been released after their bodies broke down. It wasn't a judgement against them; they just didn't have the strength and capacity to work their bodies hard day after day. And it was no surprise that a few people from each platoon had been rejected or forced to leave the program. Those that remained looked strong and ready for just about anything.

"I guess we're through slumming it with the enlisted personnel," Lyla said as she settled down into the seat beside Cage.

"That's not how I would put it," he replied.

"Oh, I know," Lyla said, as if he were a simpleton. "I didn't mean to upset your delicate sensibilities."

"You should take this more seriously," Cage said. "We're no better than the enlisted personnel. We're not officers yet, and we may not be. We still have to complete OTS."

"Don't remind me. More training. Sometimes it feels like it will never end."

Cage ignored her. Lyla had done the least amount of work to get by. After dropping out of the marathon run on the very first day, she had developed a chip on her shoulder, as if she were too good to be training with everyone else. He hated to think of her being in charge of other people, but that wasn't his decision to make. Instead of worrying about Lyla, he searched the auditorium for Felicity.

The recruits had spent their last few days of basic training getting ready for their one day off. Cage had gotten his hair cut again. He was beginning to like the buzz cut. That—along with the added muscle he had developed over the past two months—made him look tougher than he'd thought possible. His face was harder and more angular, his chin more pronounced. He wanted to see Felicity, and not just from a distance. They needed to break away from their peers and meet up. He didn't care where, just so long as he could be with her as much as possible in the time they had off.

"You know, when this is over, we could get out of here. Go someplace private," Lyla said. "What are you looking for?"

"Nothing," Cage said.

"What, do you have a boyfriend in here or something?"

"No," Cage said, trying to engage with Lyla as little as possible.

"Good, I don't need the competition. So, what do you say? Me and you, all alone," she said, running her finger down his arm. "We could have a good time."

"I've got plans," Cage said.

"What is with you? Are you religious or something?"

"This isn't a hustle for me," Cage said.

"And you think it is for me?"

"You broke the rules."

"So what? We're not just enlisted riffraff. Their rules don't apply to officers."

"I'm just not interested, okay?" Cage finally said.

"Your loss," Lyla said.

She turned in her seat, trying to get away from him, and he knew he had made an enemy. But he didn't know what else to do. Cage didn't like disappointing or hurting people, but he wasn't going to try and soothe Lyla Drucker's ego. She already thought she was upper class, even though she had seduced over half of Zebra platoon. It didn't make sense to Cage, but she obviously got some sort of ego boost by convincing men to be intimate with her. Cage doubted she even enjoyed it. It seemed as if she thought all men only wanted one thing from her. She treated her partners like conquests, and Cage was determined not to be one.

The lights dimmed and a spotlight came on as General Haley walked across the stage. Someone with a commanding voice shouted loud enough to be heard all through the auditorium. "Ten-hut! Commander on deck!"

Everyone jumped to their feet and immediately stiffened to attention as the general took his place behind a wooden podium. He cleared his throat, then said softly, "You may be seated."

Everyone sat down. Cage felt his excitement building. He was proud of what he'd accomplished in basic training. He had learned a lot and risen to every challenge, thanks in no small part to Felicity's love of exercise. Yet it wasn't just completing basic training or starting officer training that had his heart beating faster; it was knowing that he would soon be with Felicity again.

"You have all completed your basic training. Congratulations," the general said, pausing while the recruits clapped and cheered.

Cage was reminded of high school. Graduating wasn't so much an accomplishment of effort or even intellect as much as it was of perseverance. The general gave the recruits a moment to celebrate, then raised his hand to quiet them down. When the crowd hushed, he continued.

"You are all now officially part of the MCM mission to the Fortuna system. First deployments begin in four weeks. From this day forward, you are all officially privates in the militia."

He waited as more cheering erupted.

"When you return here tomorrow, by 1200 hours at the very latest, you will begin training in your specialized areas. I urge you to focus your mind on the task at hand and give it all your effort. When we leave the Sol system, we will be entering uncharted territory. Such an endeavor is never without risk. As I look around this room, I realize that even if everything goes smoothly, some of you will not survive the initial enlistment period. Mistakes cost lives, people. Let's be professional and ensure that we make as few mistakes as possible.

"From this point forward, you will all have a little more freedom. Your time off will be your own. If you choose to spend it off of MCM property, keep in mind that you are still under contract. Trouble with the law will not be tolerated. Arriving late to your assigned classes and exercises will result in financial penalties and increased PT, regardless of the reason or excuses. Failure to show up for your assigned classes will result in immediate dismissal from the MCM.

"We are embarking on an historic venture, and you are all

a vital part of it. We need you. We need for you to be at your very best. It is time to enjoy the fruit of your labors and return ready to give one hundred percent to the role you've been selected for. Welcome to the Magellan Corporation family. Be safe. I'll see you all back here at precisely 1200 hours."

There was a whoop of joy from the graduating class of recruits. Cage would have to stop thinking of them as recruits; they were all privates in the militia now, and soon they would be leaving Earth and everyone they knew behind to carve out a new life on a distant planet. That thought made him feel small and completely insignificant.

Finding Felicity was impossible in the crowd, and even if he managed to spot her, he wouldn't be able to join her without attracting attention. So he filed out with the other graduates. Unlike Felicity, Cage had earned a salary while completing his basic training. It wasn't riches, since housing, clothing, and food were all considered part of his pay, but there was enough to pay for a night in a hotel.

Travel wasn't something most people did. It cost money to spend time away from their government-subsidized housing. Travel required money, and only a small percentage of the population could afford it, but there were still hotels. Most were run-down buildings that offered temporary housing. But Cage had done a little research. The Excelsior was only twenty minutes away by train. He went directly to the depot along with most of the graduates who crowded onto the platform. While his peers crowded close to the loading zone, Cage hung back. He was waiting and watching for Felicity. She appeared in the crowd and made his heart skip a beat.

He joined the throng behind her and waited until she boarded the train. He made sure to get on the same crowded train car but stayed close to the door. It didn't take Felicity long to spot him. She was with a group of girls. Most of the passengers got off on the first few stops, and when the train reached the area closest to the Excelsior, Cage stood up and moved to the doorway much sooner than he needed to. Felicity didn't move until the train came to a complete stop, then she followed the other passengers exiting the train.

The hard part was not looking back. Cage knew she would follow him and catch up when she felt safe. He walked at a casual pace, leaving the train station and strolling through the crowded street toward a tall, dark building.

"Where are we going?" Felicity said as she came up beside him.

"The Excelsior," Cage said.

"A hotel?"

"We can afford it," he said. "One night, room service, the works. Consider it the honeymoon we never had."

"It sounds extraordinary," she said.

The hotel was old, but that came as no surprise. The lobby was filled with antique furnishings that no one was sitting on. Music played from hidden speakers just loud enough to be heard over the gentle splash of a small fountain that was the centerpiece of the hotel lobby. Cage walked directly to the front desk and showed the clerk his Magellan ID.

"I'd like a room for the night," he said.

"Of course, sir," the woman manning the desk said. "Just one guest?"

"Two," Cage said, as Felicity stepped up beside him.

"We have a free upgrade for Magellan employees," the woman said as she scanned his card. "If you need anything, please use the intercom in your room."

"Thank you," Cage said.

He was so anxious that his hands were trembling slightly as he took the keycard she slid across the counter toward him.

"Enjoy your stay at the Excelsior," the clerk said.

Cage didn't reply. He was already pulling his wife toward the elevators, intent on making the most of their short window of liberty.

CHAPTER 13

FELICITY MARS

She began recon training a happy woman. Twenty-four hours with her husband had made a world of difference, and she launched into PT with her thirty-five classmates with gusto. Felicity had feared that Blake might not like that she had signed up for the recon platoon. Instead, he had celebrated her accomplishment with her and spent their time telling her how proud he was.

After a full routine of PT, the recon class was taken to the firing range and given a new weapon by their instructor, Master Sergeant O'Reilly. He was a big man with a black eyepatch that covered his left eye. The eyepatch was surrounded by pale white scar tissue that pinched the skin on his cheekbone and gave him a perpetual sneer.

"This is the Magellan Infiltrator," O'Reilly said, holding a heavy-looking assault rifle. "It's a dual weapon, with a tight-beam laser generator above a short-range plasma launcher. For the next four weeks, you will come to know and love this weapon like it's your sweetheart, because in the bush, it may be the only thing standing between you and a grisly death."

He began handing out the rifles. Felicity was used to handling weapons after weeks of basic training. She took one of the Infiltrators and began looking it over.

"He paints a vivid picture," Samantha Jones said.

"It looks like he knows that of which he speaks," Devon Al'Farrah added.

The trio had bonded on their morning run. Felicity didn't like pacing herself to ensure that everyone kept up. She had long, strong legs that liked a big stride. Sam and Devon were the only other members of the class who even tried to keep up with her.

"It's rugged," Felicity said, referring to the weapon.

"Simple," Master Sergeant O'Reilly declared. "The laser generator is self-contained. Drop it in the water, throw it off a cliff, carry it through a sandstorm, and it still works. The only weakness in its design is right here."

He pressed a tiny button on the side of the rifle, just under the scope. The laser generator popped off, and he held it up. There were two silver diodes on the bottom side.

"This is the power conduit. It has to be cleaned regularly to ensure good contact," the master sergeant said. "Battery acid will ruin the laser's ability to fire. You will check and clean this connect every single day."

"Yes, Master Sergeant!" the class replied in unison.

"Above the laser is a Pendleton all-terrain optics scope. It has night vision, thermal, and will zoom to one hundred times its natural magnification. It's also the most vulnerable piece of hardware you will carry. I suggest you keep it stored in a safe place when you don't need it."

The master sergeant removed the scope and put it in the

pocket of his fatigue shirt. The entire class followed suit. Their sweatpants and T-shirts had been traded for gray and brown fatigues. Felicity wore an undershirt beneath the bulky fatigues. The pants were stretchy and form-fitting with cargo pockets on the front thighs. The fatigue shirt was almost like a smock. It hung on her, the sleeves too big, the shirt tail hanging well past her waste. It felt more like a lightweight jacket than a shirt. The material was a synthetic that was designed to retard penetration. It was water-resistant and while not bulletproof, it would stop a knife or the bite of an animal.

The fatigue top had several pockets, and Felicity removed the scope and put it into one of the pockets. The master sergeant had turned his rifle upright so that the class could see the lower barrel.

"This is a simple, mechanical firing system," O'Reilly declared. "Its design has been used since firearms were invented."

He held up a plasma cartridge. It was encased in a hard plastic shell the size of Felicity's thumb.

"Inside this shell is a delicate cartridge that degrades quickly from friction in the air or impact. Once the airtight cartridge is compromised, the gas inside is triggered by a chemical reaction through contact with oxygen. It then expands exponentially and rapidly, producing a tremendous amount of heat in the process. A person hit with one will be burned to death, his flesh boiled to atoms, his bones reduced to ash. Let's go try it out."

They spent the first half of the day training with the Magellan Infiltrator. They fired them, cleaned them, took them apart, put them back together, and did it all over and over again. By lunch time, Felicity felt like an expert. She wasn't the fastest member of the class to disassemble and reassemble the rifle, but she could do it with her eyes closed.

In the afternoon, the class was split into two groups. Captain Choi took one group, and Captain Sullivan the other. They began explaining and demonstrating formations used in the recon exercises.

"You can march," Sullivan said, "but you can't march through heavy foliage in the bush. Recon platoons must be able to move silently through any terrain. At times, we run the risk of being caught out on patrol with no backup. In those instances, a recon platoon must fight together with the strength of an entire battalion. Finally, in the rare instances where our team is spotted by the enemy, we must understand the concepts of escape and evade to get safely back to the main body of troops. We have one week to learn each of these techniques, and by the end of recon training you will be ready to carry out whatever orders Major Tarantino gives us."

Later that same day the class was divided into small groups. Some were assigned to vehicle training. Recon had armored platoon carriers for long-range missions. The carriers were essentially a box on repulsors with weapons and supplies. A platoon could be transported by connecting their battle armor to the sides of the carrier. Others were trained to become HeWEs—Heavy Weapons Experts. They carried large repeating cannons that were mounted on harnesses to make them easier to carry. There were snipers, troopers, and radio operators too. Felicity was in the smallest group that was designated as scouts.

Her scouting instructor was a staff sergeant with gray hair and dark skin. He was short and thin, and Felicity could tell just by the way he moved that in the right circumstances, he was a ghost. Her father had similar movements—a grace to the way he walked, with no wasted motion and precision in every step.

"Being a scout is more than just forging ahead of the platoon," Staff Sergeant Prater explained. "You must move carefully, observe everything, and become one with your environment."

They practiced walking quietly in various terrains, making camouflage from whatever was native to their surroundings, and precise reporting. The weeks flew by in a blur. The Magellan property had converted several old hangars into unique terrain simulations. The first time Felicity stepped into one of the habitats as the hangars were called, she was floored by all the greenery. She had lived her life surrounded by concrete, glass, and steel. She had never seen a real tree or even a grassy field apart from television and movie portrayals.

They hiked through the habitats, sometimes in platoon groups, other times just with their specialist teams. There were only four scouts, two for each platoon. Basic training had been taxing, but recon school was grueling. They worked sixteen hours a day and fell into their bunks exhausted each night. When the training was finally over, Felicity was trained to kill with ruthless efficiency. She could also move into an area, identify the targets, give an accurate report, and disappear without the enemy even knowing she had been there.

In many ways, she felt like her father had been training her to be a recon scout her entire life.

CHAPTER 14

BLAKE CAGE

Unlike his wife's training, OTS was much easier than basic training. It was all done in the classroom—three hours in the morning and three in the afternoon. He was done every day before dinner, and even the book work was simple. At least, in Cage's opinion it was easy. He had studied military history in his online university classes and already had a working knowledge of most of the battles the officers in training studied in their strategy and tactics classes. They also studied logistics and management. Cage had a good memory and soaked up the information like a dry sponge. His classmates weren't as fortunate.

Cage had no idea how the others were selected for officer training, but he could tell they weren't scholars. Only a few even had a passing interest in the material. There were times when Cage was the only student engaged in the lectures. Lyla was the worst performer of the group; she hated the class work and spent most of her time complaining. There was no PT element to OTS—they were expected to keep up their physical fitness on their own. Cage spent each morning running, and when the classes wrapped up at 1500 hours, he utilized the weight training area. Exercise was an excellent way to burn off the excess energy he had after sitting in a climate-controlled classroom all day. It also helped relieve the stress of not getting to see his wife.

He did occasionally see Felicity, but she was usually hurrying to a training exercise on another part of the base. Her PT was often complete before he even got out of bed, and the recon class ate their lunch and dinner in the field, just as they would on assignment. One day, during the final week of his OTS, as Cage was preparing to head to the mess hall for lunch, the tablet computer he'd been assigned beeped with a priority message. The tablets acted as reading, video, and writing devices. They didn't have access to the internet or messages outside the MCM, but his classmates could send him notes. So far he had never gotten a message from anyone other than his teachers.

The message was simple enough: He was ordered to report to Major Tarantino's office in the admin building. They had an hour for lunch, but Cage rarely spent more than ten minutes eating his midday meal and saw no reason why he shouldn't go straight to the major's office. While his classmates shuffled off to the mess hall, Cage went to the admin building. It took him only a few minutes to find the major's office, and she didn't keep him waiting.

"Ensign Cage, it's nice to meet you," Major Tarantino said. She didn't have a secretary or assistant and opened the door to her office herself.

"Thank you, Major," Cage said.

"Have a seat," she said, waving him to a chair.

It was just a simple, plastic chair. The office was small.

There were no plaques or awards on the walls—just a desk, computer, the major's chair, and two guest chairs. Cage sat down and the major sat beside him on the same side of her desk.

"I've been going over your coursework," Tarantino said. "You've gotten excellent marks, and your teachers are impressed with your effort and attitude."

"Thank you—that's good to hear, Major," Cage replied.

"Have you thought about what you want to do when you finish OTS?"

"I wasn't aware I had a choice."

"Well, there are several areas of need within the Fortuna project. That's where you've committed yourself for the first five years. After that you'll have more opportunities if you remain in the MCM. For now, I'd like you to consider helping me with recon platoon Bravo."

"Recon?" Cage said, caught off guard.

"That's right. You'll be a second lieutenant when you finish OTS, and recon will require you to do some catch-up, but we like to have two officers with every recon platoon. The Fortuna project will have two, Alpha and Bravo."

"So I'd be working with another officer?"

"Yes. Captain Walter Sullivan is the CO of Bravo platoon. He's solid, and you'd learn a lot. Recon is an important part of the militia. We take only the best. From what I've seen, that's you, Cage. What do you say?"

Cage forced himself to hesitate. He was ready to say yes the moment he heard the word "recon." All he wanted was to be near Felicity, and working as an officer in her specialty would be the perfect opportunity.

"I accept," Cage said. "And thank you for the opportunity, Major."

She smiled and sat back in her chair. He hadn't realized how much she was hoping he would say yes. It was a little surprising, but he didn't think it was bad. She needed someone and was hoping for a volunteer rather than a consignment, he told himself. But it didn't feel right just the same.

"Good. I'll be sending you extra reading material to get you up to speed on our jargon and tactics. We'll have two days before we're sent up to the convoy. We'll use that time to run you through a crash course in recon weapons and tactics. That will cut your liberty down to just one day before we leave Earth. I hope that's okay."

"That's fine, Major."

"Good man. Then I'll see you on graduation day, Cage. Welcome aboard."

They stood up, shook hands, and Cage left the major's office. He walked out of the meeting feeling strange. So much was happening so fast, and yet Cage felt as if the separate pieces of his life were coming together. He and Felicity would both be in the recon platoons, which meant they would leave Earth together.

As part of his officer training, he had been briefed on the specifics of the Fortuna project. They were going to a planet that was being called Magnificus Prime. The initial results of the survey done by unmanned probes was that the fourth planet in the Fortuna system wasn't just in the Goldilocks zone; it was a vibrant planet with liquid water, breathable atmosphere, and indications that it was immediately habitable. No terraforming was required—all they had to do was establish a colony and let it grow. That was excellent news for the militia. Their allotment of land upon completion of their enlistment period would be much more valuable than on a world that might take decades to develop optimal living conditions.

There would be a convoy of ships leaving Earth and arriving in the Fortuna system. The first would be a ship with supplies and both recon platoons. The other ships would arrive later on a carefully planned schedule. Cage had worried that with Felicity on the recon vessel, he might be assigned to a ship arriving much later. He didn't want to spend weeks, maybe even months without her. Even once they were both in the system, there was no guarantee that they would be in the same vicinity. It was possible that he could be assigned to a ship in orbit while she was on the planet, and they might have never seen each other.

But his new assignment to the recon platoon eliminated his worry. He would be with—or at least near—his wife, hopefully for the duration of their enlistment.

Unlike basic training, which only required participation, officer training ended with a series of tests. Some were simple enough, but others more demanding, such as the strategy and tactics test. Cage and the other ensigns spent their final few days of OTS studying for the examinations. The morning of their graduation was taken up with a short ceremony. A single gold bar was pinned to the collar of his shirt, and he was officially a second lieutenant in the MCM. General Haley gave them three days of liberty before returning to begin work on the Fortuna project, which was scheduled to launch in one week's time.

"Congratulations, lieutenant," Major Tarantino said as the little ceremony ended.

They were in a small room inside the admin building. There were large silver coffee pots and finger foods on a buffet table, mostly sweets. Cage guessed that the officers attending were just those who'd happened to be in the building when the ceremony was announced. No family was present, and no grand speeches were given—just a few words from the general about duty and honor. Most of the attendees were more interested in the buffet than the newly commissioned officers.

Major Tarantino had ignored the food and gone straight to Cage. She was all business, but Cage respected that. Reconnaissance was a difficult and sometimes dangerous affair. Recon platoons Alpha and Bravo would be the first humans setting foot on Magnificus Prime. He liked thinking the troopers would be all business, just like Tarantino.

"Thank you, Major," Cage replied.

"You finished top of your class," Tarantino went on, speaking quietly, "and kept up your PT. I respect that. Not everyone shares your sense of responsibility."

She glanced over to where his classmates had joined the other officers around the buffet table. There was a look of disgust on her face. Cage wasn't sure what to say. He knew most of his fellow graduates were just celebrating their good fortune, but he also knew that he didn't want them by his side in a fight.

Cage didn't like violence, but he had been in his share of conflicts. One thing he loved most about Felicity was that she didn't shy away from danger. She was just as strong as he was and a much more highly skilled fighter. Cage had approached his training in the MCM the way he thought she would.

"Do you need to do anything before I take you over to the recon training area?" Tarantino asked.

"No, Major," Cage said. "I'm ready."

She nodded. "I knew you would be. Let's get out of here, and I'll introduce you to you to Captain Sullivan."

CHAPTER 15

FELICITY MARS

Felicity was with her platoon mates. She had just been assigned to recon platoon Bravo, and they were prepping gear in the equipment room. Everything was being checked and cleaned before being packed away for their eighteen-year journey to the Fortuna system, but spirits were high. They had been promised seventy-two hours of liberty: one last hurrah on planet Earth before going aboard an interstellar spaceship and being put into cryogenic sleep that would keep them from aging on the eighteen-year journey to a new solar system.

"Three days," Porter Bailey said, handing her a portable solar recharger. "You got plans in the real world, Mars?"

Her platoon mates had quickly begun using her last name when they saw how proficient she was in hand-to-hand combat. Porter Bailey was the other scout in Bravo platoon. A tall, thin boy of nineteen, he had been a dancer and could move through almost any environment without making any noise.

"Seeing my family," she said. "You?"

"My folks wrote me off the minute I enlisted," Bailey said. "I'll be seeing some old friends, though."

"Here's the last of the spare battery packs," Samantha Jones said. "Is that everything?"

Felicity looked at the hard case—it was full. She closed the lid.

"Looks like it," Felicity said. "We can check with Captain Sullivan, but we should be done."

They flipped the latches on the hard case and started toward the tiny office where Captain Sullivan was working. There were already several people standing outside the small room. A window allowed the occupants to see what was going on in the equipment room and vice-versa.

"What's going on?" Porter asked.

"New blood," Grant Laubin said.

"Gotta be the new officer," Samantha replied. "I heard the captains talking about it."

There were three people in the room. The window had blinds that made it difficult to see through, but Felicity moved until she could see enough. Her breath caught in her throat. Not normally given to reactions people would describe as girly, she almost squealed with delight.

"There's going to be a new officer?" Porter asked.

"A second lieutenant," Grant said. "Probably won't know what he's doing half the time."

Felicity fought the urge to defend her man. Somehow Blake had managed to get them in the MCM, earn a commission, and still join her in the recon division. If that didn't reveal how driven and capable he was, nothing did. But she couldn't tell anyone. She couldn't even act excited or risk giving away the fact that they were more than mere acquaintances.

The door to the office opened, and the group stepped back. More of the platoon had gathered outside the office, and the rest were still working on loading weapons and gear to be hauled up to their ship in orbit.

"Officer on deck!" Staff Sergeant Wyatt Dole shouted.

The entire room stiffened immediately to attention.

"At ease," Major Tarantino said as she stepped out of the office.

Felicity could feel her heart hammering in her chest as Blake followed the major and the captain out of the little room. He looked dashing in his fatigues, which were different from the clothes the recon platoon was wearing. He had khaki pants, polished shoes, and a simple, gray button-up shirt with short sleeves. On his shirt collar was a golden bar signifying his rank as second lieutenant. Felicity wanted to throw her arms around his neck and smother him in kisses, but she did her best to seem completely uninterested. The only reaction she couldn't hold in check was the tears stinging her eyes. She was proud of her man.

"Bravo platoon," Captain Sullivan said. "This is Second Lieutenant Blake Cage. He's joining us and will spend the next two days learning how we do things. I need three volunteers to help."

Felicity wanted to jump at the chance, but she also wanted her three days off—and she didn't want to appear too anxious.

When no one replied, Major Tarantino added, "I have an extra two thousand credits for any volunteers."

Felicity elbowed Samantha Jones, who glanced at her and nodded. They both raised their hands as the same time.

"We'll volunteer," Sammy said.

"Excellent," Captain Sullivan said. "Anyone else? You can volunteer or I can assign you."

"I will volunteer, Captain," Devon Al'Farrah said.

"That's three," Tarantino said. "You're all immediately promoted to corporal in the MCM. I'll have your bonus checks waiting for you in the admin office by end of day."

Tarantino said something quietly to Blake; Felicity couldn't hear what it was. The room was buzzing with quiet murmurs. Most of the other troopers wandered away as Devon joined Sammy and Felicity next to Staff Sergeant Dole.

"Are you all finished loading your equipment?" Dole asked.

"Yes, staff sergeant," they all replied.

"Very good. Lieutenant Cage is already familiar with the makeup of recon platoons, but we need to practice formation movements," the staff sergeant explained. "Lieutenant Cage, this is corporal Al'Farrah, our sniper."

"Pleasure," Blake said, shaking Devon's hand.

"Corporal Mars is one of our scouts," Dole continued making the introductions. "And Corporal Jones is a trooper."

"Call me Sammy," Samantha said. "Everyone does."

"Sammy, got it," Cage said.

"All right, let's get on over to the habitat building and get started," the staff sergeant said. "We're burning daylight."

They left the equipment room and started for the habitat building. Captain Sullivan and Cage stayed behind so that he could get out of his officer uniform and into recon fatigues before joining them.

"At least he's cute," Sammy said.

"I am not sure that is an appropriate observation," Al'Farrah said. "He is our superior."

"A cute superior," Sammy said. "He can order me around any day."

Felicity felt herself blushing. She'd never heard anyone talk about Blake so openly. Of course she thought he was handsome, but she didn't know how to respond. Fortunately, Staff Sergeant Dole spoke before she got the chance.

"My experience is that most officers aren't worth the time," he said in his southern drawl. "They shuffle through recon pretty quick."

"Is that common?" Felicity said.

"Oh yeah," Dole explained. "Officers get promoted and assigned to other units or even sent back to Earth all the time. If the lieutenant is even halfway competent, he'll be out of here in six months or less."

"Six months is plenty of time," Sammy said.

"You joke too much," Devon said. "You are a corporal now."

"Oh yes, I need to set an example for the platoon," Sammy teased.

Felicity was speechless. She had been excited for Blake when he'd been selected to become an officer, and she was thrilled that he had found a way to join her recon platoon. But if what Staff Sergeant Dole said was true, she feared he might be promoted and sent back to Earth. She didn't want to be apart from him for the next five years, but if he was sent back, they would be separated for half a lifetime.

She had known early on in their relationship that he was the one for her. It didn't matter that they had different backgrounds or even different colored skin. He was smart, loyal, and mentally strong. She had always imagined them building a life together. He was her best friend as well as her lover, and she didn't want them to be apart. Her mouth felt dry, and a knot formed in her stomach.

"All right," Dole said as they approached the habitat. "We've got about five minutes to get everything set up. Al'Farrah, turn on the fog generator while Mars, Sammy, and I set up the check points and trip wires."

"Yes, Staff Sergeant," Devon said.

When Captain Sullivan arrived at the habitat building with Blake, everything was ready. The old hangar was filled with dense foliage that mimicked a rain forest. Just inside the doorway, there was enough room to stage a platoon. They spent the first hour going over formations so that Blake could see and understand how a recon platoon maneuvered through unfamiliar territory. Then they spent two more hours on exercises. First Blake was just one of the troopers, but it didn't take long until he was giving the orders.

Felicity welcomed the exercises. She needed something to focus on other than the possibility of Blake leaving her. To everyone's surprise except for Felicity, Blake picked everything up quickly. After their maneuvering exercises, Sammy volunteered to take Blake to the gun range and teach him all there was to know about the Magellan Infiltrator. It was midday, so Felicity and Devon were sent to fetch lunch for the group.

"You do not like our new lieutenant?" Devon asked as they walked across the Magellan Corporation complex of buildings toward the mess hall.

"What makes you say that?" Felicity asked.

"You have been very quiet with your opinions. It is not like you."

"I guess I don't really know what to think," Felicity said.

It was an honest answer. She felt both worried that Blake might leave and fiercely protective of him at the same time. Sammy was her closest friend, and yet she was suddenly jealous of her. It didn't seem fair that Sammy could talk openly about her feelings for Blake but Felicity couldn't.

"He seems capable," Devon said. "A very fast learner."

"He is," Felicity said, then immediately wished she hadn't. She was speaking from her past knowledge, but fortunately, Devon thought she was going on the past three hours and what she had seen in their recon maneuvers.

"I think we are lucky to have him," Devon went on. "He had no sense of superiority, I think. Where I am from, a teachable person is wise."

"I get that," Felicity said. "I guess I'm just having trouble trusting him at the moment."

The thought of Sammy shamelessly flirting with Blake flashed in her mind. Sammy wasn't Blake's type, but she wasn't unattractive. She had sandy brown hair and a round face with freckles across her nose. Blake didn't like freckles, she suddenly remembered, feeling a little less out of sorts.

"It will come in time, never fear," Devon said.

"I'm probably just regretting that we didn't take our leave," Felicity said. "It's hard to think about everyone else having fun."

"We will have the last laugh, I think" Devon replied. "We have the bonus and a promotion in rank. A little discipline now will pay off in the long run, will it not?"

"Yeah, sure," Felicity said. "I know you're right. Just ignore me. I'll shake off this funk I'm in. Probably just hungry, is all."

"I believe the term is 'hangry,'" Devon with a chuckle.

Felicity tried to laugh with him, but it wasn't sincere. She tried to be happy, but for some reason she couldn't. The truth was, she was sick of pretending she didn't know Blake. And perhaps seeing him every day and being in the same platoon with him would be even harder, if that was possible. Something needed to change—and soon—or she felt like she was going to lose her mind.

CHAPTER 16

BLAKE CAGE

That evening, Cage was assigned a temporary berth in the officer's housing building. After training all day he was exhausted, but he was also relieved to have seen Felicity. He had thrown caution to the wind and volunteered for scout training, knowing that she would be given the charge to show the newly commissioned second lieutenant the basics. He had easily avoided Corporal Jones' flirtations. She was friendly and in many ways hilarious, but subtlety was not a skill she possessed. Even if Cage hadn't been a faithful husband, Sammy simply wasn't his type.

After learning to use the Infiltrator, which was a superior weapon to most of the firearms he'd used in basic training, they had spent the afternoon going over the different specialties of a recon platoon. Cage would be the second radio operator, but he needed a familiarity with every position, weapon, and piece of equipment. After three hours practicing with the radio and satellite equipment, he was ready to move.

"Corporal Mars will show you the ropes," Staff Sergeant

Dole had said. "Nothing too heavy, Mars. We don't want to lose our new LT."

"Yes, Staff Sergeant," Felicity had replied.

"Scouting takes a certain physical skill set that most people don't have," Dole continued explaining to Cage. "All you need to know is what Mars and our other scout Bailey are capable of."

"Roger that, Staff Sergeant," Cage said, his heart racing at the thought of being alone with Felicity.

"We'll see you back here at 1730 hours. We still need to go over the platoon. A good commander knows the strengths and weaknesses of everyone in his unit."

"I agree," Cage said. "An hour and a half. I've got it."

Felicity led the way out of the platoon's series of rooms that were used to store gear, prep for exercises, and debrief after lessons. Captain Sullivan was back in his office. Cage had to admit the captain knew his stuff, and yet it seemed he preferred to be in his office than in the field. That was okay, in Cage's opinion, but as much as he loved reading, nothing compared to being out in the field with members of the platoon and leading a combat operation.

"So," Cage said as they strolled toward the big habitat building. "How do you like recon?"

"Don't patronize me," Felicity said. She was a step ahead of him, and he recognized her vigilant gaze sweeping back and forth, on the lookout for threats.

"I didn't mean to," he said.

"Then don't talk to me like we don't know each other," she said quietly.

"Are you angry?"

"I don't know," she replied.

"I thought you'd be happy to see me," Cage said.

"I am happy to see you," she said as she opened the door to the habitat building. "Now stop talking, and let's get started."

She gave him a few pointers on how to move through the dense foliage without making noise, and then they set off. The building was huge and filled with trees and large, leafy plants. They walked deep into the foliage for several minutes before Felicity whirled around. She threw her arms around his neck and pulled him close. They kissed feverishly for several minutes. In the back of his mind Cage knew they would have to stop, but he didn't want to. He had missed her so much; her touch and kisses were like food to a starving man.

When they finally pulled apart, they were both breathing heavily but completely hidden in the dense forest inside the old hangar. It was as safe a meeting place as they could have on the Magellan Corporation property.

"How'd you do it?" Felicity asked. "Tell me you didn't make some awful deal to get assigned to recon platoon."

"I didn't," Cage said. "Major Tarantino approached me. She just offered it to me."

"Do you think they know about us?"

"No," Cage said. "I think we just got lucky."

"I don't believe in luck," Felicity said.

"Well, for whatever reason we're together now. That's all I care about."

"Blake, it's so hard. I never dreamed it would be this difficult."

"Me neither," he said, pulling her close again. "But at least we'll get to see each other every day."

"I want more than that," Felicity insisted.

"So do I," Cage replied. "Just give me some time to get the lay of the land. Then we'll figure something out."

"Staff Sergeant Dole said officers come and go from recon

all the time. He said if you're halfway competent, they'll send you back to Earth."

"They can't," Cage said. "I'll refuse. I'm not leaving you."

"Promise," she begged.

"I promise," he replied.

Leaving the habitat and Felicity was difficult, but Cage threw himself into his studies. It was late by the time he was escorted to his temporary room inside the officer's building. His mind was full with the names of and notes on each of the members of Bravo platoon. Staff Sergeant Wyatt Dole was a twelve-year vet from the Texas Metropolis who was on his third deployment. The rest of the platoon were all new enlistees, but they were the strongest candidates. He knew their names, where they were from, and what their specialties were —he had gone over all the notes in their files. Not a single one had dropped out of the marathon run on their first day, and they had all willingly volunteered for recon.

His room was small—just a bed and a locker. There was a community bathroom down the hall. He showered and shaved without seeing anyone. When he got back to his room, he checked the clock on the bedside table; he could get six hours of sleep if he was lucky. He lay down, closed his eyes, and before he knew it, his alarm was beeping. He groaned and rolled out of the little bed. The last month in OTS had spoiled him. Even with his PT and the weight-lifting program, he wasn't really prepared for the long hours and intense work preparing himself for recon.

He dressed quickly, pulling on the snug, stretchy pants that recon platoon troopers wore. His fatigue shirt crossed over his stomach like a karategi. Part of his equipment was a thick, Kevlar belt with ammo loops, a holster for a multi-tool, and a sheath for a bush knife. He strapped the belt on, laced up his boots, and pulled on the recon navy blue beret that clung to the stubble on his head. After brushing his teeth, he looked at himself in the mirror. What he saw wasn't bad. The uniform was functional, but it looked good too.

Eventually he would add a sidearm, battle armor, and a field pack, but for his last day of training, he had all he needed. The day flew by. He learned sniper skills from Devon, joined Felicity on the heavy weapons range, and then spent the afternoon learning to drive an RPC, or Recon Platoon Carrier. That night, he met with Captain Davis and the two of them pored over reports on the planet Magnificus Prime. The probe reconnaissance had done basic scans of the planet's terrain, focusing on what it deemed the most ideal areas for human colonization. Two sections had been picked out on opposite sides of a mountain range. There was abundant water, the climate was ideal, and both sites were sheltered from storms and dangers that could be reasonably assumed to exist on the planet. Alpha platoon would explore the first site, which was on the eastern side of the mountains and only a few hundred kilometers from the shore of the planet's largest ocean body. Bravo platoon would explore the second site. Once both sites had been assessed, one would be selected as the best fit for colonization, and the other recon team would head to the selected site before the first of the supply ships hit orbit and began dropping the heavy equipment necessary for clearing the land and building the colony's primary structures.

When Cage finally called it quits for the night, he was tempted to go find his wife, but they had made their plans. She was spending the night with her family. He would join her the next day, and they would say their final goodbyes before spending the last night of their leave together in a hotel near the Magellan Corporation complex. Returning to his tiny room was a bit depressing, but he was tired and knew that a good night's sleep would put him in the right frame of mind to say his goodbyes the next day. It would be an emotional day, and the best thing he could do was get his rest.

When he got to his room, however, he found the door open. He stood in the hallway, his stomach tense, wondering who could possibly be inside. When he pushed the door open, his heart dropped.

"Hello, stranger," Lyla said. "I was beginning to think you weren't ever coming home."

She was stretched across his narrow bed, propped on one elbow. She wore his recon fatigue shirt, and from the looks of things, nothing else.

"What are you doing here?" Cage asked.

"Waiting for you, of course," she said. "Recon wouldn't have been my first choice, but since you're leaving soon, I decided to give you a going away present."

She pointed at him, then patted the bed beside her.

"No," Cage said.

"Oh, come on, lieutenant. We aren't breaking any rules now."

"I'm married," Cage said.

Lyla giggled. "So? You're leaving. Your wife will move on the moment you board that ship in what, thirty-six hours? Come on, live a little."

Cage wasn't made of stone. He was a man and seeing a half-naked woman in his bed was tempting, but there was nothing about Lyla Drucker that Cage found appealing. She was crass, belittling, and without honor. He wanted nothing to do with her. As tired as he was, he knew there would be no getting her out of his room without causing a scene. The only hope he had was in out-maneuvering her.

Stepping into the room, he closed the door behind him. Lyla smiled, thinking she had won him over. Instead, Cage grabbed his bag. It already had a change of clothes inside. He slid his toiletries into the duffle and headed for the door.

"Don't you dare," Lyla hissed. "Do you have any idea what I gave up to be here tonight?"

"I'm not another conquest for you to brag about," Cage said quietly before slipping out the door and closing it behind him.

He could hear Lyla cursing him. She decried his manhood, but fortunately she wasn't loud enough to cause trouble. Cage didn't stick around for her to come after him. Instead, he hurried out of the building and headed across the complex toward the recon building. It was dark, but that was okay with Cage. He went inside, lined up some of the chairs in the briefing room, and lay down.

Sleep was beckoning him, but before he fell asleep, he couldn't help but wonder how many men had done a similar thing to his wife. Cage trusted Felicity, but the very thought of some other man trying to seduce her the way Lyla had with Cage made him angry. He didn't want to think about it, but the terrible thoughts followed him into his dreams.

CHAPTER 17

FELICITY MARS

After a bittersweet goodbye to their families, Felicity and Blake had their one last night together before reporting back to the Magellan Corporation for the Fortuna project. The hotel they stayed in had a restaurant on the roof, and they splurged on a meal late that night, sitting out on the balcony high above the noise and chaos below. The stars were dull and veiled in a haze of smog, but it was all they had ever known. They did their best to memorize all the sights, sounds, and smells of their home world. Returning to their room they lay in each other's arms, thinking about the future, and talking about the past. The hours flew by, but they both did their best to take it all in before they left the only home they had ever known for a grand adventure eighteen light years away.

Blake left the hotel early the next morning, and she hadn't seen him since reporting back. The officers seemed busy, and Staff Sergeant Dole barked orders at the platoon, getting them on the shuttle that would take them out to the launch pad on an island in the north Atlantic.

Most of her platoon mates looked bleary-eyed and sick, evidence that they had partied hard their last night on Earth.

"What'd you do?" Sammy asked her as the shuttle left the Magellan Corporation complex.

"Aren't the officers coming with us?"

"I think they already left," Sammy said.

"They will meet us on board the spacecraft," Devon said.

"So?" Sammy asked. "Did you have a good time?"

"Family," Felicity said. "I spent the night with my family."

"It was your last night on Earth, and you stayed in? You know we'll never get a chance to go to a club ever again."

"That's not my thing," Felicity said.

"Oh, hot guys and mixed drinks aren't your thing? Are you crazy?"

"She is a woman of principle," Devon said.

"I'm beginning to think she's a robot," Sammy replied.

"I'm not a robot, but I love my family. I'll never see them again."

"That's not true—I'm sure they'll send messages," Sammy said.

"That's not the same," Felicity said.

Emotions were welling up inside her, making it hard not to break down. She couldn't help but wonder where Blake was. She had thought they would be leaving together. She had thought it would be easier. Knowing that she was following her dreams and making a life for herself that she couldn't have any other way wasn't easing the pain of never seeing her parents or brothers again. Even Blake's family, as different from her own as they were, would be missed.

The shuttle was just a big, boxy transport with rows of seats, but it was the first non-public transportation Felicity had ever taken. It was more comfortable than the trains she had used for most of her life to travel through the city, and there were large windows. She watched as the shuttle cleared the city, which extended several miles from the coast out onto the ocean. Felicity wondered if Earth would eventually become one enormous city.

When the ocean appeared, dark and choppy beneath them, the platoon of recon specialists fell quiet. Most had never seen open spaces, much less a natural wonder like the ocean. Felicity thought it was beautiful. They could see for miles, and the open expanse of the sea made her feel small again, like a child.

It didn't take long to reach the area that had once been St. John's Nova Scotia. The city, along with the Avalon Wilderness Reserve, had been converted into the North Atlantic Launch Station. The shuttle set down on a small landing platform, and Staff Sergeant Dole ordered everyone out. Felicity collected her rucksack. It had everything she owned inside: her fatigues, toiletries, and the small collection of keepsakes from her family. There was even an old-fashioned photo printed on paper. Just knowing she had it made her feel a little stronger.

Recon platoons Alpha and Bravo marched across a wide, flat section of hard, packed ground. Their boots crunched on ancient concrete that had long ago crumbled into tiny fragments. In the distance they could see the Magellan ship that would carry them up into orbit to dock with the interstellar vessel, which would transport them to the Fortuna system.

The walk helped calm Felicity's nerves, but she still felt strange leaving without Blake. She had gotten used to the idea of the two of them being together. His absence was like a missing tooth. She kept looking up, expecting to see him at the head of the column of soldiers.

"This is it, I guess," Sammy said. "Goodbye, Earth."

"We are making a way for humanity to expand," Devon said. "We will be remembered in the annals of history."

"I doubt anyone is writing down our names," Porter Bailey chimed in.

"Perhaps not our names, but our deeds," Devon insisted.

"You're quiet," Sammy said to Felicity.

"I'm just thinking," Felicity said. "It's a bit more emotional than I expected."

"The woman who can break a man in half is getting emotional?" Sammy said. "I don't know why. This place sucks. You can't do anything here. Everything is old, dirty, and broken."

"But don't you feel a connection to Earth?" Felicity asked. "This is our home. It has been our home for thousands of years."

"But it is not our only home," Devon pointed. "There have been human colonies on other worlds longer than we have been alive."

"Yeah, listen to Dev," Sammy said. "This is a new world we're going to, but within a few years it will be bustling with people."

"And in five years we'll own a piece of it," Porter said.

"Your people own more than a piece of this one," Grant Laubin said.

"Yeah, well, I'm carving out my own place on the new planet," Porter said. "Something that's mine, with no strings attached."

"There's always strings attached," Sammy said. "You know the Magellan Corporation is going to make a fortune from every person that sets foot on the new world."

"At least we'll have a chance to make something for ourselves," Porter said. "Something we can be proud of."

Felicity wondered if she would be proud of the choices that she and Blake had made. Would they be happy on the new world? She couldn't imagine it being any worse than the conditions they had lived in on Earth.

"Would you look at that?" Lucinda Fuego said. "That's a big ship."

"The interstellar vessels will be even bigger," Sammy said.

"All right, enough chatter," Staff Sergeant Dole shouted. "Everyone get on board, stow your baggage, and get strapped in."

They hurried up the stairs that led to the side door of the passenger ship. Inside they found wide seats in rows. They shoved their rucksacks into the overhead bins and took their seats. When Felicity sat down, she thought the seat was hard and uncomfortable.

"This is worse than the train," Porter complained.

"It's an inertial absorbing cushion," Staff Sergeant Dole said. "Fasten your seat belt to activate it."

Felicity and the other members of recon platoon Bravo pulled the shoulder straps down. They crossed over her chest and fastened to a harness between her legs. As soon as the second strap clicked into place, the hard seat and back began to inflate. It wasn't like being on a balloon; the cushions inflated around her body. It felt like the seat was giving her a hug.

"That's weird," Sammy said.

"It's the most lovin' you're gonna get for the next eighteen years," Dole said. "Try and enjoy it."

A door opened at the front of the passenger cabin, and a

woman walked out wearing a Magellan flight uniform. Through the open door, Felicity could see more passengers.

"What's up there?" Felicity asked.

"First class," Dole said with a smirk. "Officers only."

"Why do they get better treatment?" Grant demanded.

"Because that's how the world works, and you better get used to it," Dole growled in reply. "If you need an explanation for everything officers do, you'll go crazy."

"Captain Sullivan is on board?" Felicity asked, not wanting to seem too concerned about their new lieutenant.

"Cap's on board, so is the LT. Once we get to the ship, we'll stow our gear and be taken straight to the freezers," Dole explained.

"The freezers?" Sammy asked.

"That's right," Dole said with a grin. "What did you think cryogenic stasis was, Corporal? They'll stack us like ice cubes in a freezer."

Felicity understood the concept of cryogenic stasis, but she preferred to think of it as sleeping rather than being frozen. The staff sergeant was clearly enjoying making his platoon mates squirm a bit.

"Does it hurt?" Sammy asked.

"Not until they wake you up," Dole said. "But don't worry, you'll live through it."

"He does not inspire confidence," Devon said.

"It can't be that bad," Felicity said. "He's done it multiple times."

The ship was secured and then began taxiing to the launch pad. The captain used the ship's intercom to remind everyone to dispose of anything in their mouths and to stay strapped into their seats for the duration of the flight.

"Why shouldn't we have something in our mouths?" Grant asked.

"Because you might choke on it," Dole growled. "Not that such an occurrence would be all bad, Laubin. At least I wouldn't have to answer your dumb questions every minute of the day."

The ship was positioned on a launch platform that slowly angled up. A countdown started, and Felicity gripped the armrest. The launch itself was sudden but not as scary as Felicity worried it might be. The ship was hurled into the air by the launch platform, and simultaneously the ship's rocket engines ignited. It would have been painful if not for the cushions absorbing the excess force of gravity as they were propelled upward. Felicity felt herself pushed back into her seat, but it was soft around her, and she didn't have trouble breathing.

For a few minutes, she could feel the ship climbing higher and higher, but soon her body adjusted. It didn't take long for the platoon members to start chatting again. The only time Felicity felt the pull of gravity was if she lifted her arm. It felt as if it weighed a hundred pounds, but if she left it on the armrest, the ride was as comfortable as taking the train far below in the massive city she had called home all her life.

In less than fifteen minutes the ship reached orbit, and Felicity felt the cushions around her recede. They weren't completely hard, but the soft, inflated seat was nothing like it had been. Still, the passengers were in zero-gravity, many experiencing weightlessness for the first time. Half an hour later, the ship docked with the interstellar ship *Bronx II*.

"All right, boys and girls, listen up," Staff Sergeant Dole said, rising up out of his seat and turning to face Bravo platoon. "No showboating. You will move off this ship in an orderly manner or I will make you regret ever being born, it that clear?"

"Yes, Staff Sergeant," Felicity replied along with the rest of her platoon.

"Very good. Let's go row by row," Dole ordered. "Slow and steady."

Felicity unfastened her safety harness and immediately began a slow rise from her seat. She held onto the seat in front of her and pulled her feet down to the floor of the transport before reaching up and opening the overhead bin. Even though her rucksack was heavy with gear, she pulled it free of the bin easily. It was the strangest experience of her life.

"This is trippy," Sammy declared.

"I know," Felicity said. "So strange."

"It is unsettling," Devon added. "I do not think I could get used to this."

"Don't worry, there's simulated gravity on the ship," Staff Sergeant Dole said. "Keep moving."

"How do they simulate gravity?" Devon asked.

"Centripetal force," Felicity said, almost declaring that her husband explained it to her the night before. Fortunately, she caught herself. "As the ship rotates, it creates centripetal force that is similar to gravity."

"So we'll be able to walk?" Sammy said.

"As soon as you're on board the ship," Dole said. "Just follow the others and don't touch any control panels. You wouldn't want to open an airlock and get sucked into space."

"He's joking, right?" Sammy asked.

"Yes," Felicity said, following her friends off the ship and into a long, flexible tube that seemed too flimsy to keep them safe from the cold vacuum of space.

But she couldn't help feeling like something might go

wrong. She felt helpless and vulnerable in space. All their training hadn't prepared her to feel so exposed. At the end of the tunnel, they passed through an open airlock and into a rotating tunnel that led to a larger room. The centripetal force increased slowly as they moved toward the room, and they walked onto the ship like normal. Felicity felt immediately more secure being able to walk. With the return of gravity—or something like it—she felt less uncertain.

A man in a naval uniform was waiting for them. He had two silver bars on his collar, and his name patch said "Nelson." Once Alpha and Bravo platoons were gathered in the big room, he gave a brief set of instructions.

"All personal belongings, including the clothes you're wearing, need to be secured in your rucksacks and clearly labeled," Lieutenant Nelson ordered. "We're on a tight schedule here, so if you'll follow me."

They walked down a long, arching hallway. Felicity felt like she was in a surreal dream. Soon they came to two doorways on either side of the corridor. Men went into one side, and women the other. The room was a locker facility. They took off their clothes, put on paper gowns, and stowed their rucksacks in metal lockers.

Once everyone had changed, the group was led to the cryogenic facility. Felicity stood in line, feeling exposed and cold in the paper gown, until Blake walked in. He was still in his uniform and spoke quietly to Staff Sergeant Dole. When he finished, he turned, his eyes locking with hers and giving her a tiny nod. It gave her a burst of confidence. She knew everything was going to be okay.

The entire platoon watched him leave. Before she knew it, the technician waved her forward, and Felicity walked to the empty cryo-chamber. It looked like a medical scanning capsule.

"Get inside and relax," the technician said in a bored voice. "You'll go to sleep. Don't fight it. Everything is normal. It's perfectly safe."

Felicity didn't feel all that safe, but she was confident that things would be okay. She reminded herself that Blake was involved, and he wouldn't let anything hurt her. She climbed into the capsule, which closed, and there was a screen inside just above her head. The interior was soft, and she could feel warmth radiating over her. A face appeared on the screen and gave her the same instructions that the technician had given her.

She felt sleepy, her eyes heavy. Soft, gentle music was playing, and her fears quickly slipped away. She couldn't even remember what she'd been concerned about. In less than a minute, she was asleep.

CHAPTER 18

BLAKE CAGE

"Bravo Platoon is in cryogenic stasis, Captain Sullivan," Cage said.

"Very good," the older man said.

Sullivan was seated at a table with a silver coffee set in the middle. He had a small, delicate-looking cup on a matching saucer near his right hand. With his left he was scrolling through news stories on his reading tablet. He seemed content, as if all the work was finished and he was content to sit and relax.

"Do you have orders for me, sir?" Cage asked.

"No," Sullivan said. "Our equipment is on board and safely stowed in the cargo section. Our work is done. Take advantage of the downtime."

Cage didn't mind downtime, but he felt as if he were cheating somehow. The platoon was in cryogenic sleep. He had double-checked each one just to get a look at Felicity one last time. The screen inside the capsule had a tiny camera in the corner. The computers that monitored the capsules and their occupants could show each person inside. Felicity looked as if she were asleep. He had burned the image of her face into his mind.

"How much time do we have, sir?" Cage asked.

"The ship will depart orbit in six hours. Technicians will be active for weeks still, until the ship reaches light speed. Then they'll go down. The ship's officers will spend the next thirty-six hours bringing the ship to full capacity and putting every system in standby mode. Once they've completed their work, they'll go into stasis along with the rest of us. If you want to take the day, feel free. We'll be synced to Earth's internet until we break orbit."

Cage nodded. He didn't want to surf the web, read the news, or check his banking account. What little money he had earned over the past four weeks would be there, growing while he traveled through space. It was hard to make the adjustment. He left the wardroom and went to the observatory. A reinforced panel of transparent material gave a view of what was happening outside the ship. The *Bronx II* was always turning, and the view changed constantly. In the distance were other ships, many preparing to make the same journey his own vessel was about to undertake. There were various space stations in view at different times as well. Light flooded the observation room as the glow from Earth appeared. Cage stood, staring at his home world. There was still plenty of blue from the oceans, and there was the white swirl of clouds—but the land was no longer green. It had been covered with gray, partially from all the concrete and partially from the smog that hung over the cities like a thick blanket, slowly choking the planet to death.

Cage reminded himself that what he was doing would help. A world like Magnificus Prime would be a haven to humanity. Once the colony was up and running, more people would come. Tens of thousands, maybe even hundreds of thousands, would flock to a pristine world where land was cheap and a person could make a life of their own choosing. Would it make a dent in the ever-growing population of Earth? Cage didn't know, but the more planets that were available to humanity, the greater were their chances of saving their home world.

Knowing he would never see Earth again was bittersweet. None of it was his, and yet he identified with it strongly. Earth was the home of humanity, their refuge. She had endured all of humanity's follies and failures. He felt as if he were turning his back on her, discarding the planet like an old, soiled garment. He put his hand on the window as the ship spun around and the planet drifted out of sight.

There was no sense in getting emotional. He knew what he was doing was the right thing. Staying on Earth didn't help anyone. Branching out was their future, and he was part of that. He left the observatory and made his way to the cryogenics department. One of the technicians showed him to the capsules reserved for officers. Unlike the booth his wife was in, Cage's capsule had a slot for his clothes and boots. He disrobed and slipped on a paper gown. He folded his uniform carefully and stowed everything in its proper place before climbing inside. The technician at a console on the other side of the room activated his cryogenic chamber. He felt it warm. The screen came on and gave him instructions. Cage closed his eyes. He felt warm, relaxed, and safe despite being on a ship where every soul on board would soon be in a similar state of cryogenic stasis. The ship would be flying itself, which might have unnerved him had the capsule's muscle relaxers and anti-anxiety meds not been coursing through his bloodstream. He was drifting toward the darkness on a warm current of narcotics that would prepare him to be preserved inside the capsule for eighteen years while the ship traveled to their new home.

In his mind's eye he saw Felicity, her ebony skin glowing in the light from the small display screen, her strong features relaxed in sleep. He missed the gentle curve of her lips and the way her eyes sparkled when she looked at him. Cage was the luckiest guy on the planet, he thought, even though he was no longer on any planet. It didn't matter anymore—nothing did in that moment. He was too happy, too content to simply drift away into a dreamless sleep. He couldn't see Felicity in his mind anymore, but he could feel the happiness of knowing he was hers, and she was his. And then the darkness engulfed him, and he knew nothing else for almost two decades.

INTERMISSION

18 Years Later

CHAPTER 19

BLAKE CAGE

Cold. He felt it even before his mind could identify it. He felt as if he had been disassembled, like a puzzle. All his parts had been put in a box, shaken up, and poured onto a table. It took a while to get all the pieces back in the right order.

His name was Blake Cage. That was almost a revelation, just remembering his own name. And he was cold, shivering, and tired. How could he be tired? He'd been asleep for so long. But his body hadn't really been asleep—it had been in suspended animation, not sleeping. There were no regenerative processes happening for the past eighteen years, and while his body was coming out of cryogenic stasis, it was also filtering out the drugs used to relax his body before the process had essentially frozen him for nearly two decades.

He moved his hands and fingers. They were stiff but functioning. His feet moved just fine as did his legs, but everything hurt. It was like he had woken up in the middle of the night after losing his blanket. His entire body was stiff and cold. He reached up and touched the lid of his capsule. It opened automatically, and a waft of cold air made him shutter. The dim light was too much. It hurt his eyes, but he had to open them to adjust, to get moving.

Clothes! He had a uniform folded up just outside his capsule. He sat up, his hands on the side of the booth. It took nearly ten minutes to get dressed. His coordination was off. He had trouble getting his socks on his feet and pulling on his uniform, but each item of clothing felt good as it brushed over his skin. His body was trying desperately to warm itself, and the clothes helped.

He could keep his eyes open thanks to the dim lighting in the cryogenic section. Cage stood up and stretched. He could feel his blood warming. It seemed too thin as he moved, and his aching muscles quivered from the strain of just holding him up, but it felt good to move again.

"Welcome back, Lieutenant," the technician said. "We've reached the Fortuna system."

"How long?" Cage asked, his voice a hoarse croak.

"Don't try to talk yet. You need to get some fluids in you first," the tech explained. "We're two days from orbit. Every system is online and in the green. You'll be able to head planet-side on schedule."

Cage nodded, gave the tech a weak little wave, then lumbered out of the room. He felt like he might be sick to his stomach as he navigated the ship's arching corridors. The need for water was all his mind could process. He reached the wardroom and found Captain Sullivan waiting inside along with Staff Sergeant Dole.

"It's a bitch, ain't it?" Sullivan chuckled.

"Here, sir," Dole said, getting a cup and filling it with

water infused with electrolytes, vitamins, and amino acids. "Drink this."

Cage lifted the cup to his mouth and let the cool fluid wash over his dehydrated tongue. It was the sweetest thing he'd ever tasted. Once he finished the drink, the staff sergeant refilled his cup.

"I want to see it," Cage said.

"Go ahead," Sullivan said. "We'll wake the troops in a few hours. Captain Choi and I will go over the initial data, but from what I've seen, everything looks good for an immediate deployment."

"We'll all feel better once we're on the ground, sir," Dole said.

"I hope you're right," Cage said.

It was like recovering from the flu. He wanted to move, but he felt so incredibly tired and weak. The water was helping, but slowly. He wished he could spare Felicity from what he was feeling. The memory of his wife hit him almost like a physical blow. He sat up suddenly in his chair.

"Ah, yes," Sullivan said. "Memories come back in waves. Rest assured that everything is as it should be, Cage."

"The cooks are whipping up a meal for us," Staff Sergeant Dole said. "You want to walk down to the observatory and back? It might do you a world of good."

"Yes," Cage said. "I'll do that."

He struggled to his feet. They felt like he'd been slogging through mud and the soil was clinging to him, making his legs feel heavy.

"Go with him, Staff Sergeant," Sullivan ordered. "We can't have our new LT getting hurt before we even deploy."

"Roger that," Dole said, following Cage to the door.

"It'll pass, Lieutenant. It'll pass," Sullivan declared.

"Take it slow, sir, and you'll be fine," Dole told Cage.

But he didn't feel fine. He felt awkward, stiff, and weak. It was like his consciousness had been transferred into the body of a corpse. He lumbered on, reminded of the tin man in the Wizard of Oz. He had read the book in a history of literature course. The tin man, rusted in place, needed oil to lubricate his joints and move again. Cage didn't need oil, but he needed blood to infuse his muscles and fill the spaces in his joints. It was slowly working; his legs felt more reliable, but his back and shoulders were stiff. And his head still felt foggy from the drugs.

"How long have you been up, Staff Sergeant?" Cage asked.

"An hour or so," Dole replied. "It's easier for us, though. The first time's the hardest."

"Can't believe you would do it again," Cage said.

"It's like childbirth—you forget the pain," Dole said, just as they turned into the observation room. And Cage suddenly realized what he meant.

Magnificus Prime was just sliding into view. It was a great, gleaming ball of green, like an emerald. Cage was speechless, his struggles with reanimation completely forgotten. There were a hundred shades of green on the planet, with pure white clouds swirled in.

"It's green," Dole said. "Even the oceans are green. I've never seen anything like it."

"Beautiful," Cage said.

They stood staring at the planet until it was lost from view, replaced by stars that looked different. He'd never been a star gazer. The vast city was too bright to allow them to see the stars very clearly. Only the brightest could compete with the ambient light from millions of street lamps, even if half of them were burnt out. Still, the stars looked different somehow.

"Same stars, just a different perspective, that's all," Dole said, as if he could read Cage's thoughts.

"Amazing," Cage said. "There are so many."

"Indeed," Dole replied. "And nothing else in the system but us. That's a strange feeling. But don't worry, it'll fill up with ships and people before you know it."

Cage didn't know whether to look forward to the other ships arriving or to dread it. The staff sergeant certainly didn't seem to think that more people was a good thing.

"Will you stay?" Cage asked.

"Depends," Dole said. "I'm here for the first few years, at any rate."

"Depends on what?" Cage asked.

"The planet, for one thing. I've been on two others. Felt wrong to me. Like we didn't belong there. Of course, they weren't as perfectly situated as this one."

"So if the world is right?"

"If it feels right, I'll stay. If not, I'll roll the dice one more time."

Cage couldn't imagine going back. So much would have changed by the time they arrived back at Earth. His parents were still alive, but would they be in another twenty years? It was doubtful. They had both been in their fifties when he'd left Earth. Twenty more years would put them in their nineties. Even if he saw them again, he might not recognize them, and they certainly wouldn't be the same.

When the planet reappeared, Cage felt a sense of relief. It really was as beautiful as he thought it was. His head seemed to clear as he focused on getting down to the surface. That's what he wanted: to experience a new world firsthand, to be one of the first humans to walk upon the surface of a pristine world. He couldn't wait.

"You think you're ready to eat?" Dole asked.

"Lead the way, staff sergeant," Cage said.

He was determined to shake off his lethargy and do whatever was needed to get everyone ready to deploy. They ate powdered eggs and drank orange juice from concentrate, but it all tasted good to Cage. His digestive system engaged, and by the time he finished his meal he could feel his strength returning.

Recon platoon Alpha had two officers, and they were all in the wardroom eating and talking. A current of excitement coursed through their conversation. It wouldn't be long before their platoons boarded the drop ships and made the flight down to the planet. It was what they had trained for, and everyone was anxious to get moving, with the possible exception of Captain Sullivan. Cage had a hard time reading his superior officer. He was the oldest man in the room and a little heavier than the others, as well. He acted aloof in regard to the planet, as if he had been on hundreds of colony worlds. Cage couldn't tell if the excitement had actually worn off for him or if he would have preferred to stay on the ship.

Nothing could have kept Cage away. He couldn't believe they had to wait for two days before making planetfall, but he understood the reasons. There was a lot of work to do in a short amount of time. As soon as he finished his meal he stood up, anxious to get started.

"Our new lieutenant is feeling better," Sullivan said. "That's good."

"With your permission, sir, I'd like to start waking the platoon," Cage asked.

"Staff Sergeant?" Sullivan asked.

"I'm game," Dole replied.

"Fine, get them up. Take them through reanimation protocols and then get started prepping gear," Sullivan said.

"Roger that," Cage said.

"We'll have everything ready ASAP, Captain," Dole added.

They left the wardroom and headed for the cryogenic department. Cage could hardly wait to show the new planet to his wife. They had finally found a place to call home.

CHAPTER 20

FELICITY MARS

W alking to the locker room was painful. Like every other member of Bravo platoon, Felicity was shaking, her mind foggy, her body aching with every step.

"Get water," the lieutenant was calling. "Right here. This helps."

He was loud and excited. Felicity felt like a child being awakened early for school. Nothing seemed to make sense. Her body instinctively followed orders while her mind was running to catch up. She walked to where the lieutenant was handing out disposable cups of water. She took one and drank it. Her body's response was immediate. She turned up the cup and sucked it all down, then took another.

"You won't believe it," the lieutenant said.

Felicity looked up at his familiar face but couldn't place him. She knew she should recognize him, but she couldn't.

"Believe what?" a Latino woman to her right asked.

"The planet," Lieutenant Cage said.

Felicity read the name, and the memory of the handsome man before her hovered just out of reach.

"It's beautiful," the lieutenant continued, but his eyes had gone up toward the ceiling. He was surrounded by women in thin paper gowns, most of them shivering with cold, eager for the water he was handing out, but he didn't look them in the eye anymore—not after staring straight into Felicity's.

"You should get dressed," Lieutenant Cage ordered. "Then come back for more water. We'll get down to the mess hall and you'll feel better."

"Can't feel any worse," another woman with freckles said.

"Sammy," Felicity said.

"Mars," the woman said.

"My head is full of cotton," Felicity said. "I'm having trouble remembering names."

"Me too," her friend said. Sammy was Felicity's best friend. They were tight. It was starting to come back to her.

"I feel like I died and came back to life," the Latino woman said. Her name was Lucinda Fuego, Felicity remembered: another friend, but not as close.

"I feel like I'm still dead," said a thin, pale woman with black hair and puffy eyes.

Her name is Lori, Felicity thought to herself—Lori Cunningham—and she's a trooper. They all dressed as quickly as their numb fingers would allow. Felicity's skin felt dry and her head hurt, but she was starting to warm up, starting to feel more like herself.

And then, out of the blue, it hit her. It was as if her mind suddenly downloaded every memory she had of her husband: meeting him for the first time, their first kiss, the way he looked at her, their wedding, and the fact that she couldn't let on that she even knew him outside of the platoon. She stood up suddenly as the memories poured into her mind.

"You okay?" Sammy asked.

"Yeah, just a cramp," Felicity said, rubbing her leg. "No big deal."

She sat back down and finished tying the laces on her boots.

"It doesn't seem real," Lucinda said. "I mean, it's like I put my gear in this locker just last night."

"It feels real to me," Sammy complained.

"But not eighteen years," Lucinda insisted. "That's like my entire life, almost."

"You didn't miss it," Felicity said. "Everything's just been on pause."

"It all looks the same," Lori said. "My stuff didn't even shift in my locker."

"It's good to know no one pilfered through our stuff," Sammy said. "I mean, they could have and we wouldn't have known it."

"Until now," Felicity said. "And then that nosy someone would have to pay."

"You know that's right," Lucinda said.

Felicity gave the younger girl a high five. It was all coming back. She didn't feel good. Her body ached. Her stomach quivered inside her, threatening to reject anything that she ate, and her mind was still foggy, but she knew in time it would all pass. They just needed a little time and they would all be back to normal. She couldn't believe she had just skipped ahead eighteen years into the future. It was no different than going to bed and waking up to a new day, only instead of eight hours, eighteen years had flown by. And she felt horrible.

They filed down to the mess hall. Eating helped. The food wasn't good, Felicity could see that. Her scrambled eggs had a dull, grayish color and were almost soupy, but it tasted so good. She ate everything on her tray, which wasn't much—just the powdered eggs and canned fruit. Her strength was coming back, and she wanted to move. Staff Sergeant Dole ordered them down to the armory, a tiny room in the bowels of the ship. They got their weapons out and began working them. The oil was completely dried in her rifle. It was one of the only signs that time had passed while they slept.

Across the room, Staff Sergeant Dole and Lieutenant Cage were breaking down their own weapons. Felicity had a hard time taking her eyes off of her husband. It was as if she were looking at him with brand new eyes.

With their weapons seen to, the rest of their day was filled with grunt work. They carried supplies to the drop ship. Their bodies slowly worked through the pain and weariness of their long cryogenic sleep. Six hours after their breakfast, they were fed again: pasta with protein-enriched marinara sauce. The food tasted good and made her feel even better. With a little time off after the meal, Felicity found herself in the observatory along with most of Bravo platoon.

"Incredible," Devon said when the emerald planet came into view.

"I've never seen anything so green," Sammy said.

"It's beautiful," Felicity agreed. "I can't wait to get down there."

The sentiment was shared by her crew mates. They were sent to the cargo area they had just cleared out and given thin yoga-style mats to sleep on—but sleep was hard to come by. Felicity lay in the dark next to her friends, listening to the whispers from Alpha and Bravo platoons. She knew that somewhere on the ship, Blake was working or sleeping. She wished she could sneak away, find him, and feel his skin on hers.

"I can't sleep," Sammy said.

"It feels like I just woke up after sleeping eighteen years," Devon said.

"Very funny," Felicity whispered. "It's just excitement."

"There's nothing down there," Sammy argued. "What's to be excited about?"

"Are you saying that you are not filled with anticipation?" Devon asked.

"No, I'm excited," Sammy said. "I just don't know why."

"Because it's a planet full of possibilities," Felicity said. "No more restrictions."

"I'm a city girl," Sammy said. "When do the hot, young colonists arrive? When I get out of the MCM, I'm selling my land and investing in a club. Music, drinks, people doing things they shouldn't—that's what I want."

"I suppose we'll need that," Felicity said.

She hadn't thought much about what she might do on Magnficus Prime once her enlistment ended. All that had ever crossed her mind was just the freedom to do whatever she chose. On Earth, they'd had no choices. There were thousands of people for every job opening, and the government controlled everything. If a person wasn't born wealthy, they had almost no chance of ever getting ahead. Those that worked outside the government system were taxed so heavily that it was criminal. Who wanted to work hard only to have the government take ninety percent of what you earned? But on Magnificus Prime, things would be different.

"A self-defense school," Felicity whispered.

"What?" Sammy asked.

"That's what I want to do," Felicity replied. "Open a school that teaches women how to take care of themselves."

"I'm all for rolling around with other people," Sammy said, "but not women."

"You are full of humor this evening," Devon said with a chuckle.

"Anything is possible," Felicity said. "Anything at all."

At some point they fell asleep, only to be awakened by a loud clanging. Staff Sergeant Dole had discovered a metal wrench and was pounding it on a metal cargo bin.

"Up and at 'em," he shouted. "Today's the day, boys and girls."

Felicity felt a bit like a child on Christmas morning. She rolled off the mat and did some light stretching. She was stiff from sleeping on the deck, but no one cared about her comfort. The day had finally come to leave the claustrophobic confines of the interstellar ship and begin exploring their new world.

CHAPTER 21

BLAKE CAGE

Perhaps it was the excitement of going down to the planet, but with his weapons in place, Cage felt like a warrior. He had his Magellan Infiltrator hanging from a sling across his chest. His fatigues were covered with light, ceramic armor plating in Kevlar. Every loop on his belt was filled with plasma cartridge shells or extra batteries for the laser weapons.

On his hip hung a Belmont semi-auto pistol. It was a traditional pistol with hollow tip slugs. The old-fashioned pistol reminded Cage of the decorative swords worn by officers once they had become obsolete weapons of war. He also carried a bush knife on his other hip, but it was a thick blade with saw teeth on the spine, more of a tool than a weapon. His entire body tingled with anticipation as he stepped aboard the drop ship.

Captain Sullivan followed him, the last to board. They went to the seats that were behind the pilot. Recon platoon Bravo were arranged on either side of the drop ship's cargo area, seated on slings that hung from the bulkhead. In the middle of the cargo area, their initial supplies were stored in hard plastic bins. The members of Bravo platoon wore open-faced helmets with their names stenciled in white on their foreheads. The helmets had eye protection that slid up over their names when not in use. Communication links consisted of a simple earpiece connected to throat mics. Everyone was geared up with weapons and armor. The heavy weapons experts were shrouded in gear, their harnesses and auto-cannons making them look like cyborgs from a movie.

Cage passed each person, repeating their name to himself as he passed them. They were already buckled in, their five-point harnesses holding them tightly in place, their heavy survival packs stowed under their sling-type seats. When he passed Felicity, she winked at him. His heart skipped a beat. He had seen her in all types of dress, from costumes in school plays to her wedding dress the day they'd pledged their vows to one another. But he'd never seen her looking more fearsome or more beautiful than she did in battle armor. Unlike the troopers or Cage's own armor, Felicity's scout armor was thin and made from flexible sheets of pauldron. It was like plastic but completely impenetrable, and it allowed her complete freedom of movement. She carried an Infiltrator rifle and a Magellan Stinger pistol in a thigh holster. Unlike trooper armor, she didn't have a lot of ammunition in loops. There were no loose parts on her garments that might catch on a limb or snag on a sharp rock. Nothing hard was stored next to one another, so there was no chance of her gear clanking or rattling.

The platoon was watching him, so Cage couldn't respond to Felicity's wink. He continued to the back of the cargo hold and strapped himself in. Beside him, Sullivan was doing the same. Their survival packs had already been brought on board and stowed under their seats, which were padded. Cage noticed Sullivan's small pack and how the captain struggled with his rifle as he tried to strap himself into the seat.

"We're ready," Sullivan said as his harness clicked into place. "Pilot, take us down."

The pilot responded to the order and began communicating with the ship's command officers. Cage could hear everything through his com-link, but in his mind it was just noise. All he could think about was going down to the planet, being the first to set foot where no man had ever gone before. It felt heroic, and more importantly to Cage, it felt historic. How would history remember him? He had no idea, but he hoped their endeavor would be more than just a footnote lost in the flood of reports about Magnificus Prime.

The drop ship with Bravo platoon was the first to leave the ship. The shift to zero-gravity was sudden, but it wasn't long until the drop ship was breaking through the planet's upper atmosphere, and they all began to feel the pull of Magnificus Prime.

"Is it supposed to shake like this?" Private Junior Knoxx asked as the ship began to be buffeted by the thicker air.

"Just relax," Staff Sergeant Dole said. "Everything is normal."

Cage was being pressed into his restraints. It felt like he was falling and the ship was strapped onto him, pulling him down. He held onto his rifle and waited for the ship to level out.

"What happens if we crash?" trooper Joelle Cotuma asked.

"Then we die," Dole said. "Don't worry, you'll never know it if that happens."

The ship shook even harder, as if some titan had taken hold of the aircraft and was trying to discover what was inside. Cage held onto the arms of his small seat. The non-commissioned platoon members didn't have armrests. Their seats were slings, like hammocks made of cargo straps. Cage kept his eyes fixed on Felicity. She looked straight ahead, a determined look on her face. She held her rifle tight across her body and the safety harness that crossed her chest.

"Fifteen minutes," the pilot called over the com-link.

Cage hoped the shaking wouldn't last that long. He felt like his teeth were about to come flying out of his head. And then, as if some divine being had heard his request, the shaking stopped. Cage let out a long sigh. He didn't realize he'd been holding his breath.

"That's better," said vehicle specialist Hugo Webster.

"Smooth sailing from here," Staff Sergeant Wyatt Dole said, having to shout as the engines seemed to grow louder.

"Weather's perfect," the pilot informed them. "Seventy-two degrees on the ground and clear skies. The wind's out of the south at three knots. Nothing but green as far as I can see."

"Sounds like paradise," Cage said to Captain Sullivan.

The sour expression on his superior's face revealed how he really felt, but he said, "Yes, pristine."

A short while later, the drop ship slowed for a vertical landing. Using repulsors, it hovered in midair, slowly descending.

"Thirty seconds," the pilot warned them.

Cage hit the release on his harness. His excitement was overwhelming. He stood up and started for the rear hatch release. Seeing him move, Dole got up and started barking orders.

"It's time," he shouted. "Everyone on your feet. Get ready to move."

The specialists released their safety straps and stood up. The heavy weapons troopers were right behind Cage. Regular troopers would haul out the gear. Cage hit the release and the hatch started opening. Cool air blew into his face. Light from Fortuna, the system star, poured into the dark cargo hold of the drop ship. The platoon fell silent. The ship settled onto her landing struts, and the hatch extended to the ground.

"Here we go," Cage shouted, leading the way down the ramp.

The ship had landed in a field of light green grass. It was soft under his boots as Cage walked onto Magnificus Prime. He wanted to say something weighty and important, but the beauty of the world stole his words away. The troopers spread out behind him. There were mountains close by, and a wide, shallow river was flowing down from the snow-covered peaks. Everywhere he looked there was green. Waving trees lined the river, and tall, cone-shaped trees covered the lower mountain slopes.

"Enough gawking," Captain Sullivan snapped from the rear of the drop ship. "Drop that gear and finish unloading this ship. We have work to do."

How the man couldn't stop and take a moment to let the wonders of a new world sink in was a mystery to Cage. But orders were orders. He followed the troopers back onto the drop ship where they retrieved their packs. Each one was loaded with survival gear, including an emergency shelter, extra food, supplies for making a fire, first aid, solar power chargers, additional ammunition, and spare clothing. The entire pack along with its aluminum frame weighed nearly sixty pounds. Cage hefted his up and stuffed his arms through the shoulder straps. His own pack had the spare radio transmitter and the foldable receiving dish for long-range transmissions.

Once everything was out of the drop ship, Captain Sullivan signaled the pilot, who took off. They watched the ship fly straight up and then sail off away from the mountains. In the distance, across the wide-open plain they had landed in, was a forest of dark green trees that contrasted with the bright sky overhead and the light-colored grass of the plain. Cage had never seen so much open space or dense foliage in all his life.

"Let's get operations started," Captain Sullivan said. "Have the troopers launch the drones. Send the scouts to find the best place to set up base camp. There's not much shelter here."

"Roger that," Staff Sergeant Dole said. "Bailey, Mars, see if you can find us a base camp. We need shelter in case weather moves in. HeWEs, form a perimeter and stand watch. There could be any kind of creatures on this rock. I don't want to be surprised if something comes by for a visit. The rest of you, get busy launching the mapping drones."

"Private Case, check your gear," Cage ordered. "The *Bronx II* should be launching communication satellites already."

"Yes, Lieutenant," Private Amber Case replied.

She was athletic, with a round face and features that were almost masculine. She pulled out the long-range transmitter and began assembling the unit. It was made to fit in the top of her pack so that once it was put together she could carry it on her back, leaving her hands free to wield her rifle and fight.

But Cage couldn't imagine fighting in a place so perfect. He took a deep breath. The air was different, not recycled or tainted with smog. The sky was a soft green, and there were wisps of white clouds in the distance. The sun was directly overhead, and Cage guessed they had six to eight hours of sunlight left—plenty of time for Felicity and her counterpart, Porter Bailey, to find a suitable site for the base camp to be erected. Cage thought any place would do, but he understood the need to select the best of the good options. The base camp would be their home for the next two weeks when the second wave of ships arrived.

From one of the larger cargo cases, the troopers took solar-powered auto-drones. They were simple mapping drones, designed to fly out and transmit mapping data to the satellites in orbit. The explorer probe had taken initial readings of the terrain after orbiting the planet for several days, but the drones would give the colonists a growing database of the planet. It might take years to map it all, but that was the process of occupying an entirely new world.

"I've got a secure link to the *Bronx II*," Amber Case called out.

"Very good," Captain Sullivan said, "patch me through."

He gave their first situational report and in turn got feedback from the ship in orbit. The geosynchronous communication satellite had been launched. The systemwide relay buoys were going out. The weather and radar satellites were on deck.

Cage was amazed at how much technology was already coming into play on the new world. They weren't isolated explorers, but rather well-connected team members that were rapidly gaining a strong understanding of their new planet.

His thoughts were interrupted by Felicity's voice over his com-link.

"Captain, I've found a site for base camp," she said. "Three klicks northwest of your location."

"Roger that, Corporal Mars," Sullivan replied. "Mark that spot and return to this location."

"Copy, we're on our way."

Once the drones were all launched, the bin was sealed back up. Staff Sergeant Dole called out formation orders. The troopers would carry the rest of the platoon's gear, including the empty cargo bins that had held the drones. The *Bronx II* was receiving strong signals from the mapping drones. Everything was going along as planned.

Captain Sullivan was at the head of the platoon formation. Felicity and Bailey returned and led the way at the front of the column of recon specialists. Staff Sergeant Dole and Lieutenant Cage brought up the rear. The walk across the grassy field was pleasant to Cage, even in full armor with a sixty-pound pack on. His recently acquired muscle mass didn't seem to mind the added weight, and his mind was drinking in the sights of his new home.

"I never imagined it would be like this," Cage said.

"I don't reckon it's all this idyllic," Dole said. "But it's damn impressive."

They saw birds flying from the mountains. It was their first sight of native animal life. They were too high up to get a good look at, but from what Cage could see, they looked normal—as if they might have been birds from Earth. Not that he'd seen anything other than crows and pigeons before. The birds on Magnificus Prime looked bigger, but that was a matter of perspective.

"I can't believe I'm really here," Cage said. "This world seems too good to be true."

"That's what makes me nervous," Dole said. "A word of advice, if I'm not overstepping my bounds, LT."

"By all means, Staff Sergeant," Cage replied.

"Keep your guard up. This world seems perfect, and maybe it is, but in my experience when something seems too good to be true, it usually is."

"You think there's danger here?"

"I think there's danger everywhere," Dole said. "It comes from people not being prepared and letting their guard down, mostly, but there's still an awful lot we don't know about this place."

"I hear you, Staff Sergeant. Good advice. I'll keep that in mind."

Dole nodded. Cage liked the older man. He had a folksy demeanor, but he was smarter than he appeared. While Dole seemed to accept Cage, the staff sergeant was reserved in his own judgement of the young officer. Cage understood and could even appreciate that. He wanted to win Dole's respect— to earn it.

"We've got two weeks on this planet with no backup," Dole went on. "If we get in a jam, we'll have to get ourselves out."

"And until we've been here a while, we won't know what we don't know," Cage added.

"Exactly. Best to keep our guard up and not get too enthralled with the wonders of this new world. It's not new to the creatures who live here, and they may not be too inclined to let us stick around."

Cage wondered if that were true. Was it possible that the

native creatures on Magnificus Prime were intelligent? Cage had expected predatory behaviors, but not intelligence. There were no settlements on the planet and no cities, but that didn't mean the native life wasn't intelligent. He realized he had a lot of assumptions that he needed to discard until the world revealed its secrets.

But he had no idea just how incredible those secrets would be.

CHAPTER 22

FELICITY MARS

They had made it to Magnificus Prime, and it was all Felicity hoped it might be and more. It was clean, verdant, and full of possibilities. The location for their base camp was near a rugged cliff face. There were trees along the north side and a river to the south. The space between was flat, but a small berm ran along the eastern side of the clearing, with the cliff to the west.

"Excellent location," Captain Sullivan told her when they arrived. "Staff Sergeant!"

"Yes, Captain," Dole said, hurrying forward.

"Get our base camp set up. I want the command post near the cliff, but leave a little room. We can put observers up on top. That should give them a commanding view of the area, and if there's trouble they can repel down to our location."

"Roger that, Captain."

Dole began barking out orders.

"Mars, take Lieutenant Cage up to the top of that cliff," the captain ordered. "Lieutenant, let's get a communication relay set up to ensure we don't lose signal. And give me a status report once you're up there."

"Yes, Captain," Felicity and Blake said at the same time.

"You ready?" she asked him.

"Absolutely," he said, flashing a smile that made her weak in the knees.

There were two ways up to the cliff. They could have climbed straight up. The cliff was rugged with plenty of hand and foot holds, but that would take twice as long and leave them worn out. Instead, they went around the thick stand of trees and followed what appeared to be a game trail.

"Do you see any signs of animal life?" Cage asked.

"Other than the trail?" Felicity teased.

"I just mean, anything recent?"

"Well, this is the first real trail I've ever been on, but I don't see prints."

She was leading the way. Her own pack was smaller than his, without the frame. It just held extra food and the most basic survival gear. She couldn't be expected to carry a large pack and move quietly through rough terrain. Blake lagged behind with his heavier load, but he didn't complain. It was one of the things she loved and admired about him. He wasn't a negative person and didn't let hardship keep him down.

There were big rocks along the sides of the trail, and at times the path was more like stairs than a gentle slope. Once they reached the top of the cliff, they had a nice, wide plateau. There were even some trees growing near the path, and grass covered the open expanse leading out to the cliff face. They walked out to the edge and looked down. The platoon already had the frame for the command post up.

"They're making steady progress," Felicity said.

"Yeah, the captain knows his stuff," Blake said as he unfastened the belt strap on his pack and shrugged out of the heavy load.

"What aren't you telling me?" she said.

"Nothing," Blake replied.

"Don't lie to me, Blake Cage," Felicity said. "I know you too well."

"It's nothing, just an impression I got."

"About the captain?"

Blake nodded and began assembling the communications relay. It was really just a foldable parabolic dish that would act as an antenna once he ran a cable down the cliff face to the command post.

"What is it?" Felicity asked. She had two long coils of rope, which she laid down carefully in the grass.

"Can you believe this place?" Blake asked her. "I can hardly believe we're really here."

"Don't change the subject," Felicity said.

"Okay, but I don't like sharing this, so don't tell anyone else," he warned her.

"I can keep a secret," she said, giving him a wink.

"Well, there's something off about the captain. I just get the impression that he would rather be in his office than in the field."

"Really?" Felicity asked. "A recon platoon captain who doesn't like being out in the field? That's strange, isn't it?"

"Exactly, and like I said, it's just an impression I got. I'm probably wrong," he said, tightening the bolts that held the receiver rigid with a small hex wrench.

"I trust your judgment of people," Felicity said, remembering a teacher from high school who had committed suicide. Blake had predicted it beforehand. He'd also told her to watch out for a person in their building that had tried to corner her when she was alone one afternoon.

She took the ends of each rope and tied them to separate trees on the far side of the plateau. They would be the anchors if someone needed to repel down the cliff. It might have been weeks or even months before anyone saw what lay just inside the mountains if she hadn't looked up at just the right time. Her breath caught in her throat, and she looked closer.

The mountain trail ran on the far side of the trees, then headed back down the hill they were on. On one side of the plateau there was a cliff face, but the other side angled down more gently. There were a few hardy trees growing in the crumbling rock of that slope, but between them was a structure that didn't look natural to her at all.

"Blake," she said, forgetting in that moment that he was her superior and that they were keeping their relationship a secret.

"What is it?" he said, hurrying over to where she stood.

"Look at that."

She pointed through the trees, and he followed her finger with his eyes. It took him a moment to see it, or perhaps for the sight to be recognized. The structure, which was how Felicity thought of it, was mostly hidden from their view, but one side was visible—a straight line among the gnarly, irregular edges of the mountains.

"What do you think it is?" Blake asked.

"Has to be manmade," Felicity said. "It's too straight to be natural."

"You don't know that," he replied. "There's a lot about his world we don't know yet."

"Are you seriously telling me that isn't something made with intelligent planning and thought?" Felicity asked.

Blake moved, trying to get a better view, but the object wasn't close, and it was hard to see with the hills and mountains between their position and the structure.

"I can't say for certain," he replied. "It could be, but there are straight lines in nature, and maybe things we can't even imagine yet. We're on a world eighteen light years from Earth."

He headed back toward the communication relay. Felicity looked once more at the straight, clean line and then turned to her husband.

"We're not the first people to be here," she said.

"That's crazy," Blake said. "No manned craft has ever come this far before. We're the first."

"Who said anything about humans?" Felicity countered.

Blake was on one knee, bent over the relay dish. He stood up and looked at her.

"I'm just saying," she continued. "It's possible...right?"

"Anything's possible," he replied with a huff.

She knew him; his analytical, studious mind didn't like dwelling on the fantastic. Intelligent life in the universe was almost a mathematical certainty, but after over a century of space travel and nearly a dozen colony worlds, mankind had not yet encountered intelligent life.

"So why don't you believe me?"

"I don't disbelieve you," he replied. "But it frightens me just to think about it. And I don't think running down to the captain telling him we found an alien structure is going to do anyone any good."

"Are you done overreacting?" she asked, returning to the coiled ropes and making sure they could easily be tossed over the edge without tangling up.

"I'm overreacting?"

"I never said that we should tell the captain that aliens built something in the mountains," she insisted. "I'm just trying to figure this out."

"We need to get closer," Blake said. "Get a better view."

"Is that an order, lieutenant?" she said with a smile.

"No," Blake said. "I want you right here with me. I thought we could have a nice, long, uninterrupted talk. Just the two of us, taking in the sights of our new world."

"And I've ruined that," she said, feeling her own twinge of disappointment.

"No, you haven't ruined anything," he said, getting back to his feet and walking over to her. He took both her hands in his. "I've missed you so much."

She stepped closer. They were eye to eye, close enough she could feel his breath on her cheek. "Me too," she said, "so much."

"We can't," he said without moving away. "If they find out, they'll separate us."

"I don't want to be apart from you," she said.

"Then we have to be strong."

"Just one kiss."

"You know it's never just one kiss," he said, but then he kissed her. It was soft and sweet.

When he pulled back, she resisted the urge to follow him, to press him, to insist on more.

"I'll start observing," she said.

"I'll send down the radio line."

But he didn't move, and neither did she. They just stood close together for several seconds, relishing the privacy, basking in the nearness of their beloved.

When Blake finally turned away, it broke the spell between them. Felicity realized that in those exquisite seconds of intimate contact they had been completely vulnerable. Her father wouldn't approve. She hadn't gone eighteen light years from Earth just to get caught off guard and killed. She began searching the terrain beyond the base camp. She could see where the drop ship had landed. The plain stretched away in three directions. To the north and south it remained open all the way to the horizon. To the east there was a dark forest. From her elevated position she guessed it was fifteen to twenty kilometers away. There was no movement that she could see.

"Looks clear," she said.

"Roger that, let me call it in," Blake said.

"You going to mention the thing in the mountains?"

"Not right away," he replied. "If I'm right about the captain, he'll need the security of his base camp before we mention anything out of the ordinary."

"It's coming along," Felicity said.

Below them, the command post was up, and the interlocking pieces of its roof and walls were already in place. It was a Prefabricated Easy Assembly Kit, or PEAK, structure. The panels it was made of were lightweight but sturdy. The mess pavilion was going up. It was similar to the command post but without walls. Eventually they would also construct an emergency field hospital and a barracks building, but that would be after the heavy cargo drops. The *Bronx II* would fire large crates with everything from solar power arrays to their platoon carrier in vacuum-sealed crates fitted with parachutes that would open once the crates passed a certain altitude. The cargo could be dropped from orbit, and depending on atmospheric conditions—mostly wind—it would land within a hundred kilometers of their position. Of course, the crew of the *Bronx II* wouldn't begin dropping cargo until they finished launching the satellites, which would take another day, at least.

Felicity found it tempting to watch her platoon mates as they built the base camp, but that wasn't her task. She was supposed to watch for potential dangers like animal life or even foul weather. The plain was still—just a large, empty expanse—but it was beautiful. She had trouble keeping watch and not getting lulled by the sheer beauty of the world.

"This is ready," Blake said, after he had anchored the dish down using long, plastic stakes.

She looked and saw a black cable running along the grass to the cliff face, where it disappeared from sight.

"Does that mean you're leaving?" Felicity asked.

"Our illustrious leader wants me to oversee the latrine pits that need to be dug," Blake said, taking her hand.

It felt good to hold his hand, to feel his skin. It was familiar but also exciting. She loved everything about him, even the way his hands felt around hers.

"That sounds glorious," she teased. "Be sure and record it in the chronicle I'm sure you're writing."

"I must be a fool," he said.

"Why?"

"Because I'm leaving you to go dig a toilet," he said.

"Yeah, I'd say that qualifies you as a fool."

She was looking at him, and that probably saved their lives. She saw the movement out of the corner of her eye—not a thing, just movement—and she reacted without hesitation or thought. She jumped straight into him and knocked him back, then fell on top of him. The thing, whatever it was, flew past right over them.

"What—" was all Blake had time to say.

Felicity had her rifle slung across her chest. She rolled

over, took hold of it, and fired. The plasma cartridge exploded from the gun. She couldn't really see her target, but she heard the projectile make contact and saw a blue gel of burning gas spreading across the creature. It was still close and seemed to have been turning back for another attack. It wailed in agony as the gas expanded over it, burning its flesh and revealing its shape. It was unlike anything she'd ever seen before, and fortunately it fell back, away from where she lay beside Blake. They still felt the heat. Felicity raised her rifle to block the wave of heat from the plasma. Blake, his rifle on his back where he had slung it to keep it out of his way while he assembled the communication relay, had drawn his pistol and was holding his free arm up to block the heat.

"Move!" she shouted.

They both scrambled backward. The creature was moving away from them. They still couldn't see it clearly; it looked like it was covered in grass, as if it were part of the landscape. Fortunately, the plasma had scarred it, burning away its natural camouflage and revealing the size of the beast. It was a big, four-legged predator with a huge mouth. It had flopped onto its side, trying to douse the fire that was burning it alive, but the plasma wouldn't be extinguished. It continued burning until the creature finally died. There was a gaping hole in its side with smoke rising from it. The smell of charred flesh was strangely appealing to Felicity.

"Ye-yes, sir," Blake said, putting his free arm around her. "Some type of creature attacked us. It's hard to describe."

He was speaking via the com-link. Felicity could hear the captain in her earpiece, but her mind wasn't processing the words. She was a fighter and had reacted on instinct, but once the danger had passed, the fear kicked in. She was trembling all over, and so was Blake. He holstered his pistol and pulled his rifle around so that he could hold it ready.

"It was camouflaged. I didn't even see it, sir. Corporal Mars saved my life."

He tried to look at her, but Felicity was thinking about the fact that being romantic with Blake had almost killed them. She hadn't seen the creature because she felt safe. She had let her guard down, and she resolved in that very moment not to let it happen again.

"I'm okay," she said to Blake softly before stepping away from him.

He nodded, but she could see the concern in his eyes. He wanted to protect her, but she didn't know if he could. She still didn't see how it had gotten so close to them without being seen. That fearful thought drove everything else out of her mind. These things were out there, even though she couldn't see them—big, almost completely invisible predators. She couldn't let her guard down, but she couldn't will herself to see them, either. She had to focus and stay aware of what was happening in the periphery of her vision. It was only when they moved that they were visible. Perhaps it had been there beside the trail the entire time, hidden in plain sight and waiting to pounce on them when they least expected it. It made her wonder what other horrors their new home might hold.

CHAPTER 23

BLAKE CAGE

"Stay where you are. I'm sending Staff Sergeant Dole to your location with a squad of troopers," Captain Sullivan said over the com-link. "Any sign of those things down here?"

"No, sir," Cage replied. "But like I said, we didn't see it until it attacked."

He was walking closer to the beast, holding his rifle by the pistol grip. Even at close range, the unwounded portion of the creature seemed to blend right into the grass. He poked it, but the creature didn't move.

"How is that possible, Lieutenant? What were you and Corporal Mars doing up on that hill?"

"Working, sir," Cage said. "This creature has something on it. Its skin looks like the grass. I'm not sure if it followed us or was already up here. It's hard to say."

"This is highly irregular, Lieutenant. I'm not happy."

"No, sir," Cage replied.

He wasn't happy, either, and it made him angry that the captain was blaming him. But his anger came from guilt; he had been flirting with his wife when the creature attacked. All he could say for sure was that he hadn't seen it. And getting closer to the creature, he understood why. There was something about the beast's hide. It actually looked different from different angles as he circled around it.

"Once Staff Sergeant Dole reaches your location," Captain Sullivan continued, "and you've answered his questions, I want you down here in the command post ASAP!"

"Yes, sir. I'll double-time it all the way."

"No," Sullivan ordered. "Repel down. And you better have better answers for me than you just didn't see it, Lieutenant. I'm beginning to think you aren't recon material, after all. Perhaps you'd be better off overseeing the supply chain from orbit, where you won't be a liability."

Cage had to tamp down hard on his anger. Fortunately, the captain cut the connection before Cage had a chance to reply. He told himself that Sullivan was just projecting his fear onto his new, untested lieutenant. It was part of the job, being the new guy and subsequently the scapegoat. Normally hazing consisted of rowdy jokes and gags meant to embarrass the newcomer, but Cage could see how he was the easy target.

"You in trouble?" Felicity asked.

"I suppose," Cage said. "He wants me to repel down once Staff Sergeant Dole gets here."

Repelling had been part of their basic training. Some recruits hated it, but Cage didn't mind walking backward off a platform a hundred feet in the air. After the first time, he didn't have trouble trusting the rope to hold him, and he could jog down the wall without hesitation when it was his turn.

"Watch yourself, I don't want you breaking an ankle," Felicity said.

"That's the least of my worries," Cage said, poking the

beast again. "Besides, the captain is threatening to send me back up to orbit."

"That'll be hard to do without a drop ship at his disposal," Felicity said.

Cage didn't know why he hadn't thought of that, but it was true. The captain was just bluffing. He had no way of getting rid of Cage for at least a few weeks, and by that time Cage was certain he would be indispensable to Sullivan.

Staff Sergeant Dole came jogging into the clearing. The route up the hill was steep, but the staff sergeant wasn't even breathing hard. The same couldn't be said for the four troopers with him. They were puffing and wide-eyed with fear. Seeing the creature's smoking corpse didn't help.

"What the hell is that thing?" Dole asked.

"That's what we want to know," Cage replied. "We never saw it coming."

"I saw movement," Felicity said. "Right as it pounced. We got lucky."

"She pushed me down and it flew over us," Cage said. "But one shot from the Infiltrator took it out."

"Looks that way," Dole said. "That plasma is nasty stuff. I've seen it vaporize a person. Friendly fire took out a private who was being careless. Hit him in the chest and when it was done, there was nothing left of him above the knees."

"Is that true?" Sammy asked. She looked pale, her freckles even more pronounced by her fear.

"Damn straight," Dole said. "Keep your safety on, Corporal. We can't afford any accidents out here."

"Captain Sullivan is waiting on me," Cage said. "Wants me to repel down to the command post."

"Fine, we'll see what we can do up here," Dole said, pulling his knife from his belt. It was a big bowie knife with dull gray blade honed to a razor's edge. "I'm going to remove some of that hide and toss it down to you. The captain will get a kick out of that."

As Cage watched, the staff sergeant started skinning the beast. It was big, as large as the two biggest members of Bravo platoon put together. Despite the smoking hole, there was plenty of its strange hide left undamaged. Cage watched the knife cut the creature's flesh easily, and the sight made him a little queasy.

"You need help getting down, lieutenant?" Felicity asked. She was being formal but seemed a little too friendly in front of the other members of the platoon, in Cage's opinion.

"No, Corporal," he said. "I can handle this."

His armor was built onto a harness that could be used for repelling. All Cage needed to do was to snap the rope through the carabiner that was part of his belt buckle. After snapping the rope through, he wrapped it around his hips and called out the safety command.

"Belay on!" he shouted.

"On belay," someone shouted from down below.

"I guess I'm out of here," Cage said, trying not to look at Felicity.

"Let me know when you're on the ground. I've almost got this," Dole said, pulling a large flap of the creature's skin free.

"Yes, staff sergeant," Cage replied before walking to the edge of the cliff, checking his line, and leaning back.

Muscle memory kicked in, but his legs felt shaky from fear and adrenaline. He went over the cliff faster than he meant to and had to kick hard off the wall to keep from losing his balance. He righted his body at the last instant, the rope hot in his gloved hand as it slid around his body and through the carabiner. He landed on his feet, happy that he hadn't made too big of a fool of himself in the eyes of the platoon.

He keyed his com-link and said, "I'm down, Staff Sergeant."

"Roger that, LT," came Dole's reply. "Bombs away."

Cage barely had time to look up. He could see the bloody flap of hide falling at first, but then it flipped over to the skin side, and he lost sight of it. Cage had his hands up to catch the bloody trophy, and it hit his hands like a pizza dough. Blood and bits of fat spattered around him.

"Oh my God!" Peter Ormond, vehicle specialist, called out.

"Sorry," Cage said. "They'll be lowering my pack. Would you mind waiting on it?"

"No, sir," Ormond said, using the sleeve of his fatigue shirt to wipe the blood from his face.

Cage hurried around the command post and found Captain Sullivan waiting in the doorway. He held up the hide up with both hands.

"What is that?" Sullivan asked.

"Part of the creature's hide," Cage said. "The staff sergeant thought you should see it."

Cage turned it so that the flag-sized flap of skin was facing the captain. Sullivan looked at it and frowned. He reached out and poked it.

"But what is it?" Sullivan asked.

"Like I said, sir, it's got natural camouflage."

"But I can see it," Sullivan said.

"That's because it's moving," Cage said, knowing the captain wasn't being sincere.

The skin was visible, but it blended into the light green grass perfectly. And when it moved, it looked like the wind was blowing the grass. It certainly didn't seem like it could've been part of a huge predator, which was what the creature was. It had attacked them the way an animal would. They had been separated from the platoon. It made sense that it followed them up the trail and attacked the way a big predator on Earth might see a straggler as easy prey when it was separated from the herd.

"How could you not see it?" Sullivan said.

"We were working, sir," Cage replied, knowing that wasn't exactly the truth, but it was close enough. They wouldn't have seen the creature if they had been looking out at the grassy plain. "I had just finished securing the communication receiver. I stood up and asked Corporal Mars a question. She turned toward me, saw the creature rushing toward us, and pushed me out of the way. I still had my rifle slung on my back so it wouldn't be in the way while I worked on the receiver. She got the shot off, and fortunately for us both, it killed the beast."

"Well, that changes things," Sullivan said. "We'll have to double the watch. If that thing attacked the two of you in broad daylight, we won't have much chance against them at night."

"It might be easier to spot them at night," Cage said. "They may show up on thermal imaging much better than regular visuals."

"I hope you're right, lieutenant. For now, I need those latrines dug, and I want that berm reinforced. And let's get a hedge up on this side of the trees. I want this base camp secure before nightfall."

"Yes, sir," Cage said.

His hands were bloody, but there was no time to wash.

Private Peter Ormond brought his pack to the command post just as Cage was finishing up with the captain.

"Just leave it there," Cage said, pointing to the side of the building. "You and Webster grab some shovels and join me."

After scrubbing his hands in the grass, Cage spent an hour with the two vehicle specialists digging three deep holes in the ground. They covered them with boards from one of the crates that were made for that purpose. The boards had holes in the middle. With their makeshift toilets complete, the second lieutenant went to work on the hedge. It wasn't much —just a jumble of fallen limbs—but it created a barrier next to the trees that hemmed in their camp to the north.

As the sun began to set, the camp was as secure as the platoon could make it. The berm that separated the camp from the open plain was lined with the empty cargo containers, creating a makeshift fence. Lines had been strung on the far side with tiny little bells that would jingle in the night if something approached the camp. Floodlights filled the area around the command post with light. Water had been collected, and several small fires were burning. The troopers had set up their tents on the river side of the command post. They didn't have food for cooking yet—that would come down on the loads being dropped from orbit. Until then, the platoon ate MREs from dull green bags. It had been a long day, and Cage was thankful to take a break.

"Not bad for a first day," Staff Sergeant Dole said, waving Cage over to where the older man sat, his back against the support post of the mess pavilion.

There were crates inside and Cage dropped down, leaning his back on one.

"What watch are you on?" Dole asked.

"Middle," Cage said.

"That figures. You're the new guy. You'll get all the worst assignments."

"And they said being an officer had perks," Cage said.

"That depends on the officer."

"I guess I'm not a very good one yet."

"On the contrary. I've had my eye on you. I saw you digging latrines and carrying water. You're out here sweating with your troopers. In my book, that's the best kind of officer. Most of 'em don't want to deal with real work. They'd rather sit back and give orders."

"I gave plenty of orders," Cage said, stirring the stew-like contents of his meal in a bag.

"Well, that comes with the territory. But your troopers will notice that you don't pawn off the hard work on them. They'll love you for it."

Love—the word triggered something in Cage's mind, but he wasn't sure what. He was thinking of Felicity as he stared at the bag's swirling contents. It was too gloomy to see, but he couldn't help but look at it. And then he remembered: before the attack, they had seen something. Cage suddenly sat up straight.

"The food that bad?" Dole asked with a chuckle. "The latrine is that way," he pointed with his spork.

"I'll be back," Cage said.

He hurried over to where the female troopers who weren't on watch had gathered. It crossed his mind briefly that it was telling that men and women, when unable to fraternize, segregated naturally even on this new world. He shoved that useless thought away and searched for Felicity. All the women were watching him, some with undisguised appreciation. That thought wasn't useful either, and he cursed his mind for even entertaining the thought that his female troopers might be interested in romance.

"Want to join us, lieutenant?" Sammy asked.

"No, thank you," Cage said, feeling a sense of urgency. "Corporal Mars, May I speak to you a minute?"

"And there you have it," Lucinda Fuego said. "Mars wins the lottery."

"What are they talking about?" Cage asked as they walked away.

"They have a pool going on for who you'll seduce with your dreamy good looks," Felicity said. "My money is on Sammy."

Cage didn't have time for jokes. "Did you talk to the captain?"

"No, was I supposed to?"

"We have to tell him about the thing," Cage said. "The structure. I should have done it sooner, but I forgot."

"There was a lot on your mind," Felicity said. "I forgot too."

"Come on, we'll tell him together. He'll want to know what you saw."

Cage led the way. The door to the command post was closed. Cage was again struck by the fact that their captain was hiding in his office—not that Cage expected him to be roughing it with his troopers, but the feeling was there just the same. Something was wrong with Sullivan, but that too would have to wait.

Cage knocked.

"Enter," the captain called from inside.

Cage pushed open the door and was a little shocked by what he saw. The captain had a cot against one wall, a table with his food on a plate, and two camp chairs. Everyone else, including Staff Sergeant Dole and Cage himself, had been sitting on the ground, eating their food out of bags. It seemed almost obscene that Sullivan had such luxuries. The heavy cargo hadn't even been dropped yet. What necessities had been left behind so that Captain Sullivan could have his comforts?

"We forgot a detail of our report," Cage said.

"About the creature?" Sullivan asked, with just the slightest hint of fear in his voice.

"No, sir," Felicity said. "While we were up on the hill, I saw something."

"What?" Sullivan asked.

"Hard to say for certain, sir. It's in the mountains," Cage said. "But it looked out of place."

"It was a structure," Felicity said. "I'm sure of it."

"A structure?"

"We couldn't see much of it, Captain," Cage said. "And then the attack happened, and I completely forgot about it."

"You saw a structure, and you forgot?" Sullivan snarled. "Good God, man, are you that stupid?"

"Captain?" Felicity said. She shouldn't have opened her mouth, but she didn't like seeing her husband talked down to.

"Dismissed, Corporal!" he shouted at her.

For a moment, Cage thought she might knock her superior officer out cold. He could feel the rage coming off of her in waves. Cage wanted to tell her it was okay, but he couldn't do anything that might be taken as an act of kindness or affection.

"Now!" he shouted again.

Felicity turned on her heel and stormed from the command post.

"That girl is getting to be a problem," Sullivan said truculently. "Making her a corporal was a mistake. The entire service is promoting people entirely too quickly. Now, tell me what you saw."

Cage took a breath to steady himself. He was angry too, but the captain appeared much calmer now. He was quick to anger and had little self-control with his subordinates. Aggressive fury seemed to be his go-to emotion, and one that quickly passed once he had another target for his anger.

"A straight edge," Cage said. "I honestly can't say that it was more than that. But in the mountains, we saw something that looked like stone, only it was slanting down and absolutely straight."

"There are no straight lines in nature," Sullivan said.

"In the nature we know," Cage replied. "Could be different here. We couldn't get a better look at it from the hill. I could take a group into the mountains tomo—"

"No!" Sullivan said, cutting him off. "You don't really expect me to believe you saw a structure, do you? The probes did an extensive survey of this area before recommending it as a likely place for the original colony. If there was a structure, it would have been seen."

"Yes, sir," Cage said.

Cage had had the same thoughts himself. And if he was wrong, well, that thought was frankly frightening. It meant someone had been here—or still was here. Those thoughts made Cage uneasy, but he still wanted to know. Hiding from the structure wouldn't make it go away.

"We're in a new place, and you've been through a strenuous first day," Sullivan said. "You should forget about what you saw and get some sleep while you can."

"You don't think we should investigate?"

"Our orders are clear, lieutenant. We are to establish a base camp. Collect the heavy cargo. Survey the area of a potential colony site. And report our findings to the *Bronx II*. Anything outside of that is a distraction."

"But you said we should survey the site. Surely an accurate survey would include checking out something that might be a structure."

"If there is time," Sullivan maintained, "then perhaps we shall investigate your phantom structure, but the colony won't be built in the mountains, lieutenant. You need to use your mind, son. This is serious business. We have responsibilities. Thousands of people are depending on us to create a safe and appropriate site for their colony. One day, this area may be known as 'Sullivanville.' We can't let distractions keep us from our duty. You'd be wise to remember that."

"Okay," Cage said. He didn't know what else to say.

"You should get some rest, lieutenant. While you can."

Cage saluted, but Sullivan just turned back to his dinner. Leaving the command post, Cage stepped out into the cool night air. Felicity was waiting nearby, and Cage shook his head. She looked deflated and walked back toward the group of women she had been eating with.

"That as bad as it sounded?" Dole asked.

"Worse," Cage said, dropping down onto a crate. "We saw something in the mountains. A structure of some kind."

"A structure?" the staff sergeant asked.

"We could only see a corner of it, but whatever it was had a perfectly straight edge."

"And the captain isn't interested," Dole said, shaking his head.

"No," Cage muttered.

"Want some advice?" Dole asked.

Cage looked at the canny old veteran. "Please."

"You want an officer to do something, then you have to

make him think it was his idea. If you come right out and suggest it, they shoot it down every time. It's like a knee-jerk reaction. You need to learn to come about a thing from a different angle."

"I'm not very good at managing people yet," Cage said.

"You have to separate your targets," Dole said. "You don't use the same tactics for everyone all the time. Surely they taught you that in officer school."

"Something like that," Cage said.

"Well, what works on us grunts won't work on the higher-ups. We have different goals and different ideas on what's important," Dole said. "Captain Sullivan is past his prime. And he didn't rise very high in the ranks, so he's looking for a way to correct that before he retires."

"He mentioned something about the colony being named after him," Cage said.

"Well, there you go. He's shown you his goal. He wants to be the big muckety-muck here. He's thinking he'll be a local hero—maybe they'll make him the mayor when he retires from the MCM after helping establish the colony. That won't happen if they choose site A. And they won't build here if there are dangerous creatures or some mysterious structure nearby."

"You're a genius," Cage said with a grin.

"It's about damn time someone noticed," Staff Sergeant Dole declared.

CHAPTER 24

FELICITY MARS

"Spill it!" Sammy insisted.

The group of women—there were seven in the platoon—had thinned. Lucinda, Amber, and Miranda Dux, the lone female HeWE, were on watch. Only Sammy, Joelle, and Lori were left.

"What?" Felicity asked.

"Don't play coy with us," Lori said.

"Yes, tell us all the dirt. Is he a good kisser?" Joelle asked.

"I don't know what you all thought that was about, but it wasn't good," Felicity said. "The captain is on the war path."

"For what?" Sammy said. "We're out here doing all the work while he sits on his ass in his *command post*."

She said the last two words as if they were an absurdity. Felicity could see the tents nearby. They were high quality, little structures, made to keep a person out of the elements. Each one had a battery-operated pump that inflated the supports. The simple design included a heater that used solar power to radiate warmth inside the small tent. It wouldn't keep a large predator out or stand up to gale force winds, but it was better than sleeping outdoors. Still, the thought of spending the night in a tent and trying to rest in a sleeping bag on the ground made the captain's command post seem luxurious.

"Did you do something wrong?" Joelle asked.

"When the LT and I were up on the hill," Felicity pointed up at the cliff, "I was tying off the repelling lines, and we saw something."

"We know about the animal," Lori said.

"It was awful," Sammy said. "I can't believe you killed it without getting hurt."

"Did they move the carcass?" Joelle said. "One dead animal will draw more of them to us."

"It wasn't about the animal," Felicity said. "We saw a structure in the mountains."

"What did the captain say about it?" Sammy said.

"We had forgotten about it," Felicity explained. "After the attack, it completely slipped our minds. But the LT remembered, and that's why he came for me."

"So we're going to check it out, right?" Sammy asked. "I mean, if people have been here before us, that's a game changer."

"It can't be people," Lori said. "We're the first to come to this world, remember?"

"The first from Earth," Sammy countered. "We don't know that the colonies haven't sent people out here."

"Or maybe there were people already here," Joelle said. "Maybe the probe didn't see them."

"We know there aren't cities," Sammy said. "Cities would have been seen."

"There's something out there," Felicity said. "It had a perfectly straight edge. It had to be made."

"You guys are starting to give me the creeps," Lori said. "It could be anything—a past civilization or evidence of aliens. I don't like it."

"Well, we can't go home," Sammy said. "We're here now. Whoever built it will just have to deal."

"First that creature," Joelle said, "now this. It's unsettling for sure."

It was tempting to stay out near the little fire the women had built. They could see hundreds of stars overhead, and the flood lights around the command post were a reassuring reminder of civilization. On the new world, which they thought was completely untouched by outside forces or any kind of intelligent species, something familiar made them all feel a little better. But Felicity was on the late watch. She had just under six hours until she would have to get up and stand guard around the camp.

"Thanks for setting up my shelter," she told her friends. "I'm going to get some sleep."

"You sure we won't see the LT sneaking over?" Sammy asked.

"I wouldn't say no to a proposition like that," Lori said with a chuckle.

Felicity ignored them. She had already pulled her sleeping bag from her pack. She had enough food for three more days and a personal water filter still tucked inside. The platoon had ammo in one of the crates they had carried off the drop ship, and Felicity had already replaced her plasma cartridge shell. She unfastened her Infiltrator from the strap that was around her shoulder. After ensuring the safety was on, she propped the rifle up just inside her tent.

The little shelter wasn't big enough to stand up in. She removed her pistol holster from around her thigh, took off her belt with the lightweight fighting knife in its sheath, and then pulled off her armor. Her fatigues stayed on, and she crawled into the tent, neatly arranged her belongings, then zipped up the enclosure. She had to unlace her boots and pull them off. It wasn't really cold out. The temperature had fallen about ten degrees and would probably drop ten more before morning, but her sleeping bag would keep her warm. She crawled into the bag. There was just enough light from the camp that she could see inside the small shelter.

The ground beneath her was soft enough, but sleep was elusive. She closed her eyes, but the memories of the attack kept playing through her mind. And her ears heard all the strange sounds around her. Some were familiar—a voice, the footsteps of someone passing by her tent, some piece of equipment being moved—but there were other sounds she'd never heard before: strange insects humming in the darkness, chirps, twitters, and distant huffs of some type of large animal. She was on edge, and while she didn't think she was terrified, she couldn't shake off the fear.

Her father had taught her not to run from fear, but to listen to it. He had said that when she felt afraid, she needed to think, to identify what was causing her to be afraid. Was she in the wrong place? Was she with the wrong person? Was she doing something she knew was dangerous or irresponsible? The problem wasn't her thinking, it was the lack of information. They were in a place she didn't know. There were predators on Magnificus Prime that she had never encountered or even imagined. She had already come close to dying or being badly hurt by the animal that attacked her and Blake up on the hill. Those things and hundreds of imagined threats lurked in her mind. What else might be out there, just waiting in the dark to strike at the little platoon? They had weapons, but it might not be enough to stop what she felt was stalking them—especially if she couldn't see them coming.

She was in and out of sleep until it was time to get up for her watch. She could feel the fatigue, but she was ready to get out of her tent and move around. When she was sleeping, she felt vulnerable. At least with her armor and weapons she wouldn't be helpless if her fears were realized.

After getting her gear on, she headed toward the berm. Blake was there, leaning against a crate that was stacked on the small mound that bordered the camp on one side. The crate was chest-high and was perfect for stabilizing his arms as he looked through a pair of night vision goggles.

"See anything scary out there?" Felicity asked.

"Hey," he said, his voice laced with weariness. "You've got to see this."

He handed her the goggles. She leaned against the crate, propping her elbows on the top just as he had been doing a moment before. When she looked through the goggles, she could see the wide, grassy plain.

"Oh, wow!" she said in a soft voice.

"They're magnificent, aren't they?" Blake asked.

"They are," Felicity said.

She could see a vast herd of majestic creatures. They were tall and regal like horses, but they had long horns on their heads that spiraled tightly up toward a point that looked to be two or three feet above their heads. They were eating the grass and moving silently north.

"How long have they been out there?" Felicity asked.

"All night," Blake said. "I've been on watch for four hours."

"Any sign of the thing that attacked us?"

"None," Blake said. "It's been peaceful all night."

"Not for me," Felicity admitted. "I couldn't sleep."

"Too much stress," he said. "Hopefully it'll pass. It's the first night in a new place, after all."

She wanted to reminisce about their first night in the tiny apartment they had moved into after getting married. It was their first home on their own and they had barely been able to rest that night, either. The old building made noises. There were neighbors on either side, and they heard every person who walked down the hall outside their apartment that first night. But thinking of the past took her out of the present, and if their experience on the hill had taught Felicity anything, it was that she needed to stay present and focused.

The night vision goggles had other settings, as well. She could toggle between regular vision, thermal, and infrared. The thermal vision showed the stately creatures as red and yellow blobs of color. The herd was big enough that their heat signatures all blended together.

"You should get some rest," Felicity said. "You sound tired."

"I am tired," Blake agreed. "Where's your partner?"

"He's coming," Felicity said, although she had no idea where Devon was. "What happened after I left last night?"

"The captain lamented the state of the MCM and then insisted that the new colony would one day be called 'Sullivanville.'"

"You're not serious."

"As a heart attack," Blake insisted. "He doesn't want to even consider that there might be something negative to report about this colony site."

"So what are we going to do?" Felicity asked.

"I got some good advice about that from Staff Sergeant Dole. We'll work it out."

"Is there anything I can do to help?"

"When there is, I'll let you know," Blake said. "Looks like your partner is on his way."

Felicity turned and saw Devon approaching. He had his sniper rifle slung across his back and carried two steaming cups in his hands.

"I come bearing gifts," he said.

"Coffee, that's a great idea," Blake said. "I'll leave you to it."

Felicity wanted to watch him walk away. She hated pretending that they weren't married. But she forced herself to focus instead on the drink Devon held out to her.

"It will keep us awake," Devon said.

Felicity didn't think she needed help with that at the moment, but she was grateful just the same.

"Thank you," she said. She sipped the coffee. It was hot and bitter, but it reminded her of home. She handed the goggles to Devon. "Take a look at that," she told him, pointing out to the fields beyond their camp.

She liked being surrounded by familiar things, but she couldn't forget that her new home had some pretty amazing things going for it too.

CHAPTER 25

BLAKE CAGE

"Anything to report?" Captain Sullivan asked.

The captain had finally come out of his command post and was looking for coffee just after dawn. Cage had dozed for a few hours after his watch but then gotten up and done a check on the camp as the sun rose. Dawn had been spectacular. The sky had shifted from purple to red to a golden-tinged orange. The sun, Fortuna, had lifted over the horizon and shed light on their new world.

"Nothing of concern," Cage said. "There was a herd of herbivores in the fields last night."

"How many?" Sullivan said, sipping the steaming hot coffee he'd just poured from the camp's supply in the mess pavilion.

"Hard to say," Cage admitted. "Hundreds."

"Interesting. Where are they now?"

"They drifted into the woods just before dawn. There were a few stragglers, and another of the strange creatures attacked one."

"The same beast that attacked you and Corporal Mars?"

"Yes, sir," Cage said. "We saw it slinking across the field on thermal imaging."

"That's good to know. At least we're not their only food source."

"I'd guess the herbivores are their primary staple," Cage said. "And we saw no sign of the predator—Corporal Devon called it a 'stalker,' until dawn."

"Are you saying they aren't active at night?"

"Can't say for sure, sir, but the herd was unmolested until the sky lightened. The stalker went after one of the herbivores that was lingering in the field."

"But nothing came close to the camp?" Sullivan asked.

"No, sir. It was a quiet night."

"Excellent. We're in a good position here. And if we're lucky, the *Bronx II* will begin dropping our supplies soon."

"That would be good," Cage said. "What do you suggest we do in the meantime?"

"We hold this position. Continue observing as much as we can."

"The platoon wouldn't mind a little downtime after the excitement of yesterday," Cage said, hoping he could prompt the captain into giving him an order that would allow him to leave their camp. "We'll keep rotating the watch, of course, but otherwise, the troops could lounge about."

Sullivan's face pinched together. It looked like he'd just experienced a painful thought. "Lieutenant Cage, I hope you're not suggesting that recon platoon Bravo needs to rest after just a single day of work."

"Sir? I thought it would be a good idea—"

"I've had about enough of your good ideas. We'll do PT. That'll get the blood pumping, and maybe you'll have fewer ideas. You take the first group. I want a full workout. Calisthenics and a run. You lead half the platoon, and Staff Sergeant Dole can lead the second group. Full weapons and armor. Let's do this right."

"Yes, sir," Cage said, hiding the smile he felt.

Cage had never enjoyed manipulating people, but he knew in some instances it couldn't be helped. And Staff Sergeant Dole had been right; Sullivan might think that Cage was lazy, but if he'd come right out and suggested leading the platoon in physical training exercises, the captain would have probably come up with a reason not to do it. Instead, he gave the opposite suggestion—and Sullivan jumped at the chance to order Cage to do what he'd wanted all along.

Sullivan took his coffee back to the command post, and Staff Sergeant Dole strolled up. He nodded and poured himself some coffee.

"You look like you're in a better mood," Dole said.

"I got some good advice last night," Cage replied.

"Good to see that it wasn't wasted. What are we doing today?"

"PT, staff sergeant. By the way, do we have anything that will record pictures?"

"The monoscopes record video in 2D. Will that work?" Dole asked.

"Absolutely," Cage said with excitement.

The monoscope was a digital viewing device. Unlike the scope of a rifle, it was enhanced with a variety of apps. It could zoom in and out, measure distance, record, and mark targets for aerial bombardment. The compact device fit easily into a loop on Cage's armor. He exchanged a magazine of plasma shells for the monoscope, and after dividing the platoon into two groups, he set out on a leisurely run.

They covered five kilometers in half an hour. Cage had led the group north out of camp but quickly turned into the mountains. They jogged upward, following animal trails and keeping close watch for movement of any kind. There were small animals in the foothills of the mountain range. Cage saw signs of them, but not the animals themselves. It seemed most were nocturnal, which made sense. Many animals felt more secure in the dark.

But Cage wasn't interested in animals. He was looking for something else—and was surprised at how easily he found it. He raised his hand and called for the column of recon specialists that were following him to stop.

"Take a break," he said, looking back at his group.

Felicity was at the rear of the column. No one looked exhausted; they were used to long runs and heavy exercise at this point. Even the uphill trails didn't seem to wear them out too much. Some of the group leaned against boulders, while others continued up to where Cage was standing on a flat ledge on the side of a larger hill. It wasn't quite a mountain, but they were easily several hundred meters above the plain where the camp was located.

"Would you look at that?" Sammy said as she came up beside Cage.

He was already looking through the monoscope, recording what he saw. It was a spectacular sight. Nestled among the mountains was a pyramid. Cage had studied the different pyramid structures built around the world. There were pyramids on every continent, with the exception of Antarctica. The most famous were the Egyptian pyramids on the Giza plateau, and the pyramid in the mountains on Magnificus Prime looked exactly like them.

"I told you," Felicity said as she joined the group on the ledge.

"You called it, Corporal," Cage said.

"LT? Are you saying you knew about this?" Grant Laubin asked.

"We saw part of it yesterday," Cage admitted.

"Wait, is that a pyramid?" Peter Ormond asked. "Like mummies and stuff?"

"Can't be," Hugo Webster exclaimed. "That's impossible."

The pyramid was different from the ones on Earth in that it looked newer. The pyramids on the Giza plateau were weathered, and their limestone coverings had mostly been carried away. But the pyramid Cage was looking at was pristine. The sides were smooth, not stair-stepped, and looked white, almost as white as the snow on the mountain peaks around them. And the top of the pyramid, Cage guessed at least six or seven meters from the peak, was gold.

"How in the hell did the probes miss that?" Grant Laubin asked.

"Yeah," Ted Ficklestine agreed, "didn't they scan this entire area?"

"The mountains," Amber Case said. "From orbit it probably blends right in."

"This is unbelievable," Albert Malone said. "What do you think it means?"

"It means we aren't the first people on this planet," Hugo declared.

"It looks new," Felicity said. "The pyramids back on Earth don't look like that."

"That could be because it's protected in that valley," Cage said. "The pyramids on Earth have been pillaged for usable materials."

"So it could be old?" Sammy asked. "Just like ours?"

"Could be," Cage said. "We won't know until we get a closer look."

"What are we waiting on?" Amber said. "Let's go."

"No," Cage said. "We're going back to base."

"Are you kidding, LT?" Hugo said. "We can't just ignore that."

"He's right," Sammy said. "We have to check it out."

"No," Cage said. "It's twelve kilometers from here. And Captain Sullivan needs to see this."

"I doubt even a pyramid is going to get him out of his comfy command post," Grant said.

"You keep your thoughts about the captain to yourself," Cage said, but not angrily. He had similar feelings about their CO himself, but he wouldn't let the troops under his command voice their insubordinate thoughts aloud. "For now, we go back."

"And just ignore it?" Sammy asked.

"No, Corporal. We start planning an expedition to check it out."

"I volunteer," Felicity said.

"Me too," said Amber.

"I want in," Grant said.

"I'm going," Ted added.

"Let's just get back," Cage said. "And keep in mind we aren't alone out here, so stay alert. Keep your head on a swivel. Watch out for any sign of movement."

Turning away from the pyramid and going back to the base camp was the hardest thing Cage had ever done. He was a student of history and had studied the pyramids in Egypt. The Great Pyramid of Giza was still one of the greatest unsolved mysteries in the world.

"What do you know about pyramids?" Felicity asked.

She, Sammy, and Amber were crowding close to Cage as they jogged back to their camp. He let his mind call up the information before he answered.

"There are a lot of them on Earth—hundreds—although a lot have been destroyed," Cage said. "And there are different kinds. That one we saw looks like the Egyptian pyramids."

"What do we know about the Egyptian pyramids?" Sammy asked.

"The Great Pyramid of Giza is the largest and oldest. Most scholars believe it was built around twenty-five eighty BCE."

"That's old," Amber said.

"What do you mean 'believe'?" Felicity asked.

"Well, there are a lot of theories, but it's hard to imagine a structure made of immense blocks of cut stones could be quarried by people with copper chisels. We're talking before the bronze age, and probably before the invention of the wheel."

"It's really that old?" Sammy asked.

"At least that old," Cage went on. "The pyramid is believed to have been a burial structure for a pharaoh named Khufu."

"Why do they believe that?" Felicity asked.

"Because of an inscription of Khufu's name on the pyramid."

"Are there lots of hieroglyphics on the pyramids?" Amber asked.

"Actually no," Cage went on. "It's surprisingly bare inside."

"There's an inside?" Sammy asked.

"Yes, the Great Pyramid has several chambers inside. There's a corridor leading from the northern side. It splits in two, with one corridor going up and the other going down into the bedrock below. The chambers under the pyramid were never finished. There's a tunnel that just ends. Inside the pyramid there is a middle chamber, the grand gallery, and the king's chamber."

"Sounds kind of creepy," Amber said.

"Wait a second," Sammy said. "You're telling me that before there where wheels or steel tools, the Egyptians built a ginormous pyramid made of huge blocks of stone?"

"Over two million blocks of limestone and granite," Cage said. "It's a fascinating mystery."

"I'd say," Sammy said. "I'm not buying."

"You're not buying what?" Felicity asked.

"That people could build something like that back then," Sammy said. "Can you imagine moving that much stone? Even with hundreds or thousands of people, it would take decades."

"How'd they do it?" Felicity asked.

"No one knows," Cage admitted. "There are a lot of theories. Moving the stones isn't impossible, but it gets pretty tricky once you get off the ground. Moving big blocks of stone that high up would be extremely difficult."

"And people believe it was a tomb? Why?"

"There are a few reasons," Cage said. "The first being that the other pyramids were tombs."

"Just like the big one?" Sammy asked.

"No," Cage said as they came out of the mountains and turned south on the wide, grassy plain. "The Great Pyramid is different. The others are built over subterranean burial chambers. They're just solid structures with tunnels that go down under them. But the Great Pyramid has chambers inside the pyramid itself, as well as ventilation shafts that go all the way to the outside."

"Why would they need ventilation shafts for a tomb?" Hugo Webster asked.

Cage glanced back and noticed that the entire group had moved close. They were all listening to his explanations, but he didn't have good answers. He knew a lot about the pyramids of Earth, but he had never heard of a pyramid on any other planet.

"All right," Cage said. He slowed to a stop and turned around to face his audience. They stopped and gathered close. "First, I want everyone on alert for danger of any kind. Second, keep in mind that we just don't know all the answers. For thousands of years, humans have been trying to solve the mystery of the pyramids with the assumption that they were constructed by ancient man."

"But there were other theories, right?" Grant said. "Aliens and stuff?"

Cage nodded. "There are other theories. One of the most prevalent is that mankind, in that early stage, couldn't have built them on his own."

"Or her own," Felicity said, earning a few high fives from her female platoon mates.

Cage grinned and continued. "So if we didn't build them, who did and why? Aliens? Gods? A race of giants? We just don't know."

"The alien theory is looking pretty good right about now," Hugo said.

"The more important question," Cage said, "is *why* were they built?"

The group fell silent. Cage turned and started running again. His mind was buzzing with the possible answers to his own question, but nothing made sense. Their find, as amazing as it was, raised many more questions than it answered.

The talk Cage had with Staff Sergeant Dole crept back into his mind as he started thinking of how to break the news of their discovery to Captain Sullivan. He needed the older man to think of the pyramid as a positive thing, not a negative. It would take a careful explanation, but Cage already had some ideas about that. He would make Sullivan realize how important their find was—not just for the colony or the company, but for all of mankind.

CHAPTER 26

BLAKE CAGE

"Sir," Cage said after knocking politely on the door of the command post.

"Enter," Sullivan shouted.

Cage opened the door. There was chatter on the radio from the *Bronx II*. The captain, with nothing else to do, had been listening in. Cage closed the door and waited for Sullivan, who was eating his midday meal even though it was still two hours from midday, to look up.

"Yes, Lieutenant?"

"Sir, I know this mission is important to you," Cage said. "It's your legacy in the company."

"It's historic," Sullivan said.

"Yes, sir, and I think it's even more historic than we realized."

"What are you going on about now, lieutenant?"

"Sir, your orders to be alert were right," Cage said, trying not to sound patronizing as he embellished what the captain had told him to do that morning. "We found something. It's going to make this colony the most important place in the galaxy."

Captain Sullivan tried to look skeptical, but there was an undeniable glimmer of hope in his eyes. He sat up a little straighter, his food forgotten.

"Go on," he said.

"We were on our run, and this is what we found," Cage said, holding out the monoscope.

The device was made to download onto a monitor. Sullivan activated the sync feature and powered on his computer tablet. The two devices linked, and the video that Cage had shot played on the tablet's high-resolution screen.

Sullivan stood up suddenly, and his camp chair toppled over behind him.

"What the devil?" he said.

"It's a pyramid," Cage said softly. "It looks Egyptian, but we won't know for certain until you explore it. You'll be the man who discovered the most significant archeological find in the history of mankind."

Cage let the thought sink into his superior's mind. The truth was, Felicity had found the structure. Cage had confirmed its existence, but the young lieutenant wasn't foolish enough to believe that anyone would care. Cage and his wife were both part of Captain Sullivan's platoon. Any discoveries would bear his name. But Cage wasn't looking for recognition: he wanted answers. He wanted to explore the pyramid and find its secrets. Not for humanity, but for himself.

"A pyramid," Sullivan whispered. "I can't believe it."

"We need to explore it and document it," Cage said. "Then you can send word back to Earth. Maybe even go back yourself and present the findings in person."

"I'll be famous," Sullivan said, completely lost in the fantasy that Cage was spinning.

"The most famous person maybe ever," Cage said.

Sullivan nodded, and Cage felt he had pushed his CO far enough. Sullivan couldn't turn back; he was too invested in the idea of his own celebrity.

"How far is it?" Sullivan asked.

"Just under twenty klicks, sir, through the mountains. If we hurry, we could be there by nightfall."

"No," Sullivan said, shaking his head. "We can't rush this. We'll make our preparations and set out at first light. The idiots on the *Bronx II* are having problems with the satellites. They haven't even launched our heavy cargo yet. We have time."

He was nodding, imagining something, but Cage couldn't guess what. His own mind started running through the list of things that needed to be done. The most important was to run a relay that would allow them to have instant communications despite being in the mountains. Fortunately, Felicity had already solved that problem. They'd set up a receiver in the trees where she had secured the repelling lines. From there, in a gap between two big, craggy hills, there was a direct line of sight to the pyramid.

"I'll get started," Cage said. "With your permission, Captain."

Sullivan nodded and waved Cage away. It seemed strange to him that Sullivan was so lost in his own world. When Cage had been introduced, Sullivan seemed sharp and capable. But ever since they had come out of cryogenic stasis, the captain seemed to be pulling away from the platoon, going deeper and deeper into his own thoughts. Cage made a mental note to keep an eye on the older man. He was only fifteen years

Cage's senior, and yet he was starting to act like someone who was losing their grasp on reality. In fact, Cage felt a little guilty for planting the seed of celebrity in Sullivan's mind. The captain seemed suddenly obsessed with the idea of it.

"What's this business about a pyramid?" Staff Sergeant Dole asked as soon as Cage stepped out of the command post.

"That's the structure we found," Cage said. "An Egyptian-style pyramid. We confirmed it on our PT run."

"I'll be damned," Dole said. "You're serious? This isn't some prank?"

"I got video using the monoscope, just like you showed me," Cage said. "Captain Sullivan has it."

"He's a cautious man," Dole pointed out. "What's our orders?"

"Prepare today, leave at dawn," Cage said. "You can see it clearly from a ledge about five klicks from here. Corporal Mars can show you where. I'm going to set another communication relay that should give us access to the base camp from the pyramid."

"What's it look like?" the older man asked, his gruff, common-sense demeanor replaced with pure wonder.

"The way the Great Pyramid of Giza would have looked nearly five thousand years ago," Cage explained. "The base is covered with polished white limestone. And the cap is covered in gold."

"Bullshit," the staff sergeant replied.

"I kid you not," Cage said. "You'll see it for yourself."

"This was not part of the plan," Dole said.

"I think we can toss the plan out the window and start over," Cage said. "It may take them twenty years to get here, but I'm guessing every historian on Earth is going to make the trip."

Dole put his arm around Cage and led him away from the command post. Then he spoke in quiet, somber tones.

"I hope you don't mind me taking the liberty to speak to you like this, lieutenant, but I hope you know that the captain is going to want to take full credit for this discovery."

"I do," Cage said. "In fact, I planted that idea in his mind."

"You don't care?" Dole asked.

"I might under different circumstances," Cage said. "But the truth is, I didn't find the pyramid either. It was Corporal Mars who found it. All I want is to find out who built it and why."

"And how they got here," Dole added. "And if they're coming back."

CHAPTER 27

FELICITY MARS

She didn't have much rest before Staff Sergeant Dole found her.

"You up for another run, Corporal?"

"Yes, staff sergeant," she replied, without really thinking. She had been trained to reply "yes" so instinctively that she didn't even consider the request before answering. Fortunately, she wasn't exhausted. Their morning run had been light with stops along the way.

"What did you have in mind?" Felicity asked.

"I need you to take me to the ridge you saw that pyramid from," Dole said.

"I can do that, staff sergeant."

"Outstanding. We'll get our calisthenics done, then we'll be ready to run."

"I'll be ready," Felicity said.

There wasn't anything to do in the base camp except for standing watch and hauling water. And Felicity liked to exercise. She'd rather be sparring or rolling on a mat practicing jiu jitsu, but running was okay, especially since she could do it outdoors on a pristine planet.

She checked her gear and did some light stretching while Staff Sergeant Dole took his half of the platoon through morning PT. She also loaded up on water, filling her small, insulated canteen with the filtered water from the river that was kept in a larger cooler in the platoon's cooking pavilion.

"We're ready, Corporal," Sergeant Dole said as Felicity approached. "You take the lead and I'll bring up the rear."

"Yes, staff sergeant!" Felicity replied.

She had her assault rifle on a sling, but if she didn't hold it, the weapon would bounce against her. She put one hand on the pistol grip and the other on the barrel sheath that ran along the bottom of the rifle. It covered three sides of the round, smooth bore barrel that fired the plasma cartridges. Her thumb made sure the toggle was set to fire the carefully constructed shells rather than the laser, which she didn't think would be as effective against the large predator she had fought off the day before.

Her platoon mates fell in line behind her. Running in formation was something they had practiced nearly every day of their recon training. Porter Bailey moved up to her left, his weapon pointing away from her. The other eight platoon members followed suit, with everyone watching for any signs of danger.

"You've seen it?" Porter asked.

They were moving at a jog, and talking wasn't difficult.

"The pyramid?" Felicity asked.

"Yeah," Porter said. "Wow, it's crazy."

Felicity hadn't given the strangeness too much thought. She was excited about exploring the structure. Blake's excitement was contagious, and she loved to see him happy.

"It's amazing," Felicity agreed. "Really beautiful."

"How long do you think it's been there?"

"I don't know," Felicity said. "It looks brand new."

"I guess it could be," Porter said. "I mean, we don't know what's been happening here. The probe we sent was over thirty-five years ago. Anything could have happened in that much time."

"I suppose," Felicity said. She had assumed the structure was old because the pyramids on Earth were so old.

"You nervous about it?" Porter asked.

"No, why?"

"Well, you're usually more talkative," he said. "I know some people are pretty frightened."

"Of what?" Felicity asked.

"The pyramid, aliens, dying alone out here on this strange world—you name it."

Felicity could relate. Her own brush with death had shaken her up. She continued scanning the area ahead of them for any sign of the stalkers like the one that had attacked her and Blake. Her fear was that she could pass right by one and never see it. Fortunately, they were big creatures. They might blend into the grassy meadows, but if she saw a lump or small berm, she would notice it—at least she thought she would and had herself convinced that she didn't need to be afraid.

"You believe in aliens?" Porter asked.

"I guess so," Felicity said. "It's hard to believe we're the only intelligent life out here."

"I suppose to the creatures on this planet, we're the aliens," Porter said. "Funny how that—"

Felicity grabbed his arm and held her other up in a fist to halt the column of soldiers. There was bumping and jostling, but the platoon quickly fell silent. Everyone was on high alert, especially Felicity. She had seen something. It looked like a shimmer or refraction of light, but not just one. There were three distinct spots where the area ahead of them seemed to move.

"You got something, Corporal?" Staff Sergeant Dole asked as he came up beside her.

"Movement," Felicity said. "But I've lost it now."

"Where?" Dole asked.

Felicity pointed, then took hold of her gun again. She kept her finger off the trigger but held it ready just in case.

"All right, form up around my position," Dole barked. "Plasma rounds only, watch for any signs of movement. Mount your scopes and switch them to thermal imaging."

The rail on the top of the assault rifles could accommodate a variety of accessories. Most of the platoon had basic firing scopes, which were square optics used for long-range targets. But Felicity and Bailey, being scouts, had monoscopes, which were fully digital devices that could record up to six hours of high-resolution video.

Felicity pulled out the scope, snapped it onto her Magellan Infiltrator assault rifle, and powered the device on. A tiny dial on top toggled the monoscope through the different settings. She twisted it to the thermal setting and looked through the scope. There were three dark red blobs slowly moving straight ahead of them.

"I see three," Felicity said.

"Got 'em," Porter added.

"All right, Mars, you shoot the one in the middle," Dole ordered. "Bailey, you take the one on the left. I've got the one on the right. Fire on my mark."

Felicity settled the scope's sights on the middle blob. The

scope told her the creature was eight meters from her. If it charged, it would be on her in seconds. She moved her finger to the trigger and waited for the command to fire.

"Three, two, one, mark," Dole said.

The three rifles boomed simultaneously. Felicity looked away from her scope. The plasma round was bright white in the thermal vision. She kept her weapon trained on the beast but looked over the sights. Fire and smoke were erupting from all three creatures, which bellowed and roared. They instinctively rolled on the ground, hoping to extinguish the fire, but the plasma clung to them, burning through the creatures' flesh and boiling their blood as it sent up dark clouds of oily smoke.

"Got all three," Bailey said.

"There could be more," Dole said. "Hold your position. Keep scanning."

Felicity saw the three they had shot flopping on the ground. She couldn't tell if they were dead or dying. The only parts of the creatures she could clearly see were the wounds. Their hides blended in perfectly with the ground and grass of the plain, but the wounds were dark, smoking holes. The smell of scorched flesh was nearly overwhelming.

"I don't see any more," Felicity said.

"Me neither," Dole said. "Good eye, Mars. Let's stay alert, people. There could be more of those creatures out here. Secure you're weapons and form up."

Felicity didn't like flipping the safety on her rifle, but she didn't like the idea of people running behind her without their safeties on, either. She decided it was better to take her chances with the stalkers than get shot with a plasma round. Leading the column forward, they jogged past the corpses of the big predators. Felicity couldn't help but marvel at the way their hides seemed to shift and flow right into the background. It was difficult to make out any detail of the creatures.

"That was close," Bailey said. "We could have run right into them."

"Yeah," Felicity said, her anxiety rising. That was her worst fear—that she run headlong into the camouflaged predators—but she reassured herself that she was good at spotting them. In both of her encounters with these creatures so far, she had seen something that alerted her to the danger. As long as she stayed alert, there was no reason to think she wouldn't see them in the future.

"So," Bailey said as Felicity turned onto a game trail that led into the mountains, "aliens. Do you think they would be benevolent or set on total domination?"

"I'm hoping benevolent," Felicity said. "But I would settle for long gone."

"I don't guess there's any chance that a past civilization on this planet just happened to build a pyramid similar to what the ancient Egyptians built on Earth."

"That's too much of a stretch for me," Felicity said. "And if that's the case, why haven't we seen other signs of their civilization?"

"Yeah, I agree. I think we're the only people on this planet."

That thought, which her counterpart meant as reassuring, had the opposite effect for Felicity. She glanced back over her shoulder. There were eight other recon troopers behind her, and yet she felt like they were incredibly alone. If something happened, who would be able to help them? They were the only people on the planet.

Of course, that wasn't true. Recon Platoon Alpha was somewhere on the other side of the mountains. And there were people in the *Bronx II* somewhere in orbit with drop ships that could take them off-world if necessary. But for some reason, those facts didn't make her feel any better.

The trail into the mountains was steep at times. Felicity's strength was in her legs. She had run stairs most of her life. For most people on Earth, there wasn't a lot of extra money that could be used for gym memberships. Felicity's father had her running stairs in their apartment building from the age of six. She hadn't taken an elevator until she moved into public housing with Blake, and then only because they lived on the forty-second floor. She could climb that many flights and sometimes did, but it took too long in most cases. So jogging up the game trail in the mountains on Magnificus Prime wasn't all that taxing for her, and when they reached the ledge where the pyramid came into view, it was all worth it.

"Holy crap," Bailey said.

"That's amazing," Junior Knoxx said.

"Magnifique," Jean Pierre Seine declared.

Staff Sergeant Dole pushed through the group and looked out across the valley toward the pyramid, but he didn't say a word. He just stood there, drinking in the sight of the perfect structure. It was brilliantly white, and the limestone-covered blocks were polished smooth and looked like they were covered in fresh snow. But there was no snow this low in the valley. Felicity couldn't be sure, but she felt that it was at least sixty-five degrees Fahrenheit. The shiny crown of the pyramid, covered in gold, was almost like a second sun, and the valley was quiet.

"Doesn't seem real," Bailey whispered.

"We'll find out tomorrow," Staff Sergeant Dole said. "We've gawked enough. Corporal Mars, take us home."

Base camp wasn't home, but it was becoming familiar.

After their run back through the mountains, they passed by the carcasses of the big predators and stopped long enough for Staff Sergeant Dole to harvest a large haunch.

"What are you planning to do with that, Staff Sergeant?" asked Lucinda Fuego.

"Bar-B-Q," Dole replied.

"You really think that's safe to eat?" Billy Oberton asked.

"Only one way to find out," Dole replied.

They ran back to base camp. Nothing had changed. They were still waiting for the heavy cargo to be dropped from orbit. The platoon was either on watch duty or trying to look busy so that they weren't given some dirty job to keep them busy.

Felicity found an empty crate to rest on. She sat down and drank the rest of the water in her canteen. It was lukewarm and tasted like the plastic it was held in, but she was too thirsty to care.

"You look tired," Blake said as he joined her in the shade of the cooking pavilion.

"I'll sleep well tonight," she said.

"Good, I've made sure that you don't have watch tonight. Any trouble out there?"

"Three stalkers," she said. "But we saw them coming."

Staff Sergeant Dole approached with his bloody chunk of meat. "Lieutenant, care to join me in a culinary experiment?"

"I would be honored," Blake said.

"Good," Dole said. "You get the fire going, I'll make a spit."

"Yes, Staff Sergeant," Blake said.

Felicity felt a tinge of regret. She wanted more time with her husband, but they were constrained by the job. In time, once the colony was up and running, their lives would be more routine and then they could be together—at least that had been the plan until Felicity had found the pyramid. She couldn't have seen it and not said anything, yet she suddenly wished that she could take it all back. The longing for normalcy was growing by the day, and odds were good that they might not get a chance to be together anytime soon—not if the pyramid was as big a discovery as she thought it was.

But feeling sorry for herself didn't help matters. Her father had told her that so many times growing up. She could change things with hard work, not with wishes. She got up, weary legs protesting, and walked out to the grove of trees where Blake was gathering firewood. It wasn't what she wanted to be doing—and it certainly wasn't the kind of time she wanted with her husband—but at that moment it was all that was available to her, and she decided to take it.

CHAPTER 28

BLAKE CAGE

Just about everyone who wasn't on watch was gathered near the fire. The only notable exception was Captain Sullivan, who hadn't been outside the command post since getting his morning coffee.

After getting firewood gathered from the fallen, dried tree limbs, Cage and Felicity carried the fuel to a pit that Staff Sergeant Dole had ordered Hugo Webster and Peter Ormond to dig. It was a wide, shallow pit. Cage arranged nearly half their load of firewood and got it burning. Soon, Staff Sergeant Dole had a support stake on either side of the pit and the chunk of meat on a long spit that he was slowly turning over the fire.

Soon there were more questions about the pyramid, and Cage was trying to remember everything he'd learned about Khufu's pyramid, the largest of the Giza monuments.

"What I want to know is how they built them," Grant Laubin said. "How are we supposed to believe that humans built something like that?"

"Most Egyptologists agree it could be done," Cage said.

"In what, twenty-five hundred BCE? Are you kidding me?" Grant argued. "How many stone blocks were used?"

"Around two point three million," Cage said.

"That's absurd," Grant said. "How long did it take to build?"

"The Great Pyramid has Pharaoh Khufu's name inside," Cage explained. "He ruled for twenty-three years, and most researchers agree that it was built during this timeframe."

"Listen to this guy," Billy Oberton said. "It's like he's a professor or something."

"Okay, well, I'm no math wizard," Grant said. "But I calculate that moving two point three million blocks over twenty years means they had to place over three hundred stone blocks a day."

"How much do the blocks weigh?" Felicity asked.

"They vary," Cage said. "The majority are limestone blocks that weight between six and eight tons. But the smaller blocks are only a little over one ton."

"How'd they get all that stone?" Junior Knoxx asked.

"They quarried them," Cage said.

"With what?" Miranda Dux asked.

"Copper chisels and wooden wedges. They would chip out a notch in the stone with their chisels, hammer in the wedges, then pour water on the wood."

"Water?" Sammy asked.

"Makes the wood expand," Staff Sergeant Dole said, his accent stretching the word into two: *ex-pand*.

"The wood expands, splits the rock, and they could shape the blocks up and ship them out."

"You're kidding, right?" Porter Bailey asked. "Last time I checked, rock was harder than wood."

"That's the prevailing theory," Cage said. "They either shipped the rocks from the quarry via canals or on sleds across the sand."

"Can you imagine pulling a six-ton block of stone?" Felicity said.

"Impossible," Grant said. "How is that easier to believe than aliens?"

"There is a painting of the Egyptians pouring water on the sand in front of sleds with huge statues on them," Cage said. "Turns out, water on the sand makes it slick and easier to pull."

"Still, the numbers don't make sense," Grant said. "Over three hundred stone blocks a day? No way. How many slaves were used to build it?"

"Not slaves," Cage said. "The pharaoh conscripted workers from across his kingdom. They worked in three-month shifts. About fourteen thousand people at a time."

"You're telling me," Grant complained, "that in ancient Egypt, before any kind of agricultural improvements to the land, that there was enough food to feed fourteen thousand workers every day for twenty years? I'm telling you, they didn't build that thing."

"What does the pyramid say?" Billy Oberton asked. "They've got that picture language all over it, right?"

"Hieroglyphs," Cage said. "But no, there is no writing in the Great Pyramid except for a few names."

"No writing after all that work—it doesn't jive," Lucinda said. "If we built something like that, we'd have the names of the architects, engineers, and financiers all over it."

"And it was built as a tomb, right?" Grant asked. "That's what people think?"

"Correct," Cage said.

"All that for a tomb?" Billy asked.

"A monument to the greatness of the pharaoh," Felicity said.

"That's crazy," Billy replied.

"But it was empty, right?" Grant said. "I read something about it. The entire thing was empty."

"Except for a sarcophagus in the king's chamber," Cage explained. "Grave robbers are believed to have looted the pyramid."

"They took everything?" Grant asked.

"Yes," Cage said.

"Even the body?"

It was a good question. Breaking open the sarcophagus to see what treasures had been buried with the body was understandable, but why move the body? It was a huge structure, and the body of Pharaoh Khufu would have been preserved; it was the Egyptian way. Yet there is no report of anything being found in the pyramid that Cage could remember.

"I don't know," Cage said. "We're talking nearly five thousand years. Anything could have happened."

"How'd the grave robbers get in?" Billy Oberton asked. "They find a secret entrance or something?"

"They cut their way in," Cage said.

"You mean the pyramid was sealed up?" Lucinda asked.

"Yes, there were plugs built and set in the entrance," Cage said. "In fact, there have been several hidden chambers that have been discovered."

"Why hide the interior chambers if the entire structure was sealed off?" Grant asked.

It was another good question that all of Cage's studies hadn't answered. Who knew what went through the minds of the ancient Egyptians, or why they did anything at all?

"I know," Grant went on. "It's because there was something bad about it. Something dangerous."

"Ooohhh," Felicity said. "Scary!"

"I'm serious," Grant said. "I don't think they built it at all. They copied it with the others, sure. But the other pyramids aren't like the big one, right?"

"None are as big," Cage said.

"And they have markings, right?" Grant asked.

"Most do, yes. Most Egyptian tombs are full of decorations on the walls. Stories of their mythology, mostly."

"I read a book about all this once," Grant said. "Some people believe that aliens built the Great Pyramid, which is why it is so precise. I guess they were right."

The group fell silent, lost in thought. Cage couldn't deny Grant's theories. They may have been rejected by scholars, but he had seen the pyramid in the mountains and couldn't deny that it looked precisely like the Great Pyramid of Giza.

"Now what?" Billy Oberton asked.

"First," Staff Sergeant Dole said, pulling the large chunk of meat from the fire, "we taste this. Tomorrow, we go get answers."

They followed Dole to the pavilion. Only Cage, Felicity, and Sammy lingered near the fire. The roasted meat smelled good, and Cage could only imagine how much better it would taste than the packed meals they were surviving on. But his mind was too busy to think much about food.

"What is it?" Felicity asked, then quickly added, "Lieutenant."

Cage waved off the breach of protocol and didn't notice the wink that Sammy flashed Felicity. He was thinking about what they might find.

"If the pyramid on Earth was made by aliens and sealed

up by humans," Cage said, "the one on this world might not be sealed."

"Is that bad?" Felicity asked.

"I don't know," Cage admitted.

"If it is sealed up, we won't learn much," Sammy said.

"And odds are we'll have to wait to break in," Felicity said.

Cage was torn. He didn't want to open a Pandora's box, and yet the thought of the mysterious pyramid being sealed off was maddening.

"Hey!" Billy Oberton called to them. "It's good. You've got to try this."

He was waving them over.

"Go ahead," Cage said. "I'm going to make sure this fire is put out."

The girls nodded and moved off to get their cut of the stalker meat. But Cage didn't bother with the fire. It was dying down and he was too distracted. Some people had gone insane with obsession over the mysteries of the ancient Egyptians. He understood their desire to discover the secrets held by the massive pyramids. The last thing he wanted was to lose perspective and fail his platoon, but the need to know had taken root inside of him—and he didn't think it would be able to let it go. All he could hope for was that it wouldn't take him to some place he could never return from.

CHAPTER 29

FELICITY MARS

Felicity stood watch all afternoon. The temperature had warmed into the low seventies, and standing out in the sun all afternoon sapped what remaining strength she had. Once she was relieved, Felicity gathered with the other women near a small fire next to their tents. It was comforting to have the company of other women who were sharing her experiences, but what she really wanted was time alone with her husband. No one knew her the way he did. She could be completely honest with him, knowing he would never hurt her or use what she shared against her.

The ground was covered in soft grass, and there was no need for a barrier between her body and the soil. Felicity took off her armor and stretched out near the fire, propping up on one elbow and trying to let her muscles relax.

"It's not like I thought it would be," Sammy said. "I imagined an empty world."

"Me too," Amber agreed. She was heating water for tea over their little fire.

"I mean, it's exciting," Sammy went on. "This place is paradise, if you don't mind fighting off big, invisible predators every once in a while."

"Tell me about it," Felicity said.

The girls laughed softly.

"But I won't lie," Sammy went on. "That pyramid scares me."

"The pyramid, or what Grant said about it?" Felicity asked.

"Both, I suppose," Sammy said. "It's strange to find something like that out here. And to think there might be a purpose to seal it up makes it even worse."

"I think we can handle a few aliens," Miranda Dux said. She was a HeWE and loved it. All the other heavy weapons experts were men, and Miranda was proud to be the only woman in her specialty.

"You really think that's who built it?" Lucinda asked. "Aliens?"

"Are we talking little green men, or the kind that eat your face off?" Amber asked.

Felicity couldn't stop the little tremor of fear that ran down her body. She was suddenly feeling cold.

"That's not funny," Sammy said.

"No, it isn't," Miranda said. "But it's not like we're helpless here. And there's no sign of whoever built that thing. It's probably no different than the one on Earth. I'm guessing that we won't learn much from it."

"You think?" Sammy asked.

"Sure," Miranda explained. "Whoever built it is long gone, even if it's only a couple of decades old. They've been here, built their monument, and moved on. I mean, look at how old the one on Earth is. We've never been contacted by aliens in nearly five thousand years. If they didn't bother us on Earth, I don't think they'll bother us here."

The girls all seemed content with that thought, but secretly Felicity couldn't escape the possibility that the pyramid on Magnificus Prime was different. It might not be sealed off. And if the one on Earth had been sealed off because of some danger, would exploring the structure she had found put them in harm's way? She didn't know—and wouldn't until they got to the pyramid, which would probably take them a full day.

"When the colony gets built," Amber said. "There will be a flood of interest in this world."

"We'll be busy exploring it for the next five years," Lucinda said. "There's no telling what we'll find."

"I hope I find a man," Sammy said.

That made them all laugh again.

"Speaking of men," Miranda said. "What do you think of Grant? He's cute, right?"

"I guess," Amber said. "But he's pretty full of himself.'"

"It's not like we have a lot of choices," Sammy said. "I, for one, do not like sleeping alone."

Felicity thought of her tent. It was a one-person structure, but she imagined two people could squeeze in, as long as they didn't mind being wrapped up with one another.

"I think a few of the guys are cute," Sammy said.

"But they can't keep a secret," Lucinda said. "You get with one of them, and they'll be bragging about it. Every last detail will be public knowledge."

"True," Amber said. "And there isn't much privacy out here to begin with."

"Once the heavy cargo drops, things will be different," Sammy said. "This place will be more of a base and less of a camp, you know?"

"I can't wait," Amber said.

"A hot shower and a real bed would be welcome," Miranda said.

"Speaking of bed," Felicity said. "I'm going to mine."

"Already?" Sammy asked.

"She ran both groups out to the pyramid," Amber said.

"Yeah, I'm beat," Felicity added. "I also didn't really sleep much last night."

"Too busy with Lieutenant Cage?" Sammy asked.

"No," Felicity said, but she said it a little too fast. Her friends rolled their eyes and giggled.

"You won the lottery, Mars," Lucinda said. "He obviously has a thing for you."

"Yeah, you should hit that," Miranda said.

"And then give us all the details," Sammy said. "I'm talking play-by-play of the whole thing."

"You guys are gross," Felicity said, but she couldn't stop grinning.

They all laughed as she walked away. Felicity didn't mind the laughter and wondered what they would think when they found out she and Blake were married. Hopefully that wouldn't happen for years, but one day she would tell them. They were bonding, and it felt good to have friends. The stress of being on a foreign planet was made worse by the pyramid. She was beginning to wish she'd never seen it, not that ignorance would make them any safer. If there was trouble, it would find them, whether they saw it coming or not.

After carefully arranging her gear, Felicity crawled into her sleeping bag. She zipped it up and let her body heat warm the bag. It felt good to be warm, almost cozy. But her mind knew the tent wasn't safe. Her father had taught her that safety was an illusion. A person could be completely safe from every outside threat and have their own body turn on them. There were too many uncontrollable elements to ever be safe. Yet as Felicity drifted off to sleep, she couldn't help but long for four solid walls and Blake by her side.

Dawn came early, but Felicity had slept well. She got up, and after a quick stretch, pulled on her armor and checked her assault rifle. It only took a few minutes to roll up her sleeping bag and make sure her pack was ready. They would be heading out soon and would be spending at least one night in the mountains, which meant everyone was breaking down their tents and repacking their heavy packs. Felicity didn't have as much to pack, and she made it over to the pavilion in time to get a small, disposable cup of coffee and refill her canteen with fresh water. By the time she finished her coffee, the entire platoon was forming up around the command post. The excitement was palpable.

Felicity caught Blake's eye. The lieutenant looked like a child on Christmas morning. She knew how much the pyramid meant to him. He had suggested they join the MCM because it was the only way for her to have a life she could really love. He was content with his books and his studies, but she needed space, adventure, and the chance to really make a difference. She loved him for his willingness to go where she needed to go and do what she needed to do to be happy. And this was his chance to combine their MCM adventure with his passion for history. She didn't think anything could bring down his spirits.

A moment later, Captain Sullivan appeared. He looked bloated, his stomach rounding out the front of his fatigue shirt.

There were dark, puffy sacks of skin under his eyes. And he looked sloppy, his armor wasn't on straight, and the straps of his rifle sling were twisted.

"Ahem, okay, you're all ready," Sullivan said. "We're going to investigate the pyramid today. But we can't abandon our base camp. Lieutenant Cage!"

Blake looked surprised. He stepped forward. "Yes, Captain."

"You'll be staying behind to protect base camp. Choose three specialists to remain in camp with you. I want watches around the clock. And do not under any circumstances contact the *Bronx II* regarding the pyramid. Until we know exactly what we're dealing with, I want no leaks and no wild theories being postulated. Are we all clear?"

Felicity wanted to object. She could see the pain and confusion on Blake's face. Nothing she could imagine would be worse to him than having to stay behind when the pyramid was explored. But she was just a lowly corporal, and the smug look on the captain's face made it perfectly clear that he knew exactly what he was doing to Blake. She was helpless to save the man she loved more than life itself, and it was agonizing.

Throwing caution to the wind, she stepped forward and even opened her mouth to argue his case, but Blake stopped her with a gentle shake of his head. The decision was made, and her wrecking her career wouldn't change it.

"Sir, a word," Staff Sergeant Dole said.

The captain stepped toward the veteran NCO, and Felicity made her move toward Blake. He looked like he might be sick, but he was doing his best to hold it together.

"Pick me," Felicity said. "If you're not going to fight his selfish order, then pick me. I'm not going without you."

"Calm down, Corporal," Blake said.

Felicity glanced over her shoulder. The platoon had shifted, and none were looking at Blake. They were like school children trying to avoid their teacher's eyes in the hopes that they wouldn't be called on. None of them wanted to stay behind, and she understood that. She wanted to find out about the pyramid as much as any of them, but she was furious that the captain had turned the tables on her husband.

"He's a snake," Felicity whispered.

"Lower your voice, Corporal," Blake said. "Take a deep breath. I'm not choosing you. I need you to be my eyes and ears."

"What?" Felicity asked.

"I've got a relay set up," Blake continued. "You can tell me what you see."

"But I don't know about pyramids," she countered, feeling horrible that she couldn't change things for him.

"That's okay, I'll be in your ear the whole time," Blake said.

"Enough," the captain said loud enough that the entire platoon heard him. "I've made up my mind. I don't need to reconsider. Lieutenant Cage, choose the three specialists to stay here with you."

Blake cleared his throat. "Webster, Ormond, Al'Farrah," he said in a firm voice.

"There, see," Sullivan said. "Now, let's get started, Staff Sergeant, before we lose any daylight, as you so often like to point out."

Staff Sergeant Wyatt Dole looked angry but didn't argue. He called out the order for the platoon to form up and check their weapons. Felicity didn't want to leave Blake. She knew he was hurt, but there was nothing more she could do without putting them both at risk. If Blake wanted her to go, she would go.

"Another day at the office, eh?" Bailey said as Felicity joined him at the front of the column.

"I want the two of you to lead the way," Captain Sullivan said. "Staggered formation, twenty-five meters. Let's try to maintain line of sight with the column at all times."

Felicity turned to face the captain. "Sir, are you sure you want us staggered? That would make the point person alone fifty meters from the rest of the platoon."

"I'm aware of my orders, Corporal," Sullivan snapped. "What has happened to everyone today? Do you think questioning my orders is your place, Mars? You're lucky I don't order you to stay behind. I want a staggered formation. Move out!"

"Yes, Captain," Felicity and Porter Bailey said at the same time.

They started walking. Bailey waited until they were out of earshot to speak, and when he did it was with a quiet voice.

"You know what he's doing?" Bailey asked.

"Making sure he doesn't run into a Stalker," Felicity said with a nod.

"I can take point," he volunteered.

"No, I'll do it. I've seen them before. I should be able to spot one if they come around again."

"I've got your back," Porter said.

"Scouts go first, right?" Felicity said, giving her counterpart a fist bump.

"Always. Keep it on a swivel, Mars."

She nodded and jogged out another twenty-five meters. The platoon was waiting as she looked around. There was no sign of movement and no more reason to wait. She pressed the activator on her throat mic.

"Looks clear, Staff Sergeant," she said.

"Roger that," Dole replied via the com-link. "Let's move out."

CHAPTER 30

BLAKE CAGE

He hadn't cried since he was a kid, but Cage felt like crying as the platoon left base camp. Staying behind felt like the hardest thing he had ever done, but arguing with his captain wouldn't have changed things. It was clear to him what Sullivan was doing. He felt threatened by his junior officer. Not only had Cage found a way to discover the pyramid, he knew a lot about it. If Sullivan had taken him along, the entire platoon would look to Cage, not the captain, in regard to the pyramid. Leaving Cage behind was Sullivan's way of insuring that he remained in control and got all the credit.

Having Cage pick the specialists who stayed behind with him was also meant to weaken his influence with the platoon. Sullivan wanted the members to hate Cage, and he guessed that robbing three specialists of the opportunity to see the pyramid up close would make him very unpopular with at least three members of Bravo platoon. It worked—Cage could see it on their faces.

"I'm sorry," Cage told them.

"Why us, LT?" Hugo Webster asked.

"I picked you and Ormond because the heavy cargo drops should be happening soon. When the captain gets back, he'll want to send out the both of you to get that equipment moved back here. I figured this way, you'll be rested."

"Well, thanks," Peter Ormond replied. "I guess."

"And me?" Devon Al'Farrah asked.

"I had to pick someone," Cage said. "I'm sorry. Look, we've got a crap job, but it's ours. You think I wanted to be left here?"

All three sets of eyes dropped down. Whether Sullivan liked it or not, Cage was popular. He was smart, fair, and most importantly, accessible. It also didn't hurt that he was willing to work while Sullivan hid in the command post. But Cage wasn't worried about his reputation. The three specialists he'd picked didn't like it, but he knew they would get over their frustration.

"So let's get busy," Cage told them. "The best place for watch is up on the hilltop. I don't want anyone up there alone. Let's work in pairs, four hours on, four off. That's the rotation for the foreseeable future."

"We could take our tents up there," Ormond said. "That way we don't waste time going back and forth."

"Yeah, we can't repel down without spotters," Webster said.

"Works for me," Cage said. "We already packed our gear, might as well get moving."

By the time they reached the top of the hill, it was clear who was pairing with whom. Cage and Devon took the first four-hour shift. The platoon was still visible beyond the trees that marked one side of their base camp. After giving the wide plain a slow, methodical search, Cage left the watch to Devon and began setting up his radio.

Hugo and Ormond, the platoon's two vehicle specialists, were sent back down to the camp to get water and a few other supplies. As soon as Cage had the radio set up, he returned to the watch with Devon.

"How is it that you know so much about the pyramids?" Devon asked.

"I got a history degree online," Cage said. "Before we signed up for the MCM."

"We?" Devon asked.

Cage felt a stab of guilt. It was only a matter of time before he slipped up, and he was letting the bitterness of being left behind make him sloppy.

"I applied with my brother," Cage lied. "But he didn't get accepted."

"That is unfortunate," Devon said. "I left my entire family in Rafah. We were very close."

"Israel? That's not far from Egypt. Did you ever see the pyramids?"

"Once, as a child on a school trip," Devon said. "But only from a distance. It must be killing you to have been left here."

"I suppose someone had to do it," Cage said.

"But not a history enthusiast," Devon replied. "It seems odd that the captain would choose you to leave behind."

"I'm the junior officer."

"On a task that any corporal could have accomplished with ease," Devon said.

Cage couldn't argue that point. He hadn't really thought about who would or should have been left to guard the base camp. In truth, he had been so excited to explore the pyramid that he didn't give it a single thought. If he was going to be a successful officer, he would have to do a better job of managing his emotions and the troopers under his command. He liked the MCM. Perhaps he would have enjoyed just about any career, but a small part of him hoped he might be able to stay on even after the initial enlistment period. He didn't want to leave Magnificus Prime if Felicity was happy here, but it was exciting to think of exploring other worlds. If she wanted to stay, then perhaps he could remain on station as an officer while she did something else.

His dream had been to build a little house and have some land outside the colony. Maybe he could teach, or perhaps write a history of the colonization of the planet. There were so many choices that he felt a little giddy just thinking about them. And yet all his plans seemed hollow and sad compared to exploring the pyramid. He tried to remind himself that just because he wasn't on the initial team that would uncover the structure's secrets didn't mean that he would never get to. But that thought was just as hollow and frustrating as his dreams had been. Finding the pyramid had changed everything, and he didn't know what he would do to settle his feverish need to explore the mysterious structure.

"You seem troubled," Devon said after an hour of staring out across the savannah.

"I wish the animals that grazed out there weren't nocturnal," Cage said. "It's so strange to see the empty space."

"I find it peaceful," Devon said. "At least there are no enemies at the gate, if you follow my meaning."

"You're a glass half-full kind of person, Devon," Cage said. "I respect that. I usually am too, but for some reason all I can see today are the negatives."

"You should take your mind off what you have lost. Tell me who you think built the pyramids and why."

"Before yesterday, I'd accepted the conventional explanation that the ancient Egyptians built them."

"Why?"

"I guess because that's what I was taught."

"And you did not question this?"

"It's a fascinating subject," Cage said, his mind digging into the lore. "One of the ancient wonders of the world, still standing nearly five thousand years after it was built. How did the Egyptians do it? Why did they do it? It boggles the mind, but so many researchers brush off any kind of supernatural explanation."

"That does not make it true," Devon said. "There are many things that we do not understand and that cannot be explained. What do you believe about the pyramids now?"

"Aliens, I suppose," Cage said.

"Why would aliens build the pyramids?"

"I don't think they built them all," Cage said. "Or that they built them by themselves. I still think the ancient Egyptians played a part."

"But under the direction of extraterrestrial beings?"

"Yeah, I guess so."

"To what end?" Devon asked.

"That I do not know," Cage replied. "I was hoping that maybe the pyramid here would shed some light on that."

"Perhaps it will," Devon said.

For some strange reason that Cage couldn't explain, the thought of finding the secrets to the pyramids suddenly made Cage's skin crawl. He tried to shrug it off, but he couldn't. Fear had taken root, and it wasn't going away easily.

CHAPTER 31

FELICITY MARS

The rotting carcasses of the slain stalkers killed by Bravo platoon had been dragged away from the kill site. Fortunately, the big predators were busy, probably feasting on their fallen, and didn't bother the platoon. Felicity didn't see them, at least, and she could imagine the vicious creatures being cannibals—she remembered that most big predators were. She had seen it on a nature program. Lions were sometimes cannibalistic. Great apes, she remembered, were cannibals when the need or opportunity arose. And grizzly bears were especially dangerous to other bear cubs.

Not that it mattered to Felicity what the animals were doing. She was certain that food chains on Magnificus Prime had developed, with some species hunting their prey and others feasting on the carrion left by predators. She found the path leading into the mountains with no problem, and after looking back to give Bailey a quick signal, she headed up the game trail. For several minutes she was alone, and there would be other times when her partner was out of sight. It didn't give her a good feeling to be alone in the wilds of an unknown world. Almost all the information they had on the planet was gleaned from a probe that had spent less than a week in orbit. But she couldn't have a safe adventure—that wasn't how excitement worked. Without risk, there was no rush, no surge of adrenaline.

Despite the fact that her husband had been left behind, Felicity couldn't deny the excitement of their mission. She wasn't all that interested in pyramids, but the structure in the mountains was fascinating for several reasons. One, it meant that someone else had been on the planet. The fact that they hadn't seen anyone pointed to a high probability that they had left. It was the first sign of intelligence outside the human race. That thought alone got her blood pumping. The second reason she was excited was for the information they'd learn— not about Earth's past, but about the future of the human race in the galaxy. If they had neighbors, cosmically speaking, she for one wanted to know about them.

Walking gave her the time to take in her surroundings better than jogging had. She wasn't scouting, not really. She wasn't exploring her way in search of an enemy. Her job was simply to lead the platoon to the pyramid, and that would be easy enough. She was hemmed in by big hills on one side and mountains on the other. All she had to do was stay between them.

When she came to the ledge where the pyramid came into view, she took her first break. A few minutes later, Bailey arrived. The game trail was only wide enough for the platoon to move in a single-file line, and they had slowed down. It gave the two scouts a moment alone to plan their next move.

"What's that down there?" Bailey asked.

"Looks like a stream," Felicity said. "But how do we get down to it?"

The stream was crowded with underbrush, but there was room on either side for troopers to walk along. If they could get down to the stream, which was thirty or forty meters below the ledge, the rest of the journey would be easy enough.

"What about that slope?" Bailey said, pointing toward a slick rock bulging from the side of a hill.

"I would enjoy seeing the captain navigate that," Felicity said. "But I don't think we could all get down without someone getting hurt."

"Yeah, the HeWEs wouldn't make it," Bailey said.

"You think this trail turns back down?" Felicity said.

"What goes up must come down," Bailey replied. "And I don't see a safe option yet."

"I'll check it out," Felicity said. "If it doesn't turn downhill soon, we'll try the slick rock."

"Roger that. I'll let the captain know."

Felicity set off again just as the first of the regular troopers reached the ledge.

"Hey Mars, you can slow down a little," Sammy called out. "We're not in a race."

"Don't go soft on me, Jones," Felicity called back.

A moment later the trail, which ran across the ledge, took her around a rocky outcropping, and she was hidden from view. It was early in the day, and there were still plenty of shadows in the mountains. All along the trail were nooks and crevices in the rock that could hide predators. Felicity slowed down, her eyes searching everywhere for danger. She was in uncharted territory, and for the moment she was all alone.

The trail dipped down, then back up another hill that seemed to be strewn with boulders. Many were lodged right on the steeply sloping sides of the hill, and she thought the platoon would need to be careful not to start a landslide. Felicity crossed over—only to be stopped in her tracks by a gray-skinned creature that looked like a spider. It had six narrow legs that spread out from its body like a spider and strange feet that gripped the steep edge of the hill. The body was thick, and a row of bulges that looked like eyes ran down its back.

It hissed at Felicity, who hadn't moved since she saw the creature except to slowly turn her gun toward it. The spider—as she thought of it—was roughly as big as she was, only with longer legs. Where the hissing came from, she didn't know; there was no sign of a mouth that she could see. Once she had her gun pointed in the direction of the spider, she chanced a look around. The hill directly ahead of her wasn't covered in rocks. There were more of the spider creatures, and they reacted to the first's hiss, standing up and slowly moving toward her.

Felicity keyed her throat mic. "Bailey, you read?"

"Loud and clear," Porter said, although his voice was laced with static.

"This way is a no-go. I've got animal life ahead."

"What is it, Mars?" Staff Sergeant Dole's voice crackled in her earpiece. "More of the stalkers?"

"Negative, Staff Sergeant. This is something new. Giant rock spiders. I'm moving back now."

The spiders were still creeping down as she moved back, but they didn't seem in a hurry to follow her. She breathed a sigh of relief as she crossed back to the first hill and took the time to raise her monoscope and get some video of the strange creatures.

When she got back to the crowded ledge, Captain

Sullivan was red-faced, sweating, and angry. He was leaning against the hill, his fatigues already dark with sweat stains. She knew the look. It was his body's way of dealing with the food he'd been devouring in boredom. Too much food and too little exercise left the body struggling to respond. She had felt the same way after the holidays, which were the only times her father gave his children a break from the nearly constant training.

"Sir," Felicity said. "The trail ahead is blocked by a number of animals."

Felicity held out her monoscope, but Sullivan didn't move to take it. After a second or two, Staff Sergeant Dole took it and looked at the video.

"Amazing," he said.

"Amazing?" Captain Sullivan complained. "Amazing? Is that what you call it, Staff Sergeant? You are aware that we are being held back from a vital mission by these creatures."

"Yes, Captain," Dole said, the skin around his eyes pinching into deep lines.

Felicity recognized the response. When Dole didn't like something, the lines appeared. They fanned out from the corners of his eyes.

"We need another route," Sullivan insisted.

"The slick rock," Porter Bailey said. "We can go down there and follow the stream."

"How do we traverse that?" Sullivan asked.

"Only one way," Felicity said. "We'll have to sit and scoot."

"Sit and scoot?" Sullivan snarled. "Have you lost your senses, Corporal? We're recon, we don't crawl around the rocks like children."

"You want to go another way?" Staff Sergeant Dole asked.

"I want to go the best way," Sullivan snapped. "And if some animals get in the way, then shoot them."

"It's an entire colony, sir," Felicity said.

"And we're an entire platoon. I say we have the upper hand. Laubin! Ficklestine!"

The two heavy weapons experts hurried over. They had their auto-cannons on their harnesses, the barrels disengaged and pointing straight up.

"Yes, Captain," they both said at the same time.

"Corporal Mars has a bug problem. Take care of it."

Grant Laubin was a handsome guy with a square jaw that had a dimple right in the center. He had bright blue eyes and dark hair that looked rugged in the short buzz cut. Ted Ficklestine was the opposite: a big, lumbering boy with acne scars on his cheeks and a doughy appearance no matter how much PT he did. He looked even bigger with the auto-cannon harness. Ted was Grant's disciple and tried to do everything his older, more experienced companion said.

"Lead the way, Corporal," Grant said, although his disdain at Felicity's superior rank was obvious.

Felicity started back down the trail, wondering how reckless it was to use their weapons on a group of animals that weren't hurting them. There was no guarantee that they would find an easier way down to the valley by following the trail. It was simply the option that required the least amount of effort, at least from Captain Sullivan's point of view.

After winding around the hillside, Felicity pulled up short of the sloping trail that led to the next hill. She could see the strange rock spiders, although they looked like stones again.

"That's them," she said. "They look like rocks."

"You sure they aren't rocks?" Grant said.

"You'll see," she told them. "Just head across the trail."

"And where are you going?" Ted Ficklestine asked. For some reason he didn't trust her.

"Nowhere, but I don't want to be anywhere near you when you start shooting those things," Felicity said.

"These babies are highly efficient," Grant said, patting the barrel of his auto-cannon.

"If you say so," Felicity said. "When I started across the path, I was blocked by one of the rock spiders. It hissed and the others started moving down toward the path."

"My guess is, once we take out their alpha, the rest will run away," Grant said.

"I hope you're right," Felicity said.

He flashed her a grin, but she wasn't impressed. It was clear that he was used to his looks getting him ahead with people, especially women. But Felicity saw through his bravado and handsome exterior. Grant was smart, but he liked to be in charge. He also liked hurting people to establish his dominance. He'd tried to hurt her in their close combat training. When she proved to be more than a match for his brute strength and cruelty, he backed off. And when Major Tarantino promoted her to corporal, the divide between them grew.

She stood back and let them pass. Grant brought his weapon online. The auto-cannon used battery power to spin the five-belt feed barrels. They could spew ten .55 caliber high-impact rounds a second. The bullets were made of brittle metal that shattered on impact. The tiny shard eviscerated whatever they hit. The cannons weren't built for accuracy. They were fired from the hip, with an augmented aiming display that was built into the HeWE helmets. When Grant lowered the barrel to the firing position, the weapon's power systems engaged. The yellow aiming display lowered over his eyes like goggles, and the barrels began to spin. Their harnesses contained two thousand four hundred rounds, enough to keep the cannons shooting for four solid minutes. Of course, that many rounds would also overheat the weapon. They were meant to be fired in short bursts.

Felicity didn't see the first rock spider confront Grant, but she saw the others rising up on their long, articulated legs. There were dozens of the bulky, gray creatures. And then the shooting started. There was a short, controlled burst from Grant's weapon, just as Ted was bringing his own cannon online. With the loud report of the auto-cannon, the spiders attacked.

Without thinking, Felicity switched off the safety of her assault rifle and toggled the firing control from plasma fire to laser. The spiders had jumped from the hillside. Grant hit two as they arced over his head, but most of his shots missed their targets. Ted opened fire and blasted three more. The rock spiders had bright blue blood. The high impact rounds blew them apart as if they were balloons at a carnival game. Their blood splashed onto the gray stones around them as their bodies collapsed and tumbled down the hillsides.

But the battle wasn't one-sided. The creatures sprayed a mist down on the two HeWE specialists. Felicity didn't know what it was and didn't want to find out. She brought her rifle up and began firing. The laser blasts burned through the rock spider bodies. Once hit, the creatures immediately dropped, their long legs curling around them. Some seemed to be trying to get away, but others were spraying the white mist as they bounded toward the boys.

"What is that?" Grant shouted.

"I don't know," Ted replied.

"Fall back! Fall back!" Grant ordered. They started back up the sloping trail. The rock spiders were on both sides—

some on the hills, others hiding in crevasses or scrambling over the summit. All told, they had killed eighteen of the creatures and only six more remained in sight. They clung to the steep hillsides, some above the trail, others below. They trembled and shook, as if they were waiting for something.

Ted was the first to succumb to the venom of the creatures. He stumbled. Felicity was shocked when Grant stepped on Ted and vaulted over his friend. It was obvious that he had no intention of stopping. Felicity was about to run to the big HeWE specialist, but the rock spiders were faster. They scurried toward him.

"Cannn't mooo!" Ted wailed, his words slurred.

Felicity raised her rifle and shot two more of the rock spiders, but a third pounced on Ted. And then Felicity saw its mouth: it had a round mouth on the bottom of its body. It landed on Ted, who screamed. Felicity was about to shoot it when Grant lumbered into her path.

"Whasss happennninggg," he cried.

"Move!" Felicity screamed. "Get out of the way."

Grant tried to obey, but his body had gone rigid. He toppled into her. Felicity swung the butt of her rifle around and flung him off. Grant dropped to the ground like a fallen tree, his body stiff. Felicity could see the residue of the mist on his clothes and the harness of the auto-cannon. She was worried that some of the toxin had gotten on her, but there was no time to save herself. Raising the rifle back to her shoulder, she targeted the spider on Ten, but she didn't fire. She could see the boy's face; it had gone white, and his eyes and mouth were wide open. The eyes were glassy and fixed, his body unmoving. He was gone. How the creature had gotten past the heavy cannon harness and Ted's armor, Felicity couldn't tell, but it was obvious that he was dead. She kept the weapon up and stepped over Grant. He was staring up at her, trying to talk, but his mouth wasn't moving.

"Hellll meeee," he cried.

"Stupid," Felicity said angrily. "This was stupid."

The rock spiders were converging on Ted's body. She wanted to kill them but feared what might happen if she antagonized them further. Instead, keeping her weapon at the ready with one hand, she grabbed Grant's collar and began pulling him back along the trail. He was heavy and while Felicity was strong, she could hardly budge him. She moved in slow, short tugs, watching the spiders.

"Corporal Mars, what's going on? Report!"

Captain Sullivan sounded like a petulant child demanding a cookie. His voice crackled through her earpiece. She wanted to rip it out, but instead she toggled her throat mic to the on position.

"Ted's gone," she said, her breathing heavy. "Grant's down. I need help."

"Hold tight, Corporal." Dole's instant response was reassuring. "Help's on the way."

She felt tears in her eyes, and her hand on Grant's collar was getting numb. She didn't know if was from the strain or from the spider venom. All she could hope was that it wasn't permanent. Fortunately, the rock spiders had lost interest in her and Grant. She kept tugging him away and hoping he didn't die.

A few seconds later Sammy, Al, and Junior came rushing toward her. There wasn't a lot of room on the trail. One side sloped upward, the other dropped off toward the ravine between the hills. Felicity pressed herself against the hill and flexed her numb hand. She could still feel it. The strain had just been too much.

"Get him out of here," Felicity said. "I'll cover you."

"Got it," Sammy shouted.

Junior and Al grabbed Grant's arms and pulled him back along the trail. Felicity followed. She wanted to scream, cry, and run away all at the same time. Ted was dead. She hadn't known him well and they weren't friends, but he was a person and a platoon mate—and she had just seen rock spiders eat him alive.

CHAPTER 32

FELICITY MARS

"Is he hurt?" Dole demanded.

"The spiders spewed some type of venom," Felicity said, "from the air."

"Is that what's all over him?" Sammy asked.

Grant Laubin was covered in the white substance. His helmet, armor, and weapon harness were speckled with it like a painter's coveralls. Grant couldn't talk, but he moaned.

"It must be a paralysis agent," Dole said. "Most spider and snake venom does the same thing."

"We can't go through on the trail," Felicity said. "We killed a bunch of them, but not enough. The rest were on Ted's body. And they may come this way."

"Orders, sir?" Staff Sergeant Dole asked.

"Will he live?" Sullivan asked.

"That's hard to say, sir. We don't know enough about that toxin," Dole said, before turning to Felicity. "How'd you avoid it?"

"I held back," Felicity said. "I didn't want to get too close while they were shooting."

She flexed her hand, confident that the contact with her skin hadn't poisoned her with the rock spider venom. She felt fine, just a little tired as the adrenaline surge subsided.

"I think it must be most toxic if inhaled," Felicity continued. "It's not affecting me."

"Well, that's good," Dole said. "Only time will tell if Grant will overcome the venom. It could be breaking down his cells or destroying his nerves. We would need to get a full body scan to know for certain."

"We don't have a body scanner," Sullivan snapped. "Don't be absurd, Staff Sergeant. The heavy cargo hasn't even dropped."

"Should we call for evac?" Felicity asked.

"Are you out of your mind, Corporal?" Sullivan demanded.

"He might be dying, sir," she said, standing her ground.

"Then he dies," Sullivan snarled. "This is the MCM. You're all soldiers. What did you think, this would be dress-up? We aren't calling for backup over one lost soldier. Besides, if he's going to die, he wouldn't make it back up to the ship. No—we push on. Find us another way to the pyramid!"

"The slick rock," Bailey said. "I'll check it out."

"Not alone," Felicity said. "We can't afford to lose anyone else."

They hurried toward the mound of stone. It was big and unlike most of the hills, there was no deterioration. The erosion had left it smooth and rounded. The two scouts jumped down from the trail and started down the sloping side of the slick rock. Felicity was the first to sit and begin scooting as Bailey charged ahead. The last two meters were almost vertical, but a slight divot in the smooth stone made a natural handhold.

Bailey grabbed onto the divot and slid down until he was dangling from the rock, but his boots were only eight or nine centimeters from the ground. He dropped onto the valley floor and turned around. It was a narrow space, but there were no visible threats. The stream gurgled over fist-sized stones, and the hills blocked the sunlight, which kept the scrub brush from growing.

"It's good," he called up to Felicity.

She keyed her com-link. "We can get down this way," she said. "It's safe."

"Roger that, Corporal," Staff Sergeant Dole said. "We're on our way."

Felicity wasn't part of the discussion that ended with Sammy and Al Malone being ordered to stay on the ledge with Grant. He was too heavy to carry, and while Felicity was confident that the rock spider venom didn't transfer through skin contact, the platoon couldn't take that chance. As the other members of the platoon scurried down the smooth rock face, Felicity directed them toward the divot, and Bailey helped them as they dropped to the valley floor. Everyone made it without incident—except for the captain. He couldn't maintain his grip on the divot and fell much harder than the others.

"I'm okay," he shouted. "Get off me."

Felicity had to wait for the captain to move out of the way before she could descend, and he had a noticeable limp as he walked away from his fall. With the way clear, she slid down and made the drop without incident.

"All right, reform the line," Staff Sergeant Dole ordered. "Scouts, lead the way."

Bailey took the lead, and Felicity didn't argue. She felt shaky, angry, and scared. In her mind she kept seeing Ted being devoured by the spiders. She heard his screams in the silence of the valley. The only sounds were her footsteps, the occasional ruffle when her leg brushed the foliage near the stream, and the gentle gurgle of water flowing over the stones. The water was clear and looked clean. The pristine nature of it helped ease her worries. And while they marched through the valley, they were fortunate not to see any more animal life.

They marched for nearly an hour before the captain called a halt. The sun was directly overhead, and Felicity sat on the ground with her back to the rock, sipping from her canteen. Amber and Lori approached and settled on either side of Felicity. Lunch was a protein bar from their packs. It was dense and hard to chew, but it gave her something to push back the gnawing hunger in her gut.

"You okay?" Amber asked after taking a drink from her canteen.

"I guess," Felicity said. "It's not like I haven't seen someone get killed before."

"Ted was a goof," Lori said. "Like your dumb kid brother or something."

"You want to know the worst part?" Felicity said quietly. "When Ted went down from the venom, Grant went right over him. He stepped on Ted and left him there."

The girls were silent for several long seconds. Felicity saw it all again in her head: the savage act of a frightened young man leaving his friend to die so that he could escape.

"You never know what you might do in that situation," Lori finally said, breaking the silence.

Felicity understood the sentiment, but she hoped that if her life were in danger, she wouldn't run over her friends to escape it. Still, they were all frightened. When they'd been training, it had seemed so fun. They were warriors, but they were safe in the habitat. Felicity knew there was a big difference between sparring and being in an actual fight. Her father had taught her to act without thinking, without letting fear dictate her actions. She had assumed that if danger struck their platoon that the training they had all done together would save them. But she was beginning to see that it wasn't enough—not for everyone. Some people—like Grant—had acted the part, but the training hadn't really sunk in. Three months spent preparing for the mission weren't enough when their lives were on the line.

"You think he's okay?" Amber asked.

Most of the girls had a crush on Grant, but they hadn't seen him when the rock spiders responded to their attack. If they had, it might have changed the way they saw him. He wasn't just a handsome soldier; he was a cruel bully and a coward.

"I don't know," Felicity said. "I guess we'll have to wait and see."

Soon they were back on the move. The day wore on, and the pyramid got bigger. Felicity knew it was large, but she was still shocked at the immense size as they approached. It sat on a rocky bluff just a few meters above the canyon floor. The stream came down off the mountains, winding around the bedrock the pyramid was built on. Felicity couldn't imagine the time and effort it would take to build such a huge structure.

The shadows in the canyon were getting long and dark as evening set in. The valley opened up as they approached the pyramid until they were on a wide expanse of lush, grassy, flat land just below the bedrock where the pyramid stood. The entire platoon was quieter than normal. Felicity guessed that they were contemplating Grant Laubin's folly and wondering if he would survive, but it could have been the pyramid itself that had put them into a reflective mood. The site at the foot of the great pyramid was idyllic and had an almost sacred feeling to it.

"This is an excellent spot for camp," Captain Sullivan declared as the platoon gathered near the base of the pyramid. "In the morning we'll begin documenting my discovery. Staff Sergeant, assign watch duty. I don't want anything taking us by surprise in the night."

There wasn't much wood for fires. They powered on the small but surprisingly bright LEDs that were built into their helmets as the sun went down. Felicity stood watch for two hours, then pulled her own sleeping bag from her pack. She and Bailey didn't have tents. Instead she slept outside, with the pyramid looming out of the darkness nearby. The white limestone reflected the starlight, which made it almost glow in the darkness. Perhaps it was seeing Ted die or being away from Blake, but she felt unsettled as she lay in the darkness. Sleep was elusive and filled with bad dreams. She yearned for morning, for the sunlight to chase her fears away, but something deep down inside told her the terror was just beginning.

CHAPTER 33

FELICITY MARS

Felicity was up before dawn, pacing to keep herself warm. She was surprised when she heard Blake's voice.

"Corporal Mars, this is Lieutenant Cage. Do you read me?"

His voice was clear in her earpiece, not laced with static the way it had been farther back in the mountains.

"Lieutenant," Felicity said, glad that she hadn't forgotten and used his first name. "I read you."

"You made it. That's good. We lost radio contact once you entered the mountains."

"We didn't all make it," Felicity said, her eyes stinging with tears as she thought of Ted. She wished she could remove the memory, but it haunted her. "Private Ficklestine was killed yesterday," she explained, "fighting some spider-like creatures."

"That's awful," Blake replied. "Was anyone else hurt?"

"Private Laubin was infected with the venom they expelled. It's like a mist. He and Ted both inhaled it. The toxin causes paralysis. We had to leave him behind with Corporal Jones and Private Malone on the ledge where we saw the pyramid."

"So you're down to twelve troopers?"

"Yes sir, that's correct," she said, feeling a little awkward calling her husband "sir."

The sun was coming up, turning the sky pink over her head. The pyramid was swathed in shadows but still had a strange glow. Felicity couldn't tell if it was inviting or frightening.

"Are you leading the search today, Corporal?" Blake asked.

"I should be."

"Good, I've isolated this frequency. The others shouldn't be able to hear it. I want you to tell me everything you see."

"Roger that, Lieutenant."

The rest of the platoon who weren't already on watch rose with the dawn. Felicity packed her sleeping bag back in her pack and ate a protein bar for breakfast. She only had six of the bars left in her supplies and four of the MREs that served as her main food source. There were more essentials at the base camp, but she guessed she had enough food to stay at the pyramid for two more days. Her canteen had its own filter, so she could fill it from the stream. By the time the captain was up, she was ready to begin the exploration.

"How do you want us to proceed?" Staff Sergeant Dole asked.

"I want pictures," Sullivan said. "Me at the base of the pyramid, myself with a few members of the platoon. Once the site has been explored by our scouts, we can go inside and get pictures there too."

"Bailey, Mars—you're up," Dole ordered.

"And you as well, Staff Sergeant. Make sure nothing gets damaged," Sullivan said.

"Roger that," Dole said. "Private Case got a temporary radio receiver set up last night. We should be within range of comms. We'll stay in touch."

"Yes, and don't take too long," the captain ordered. "I want to get this done today. The heavy cargo should be dropping soon. We'll need to procure it ASAP."

Dole nodded, and the trio set out. They climbed up onto the shelf of bedrock and approached the pyramid. They all moved a little slower than normal. The sheer size of the structure was intimidating. Felicity keyed her mic.

"Lieutenant, we're approaching the structure," she said.

"You've got the LT on the horn?" Dole asked.

Felicity nodded.

"I read you," Blake said.

"Very good. He should be here," Dole said. "He knows more about this thing than anyone."

They made their way around the entire base. The pyramid was surrounded on three sides by mountains. There were no openings that they could see.

"It's well situated," Dole said as they came back to the front.

"What do you mean?" Bailey asked.

"Mountains on three sides," the staff sergeant explained. "From a strategic point of view, it's well protected and easily defended."

"But it's not a fortress," Felicity said. "The lieutenant said the one on Earth has a single corridor and a few interior rooms, that's all."

"This one might be different," Bailey said. "It doesn't appear to even have an opening at all."

"Lieutenant, there's no way to get inside," Felicity said using her com-link.

"There should be an opening," Blake explained, "on the northern face."

"He said there should be an opening on the northern face," Felicity said.

"Not at ground level," Blake said. "You'll have to climb up several meters."

"Sir, we don't see an opening," Felicity responded.

"Wait a second," Dole said. He was running his hands over the smooth exterior. "Look at this."

The exterior was bright white in the light of day and seemed to shimmer. The sides looked smooth, and they nearly missed a series of indentations that were about a meter wide. They weren't steps, exactly; they were too shallow and too close together. In fact, they looked like wide, miniature stairs.

"What is that?" Bailey asked.

"I can't say for certain, but it looks like steps to me," Dole said.

"We found something, LT," Felicity said. "One moment."

"There's nothing up there," Bailey said.

"Nothing we can see," Dole corrected him. "We almost didn't see these stairs either."

"They could just be decoration," Felicity said.

"One of us needs to go up and have a look around," Dole said.

"I'll go," Felicity volunteered.

She didn't wait for her companions to agree. She had to turn her feet sideways, but she had no trouble ascending the staircase.

"What's happening, Corporal?" Blake asked.

Felicity felt better having his voice in her ear. "I'm climbing the stairs."

She had gone up five meters and suddenly came to an opening that sloped downward. She could see that the interior was made of more of the white limestone, which made it almost impossible to see at a distance, especially from the ground. The tunnel was dark, and Felicity felt a thrill. Here was the opening, just as Blake had said it would be, and she was going inside.

"I found the opening," she shouted down.

"Wait for us, Corporal! That's an order," Dole shouted back.

She gave him a thumbs-up. "Lieutenant, you should see the view from here," she said. "I can see the entire valley, and the mountains are magnificent."

"Use your monoscope," Blake replied. "I want to see everything when you get back."

"Roger that," she said as Dole came quickly up the stairs.

The staff sergeant had his assault rifle slung around on his back so that it wouldn't get in his way and he could use both hands to steady himself as he climbed.

"They could have made the stairs bigger," he complained as he approached.

"LT, we're going in," Felicity said.

Bailey was coming up behind Dole, but there wasn't room for more than one person at a time in the tunnel that sloped down. Suddenly, over their com-link, Captain Sullivan's gruff voice broke through.

"Staff Sergeant, what's up there? What can you see?"

"It's just a tunnel, sir," Dole replied. "We're going inside."

Felicity slung her own rifle onto her back. She activated her helmet lights and held the monoscope with one hand as she started down into the interior of the pyramid. There were more of the miniature stairs inside. The tunnel continued down several meters without any sort of markings or symbols inside. The walls and ceiling of the tunnel where smooth stone. The tunnel was small enough that Felicity had to bend over as she walked. Soon she came to a branch in the tunnel.

"Lieutenant?" she said using her com-link.

"I read you, Corporal," Blake said.

"There are two more tunnels," she said.

"One leading up and one down?"

"Yes, sir," she said.

"What's he saying?" Dole asked.

"It's the same as the Great Pyramid," Blake explained. "The upper chamber leads to the grand gallery. That's where I would go first."

"Roger that," she said, before repeating the information to Dole.

"Ask where the lower tunnel goes," he ordered.

"LT? Where does the lower tunnel go?"

"To a subterranean chamber. On Earth, it was unfinished. It had a long shaft that went nowhere—just dead-ended in the bedrock."

Once more, Felicity repeated the information.

"All right, let's go up," Dole said.

They took the ascending passageway. Just as Blake had predicted, it opened up to a tall, vaulted chamber that continued upward, while another, smaller chamber branched off but was level.

"We're in the grand chamber," Felicity said, glad that she could stand up again.

"Is there a side passage?" Blake asked, his signal starting to break up.

"Roger that," Felicity said.

"That leads to the queen's chamber," he explained. "Go up to the king's chamber. If there's something inside, it should be in there."

"The LT thinks we should keep going up," Felicity said.

"Why not?" Dole replied.

"There's nothing in here," Bailey said. "It's like a cave."

"You claustrophobic, Private?" Dole asked.

"I didn't think I was," Bailey replied, "but this place gives me the creeps."

They were in the middle of the grand gallery, still climbing the tiny steps. Felicity reached out and touched the wall. It was smooth, but it seemed strange that there weren't any markings or decorations. The pyramid was an enigma.

"Don't go touching everything," Dole said. "You're likely to trigger a booby trap and get us all killed."

"Wonderful," Bailey said.

"There's something up ahead," Felicity said. She kept climbing and suddenly entered a new chamber. The floor was flat but made of different types of stone. The dull gray limestone of the interior of the pyramid changed to huge blocks of polished red granite.

"Oh my God," Dole said. "This is unbelievable."

"Lieutenant, we're in the king's chamber," Felicity said, but there was no response. "I think I lost him."

"It's not surprising," Dole said. "The signal must be blocked by all this stone."

"It's incredible," Bailey said.

The walls, floor, and ceiling were polished smooth and reflected the light from their helmet lamps. At the rear of the chamber was a rectangular block of stone. They approached, only to discover that the stone was filled with a strange type of metal.

"Can I touch it?" Felicity asked.

"What is it?" Bailey asked. "Gold?"

"No," Dole said. "It's not gold. In fact, I've never seen anything like it."

The metal looked almost like mercury, a shimmering fluid. But when Felicity reached out a finger, she found that the metal was solid. Even more mysterious was that the metal was warm, like the outside of an oven door.

"It's hot," she said.

"We need a spectrometer," Dole said. "We need a whole damn scientific team to study this place."

They explored the chamber, which was exquisite. No dust covered the floor, and no markings graced the walls. The joints of the stone were tight, the blocks cut at perfect angles.

"I wonder where all this stone came from," Bailey said.

"This stone isn't like the rest," Dole pointed out. "It's probably granite. They used to make countertops from polished granite like this. But it wouldn't come from the same quarry as the limestone."

"Let's check the other chambers," Felicity said.

They went back down to the grand gallery, but she still couldn't make contact with Blake. She didn't think she could get more nervous, but his absence in her earpiece made her fear that something was wrong. They went into the queen's chamber but found it empty.

"Don't you think it's weird that there's no animals in here?" Bailey said.

"Not even a trace that they've ever been in here," Dole added.

"We've seen signs of nocturnal wildlife," Felicity said.

"I'm guessing they go underground in the daytime. Why wouldn't they come in here?"

"Maybe they know something we don't," Bailey pointed out.

"It's certainly strange," Dole said.

They went back down to the lower tunnel and then followed the descending passageway into the subterranean chamber. Inside they found a massive block of stone right in the center of the room.

"That seems odd," Felicity said.

"Probably a support," Dole said. "That's a lot of weight over our head right now."

Felicity touched the stone. She couldn't help herself. There were no markings, no way to know what anything was for. As she reached out with her free hand and touched the stone, there was a soft, almost inaudible hum.

"What's that?" Bailey asked.

"You do something, Mars?"

"I just touched the stone," she said.

"It sounds like the heat just came on or something," Bailey pointed out.

Dole touched the rock.

"It's vibrating," he said. "I don't think this is a rock at all."

"Where does that tunnel go?" Bailey asked.

He was pointing to a smaller, square shaft cut into the back wall of the subterranean chamber. Felicity looked at it and felt revulsion. She didn't want to go crawling through the dark tunnel, but someone had to, and she was the smallest of the three.

"Sorry, Corporal," Dole said.

Felicity pulled her assault rifle off her back and handed it to the staff sergeant. "I feel like you should tie a rope around my ankle or something," she said.

"You'll be fine. Just get down there and take a look," Dole said. "We'll be right here."

She took a deep breath and bent low so that she could crawl into the tunnel. She had to go on her hands and knees. The light from her helmet shone down in front of her, but the darkness seemed thicker in the tight space—it was more substantial, and her light didn't do as much to illuminate the strange tunnel. Her palms and knees were hurting before she reached the end, and when she did, she realized with a sense of frustration that she would have to back her way out of the tunnel. There was no space to turn around. The tunnel ended in sheer rock, but unlike the rest of the stone, it was blackened and charred. She touched the rough stone, and her hand came away covered in soot. The air was heavy and tinged with the odor of sulfur. She started crawling backward and soon her skin tingled. It felt like the air had become charged with electricity. The fine hairs on her arms and the back of her neck were standing straight out from her body.

The feeling made her scared, and she crawled faster, her knees bruising. All she could think about was getting out of the tunnel and away from the pyramid. She needed fresh air and space. A moment later, she reached the end of the tunnel and friendly hands helped her out.

"Anything?" Dole asked.

"No, just a dead end," she said moving away from the tunnel.

Porter Bailey bent down and looked in the tunnel. "Can you feel that?" he asked.

Felicity was just about to tell him to move—that what he was feeling was some kind of static electricity—but before she could speak, lightning shot out of the tunnel. It was blindingly bright. She and Staff Sergeant Dole both toppled back away from the tunnel. The episode lasted a fraction of a second but left Felicity dazed.

"Bailey!" Dole said, struggling back to his feet. "Porter!"

Felicity had spots in her vision. The light from her helmet seemed dim as she looked around the chamber for her counterpart. She saw him lying on the floor near the big block of stone that was humming. She rubbed her eyes, still trying to see, when the stench of burned flesh hit her. She nearly threw up.

"Damn it!" Dole shouted. "Get on your feet, Mars. We're getting out of here, now!"

Felicity didn't feel like obeying, but she did. In the back of her dazed mind, she could hear her father's voice: *You train so that in the moment your body knows what to do and will react without any conscious thought. It's that kind of training that saves you. And when it does, you'll look back and realize that all the hard days, every drop of sweat, every sore and aching muscle was worth it.*

She was on her feet and helping the staff sergeant drag Bailey's corpse from the pyramid before she knew what she was doing. They were scrambling up the sloping tunnel that led out of the pyramid when a flash, followed by a hair-raising pop, sounded behind them. She had Bailey's legs. They seemed fine, but his upper body was a stiff mass of melted armor, fabric, and flesh. The smell was horrific. She had to stop and retch before they reached the exit.

"Hold it together, Mars," Dole said. "We're almost there."

"Keep going," she said, her eyes flooding with tears.

She swiped her arm across her mouth and nose, picked up Bailey's legs, and kept moving forward.

CHAPTER 34

BLAKE CAGE

He cursed, which wasn't really in his nature, and adjusted the gain on the radio.

"Corporal Mars, do you read me?"

There was no answer.

"If they went inside, there could be interference," Devon said.

"No," Cage replied. "They were inside and reading me okay. Something's happened."

Just then a voice was heard over the radio, but it wasn't Felicity's.

"Recon Platoon Bravo, this is the *Bronx II*. Do you copy? Over."

The last thing Cage right then wanted was to be distracted from his wife and the pyramid. He couldn't say what had him nervous, but his sense of danger was way up. He hadn't felt such a foreboding feeling since being followed by a gang of street thugs when he was in middle school. But he couldn't ignore a call from their ship in orbit. He was a lieutenant first, at least until the colony was established and he could be with Felicity the way they wanted.

He clicked over to the appropriate channel and depressed the transmit button on the handheld mic.

"*Bronx II*, this is Bravo Platoon," he said. "We read you loud and clear, over."

"Recon Platoon Bravo, we are commencing heavy cargo drops in sixty minutes. Please confirm. Over."

"Roger that, *Bronx II*. You are dropping heavy cargo and we are standing by to receive. Out."

"How close will the heavy cargo be to our location?" Devon asked. They weren't on watch duty—that task fell to Webster and Ormond.

"Ideally they'll drop in the field close to our location," Cage said. "The computers on the ship are calculating a window of entry and will launch the heavy cargo straight into it. But the atmospheric conditions will determine where they actually land. A soft breeze once the chutes open could blow them off course by a hundred kilometers."

"How will we find them?" Devon asked.

"Each one has a tracking beacon. We'll need to get the tracking system set up, confirm touchdown of each load, and mark its location. When the platoon gets back, we'll walk and retrieve the platoon carriers. Once we have them up and running, the rest will be easy."

"We should let the captain know," Devon said.

Cage knew he was right, but he was beginning to deeply resent Captain Sullivan. He nodded, adjusted the radio, and made the call.

"Captain Sullivan, this is base camp, do you read?"

There was a moment of silence, and Cage was starting to think that perhaps his radio receiver wasn't reaching them any longer, when Sullivan's gruff voice replied, "Lieutenant, I'm quite busy at the moment."

"Yes sir, sorry sir," Cage replied. "Just letting you know that heavy cargo is dropping in sixty minutes."

"Well obviously I can't worry about that until I'm back in camp," Sullivan snapped. His condescending tone was pushing Cage's buttons.

"Yes, sir."

"Make sure you track and log each load," Sullivan went on, as if Cage were a complete imbecile. "When I return, I'll see to them. And Lieutenant, do not report the fact that I am away from base camp when you speak to the *Bronx II*."

"Of course not, sir," Cage replied.

The line went dead. It was like the older man had cut the connection before Cage could acknowledge the order, just to spite him. As much as it upset Cage to have lost contact with his wife, he knew his duty.

"We'll go back down to base camp," Cage said. "Inform Webster and Ormond. They'll have to stay on watch until we get back. Then I'll give you all an extended break."

"Roger that," Devon said.

Cage walked over to the trees where their repelling ropes were tied. When he looked out between them, he could just make out the edge of the pyramid. He couldn't stop thinking about what Felicity had told him of the attack by the rock spiders. Had they run into more inside the pyramid? Cage remembered reading stories of giant bats roosting in the Great Pyramid of Giza. He had no idea if it was true or not, but what if there were dangerous beasts inside the gleaming pyramid? It didn't seem possible, and yet it wasn't just possible; it was entirely probable. Had he lost contact with Felicity because she had been attacked?

"Should we pack up camp, sir?" Devon asked.

"No," Cage replied. "We'll be back once the drops are all logged."

He checked his weapon, making sure the assault rifle was in safe mode but otherwise ready for action, and waved to the two privates on watch. Hugo returned the wave, but Peter Ormond was busy staring out over the prairie.

"How many are they sending?" Devon asked.

"I don't know," Cage admitted. "I hope that Captain Sullivan has that in his notes. But I'm guessing it will be several loads. Long-term food for the platoon, enough structures for two barracks, a mess hall, and stationary weaponry— not to mention the platoon carriers. They'll also be sending additional structure and colony resources. I'd guess twelve or fourteen loads, all told."

They started down the trail that wound from the grassy plateau down to the base camp. Cage was frustrated with not being able to keep in touch with Felicity, but he didn't let it distract him. Any sign of movement brought his weapon to his shoulder so that he could look through his scope using its thermal setting. Perhaps he was being paranoid, projecting his fears about losing Felicity onto his own surroundings.

If Devon noticed, he kept his mouth shut. The tall, Israeli sniper wasn't a talker all the time. He would sometimes pepper Cage with a series of questions, then fall silent to contemplate the answers.

They reached the base camp without running into trouble. The stalkers seemed to be avoiding them, or perhaps the platoon having slain four in two days had cleared the area out. At the command post, Cage showed Devon how to use the tracking device. It was a handheld model that would show each load's altitude and coordinates. Once they were down, the precise location would need to be written just in case something happened to the tracking device.

Cage stayed with the radio, waiting and hoping to hear something from the camp. Instead, he got word from the *Bronx II* that the first load would be dropping. The ship made a circuit around the planet every ninety minutes. Only four loads could be launched in the window calculated to bring the equipment down near the base camp. They had to be careful not to drop the heavy cargo down in the mountains. They were being dropped in big, metal cargo containers with multiple parachutes, but if the containers dropped onto the side of a mountain, they could tumble down, damaging the goods inside and perhaps even being buried in rubble. It would take the *Bronx II* five trips to launch all the goods. Cage would be busy the rest of the day, and until Felicity reached out to him, he would have to wait and worry about her with no way to know if she was dead or alive.

CHAPTER 35

FELICITY MARS

"Help!" Staff Sergeant Wyatt Dole shouted.

Felicity had finally gotten clarity after nearly getting electrocuted in the chamber under the pyramid. She didn't know it, but her communications equipment had shorted out, and the battery packs on her Infiltrator had melted. The weapon was worthless, but Dole, who had it slung over one shoulder, didn't know that. His weapons and com-link were fried as well, which was why he was shouting.

There wasn't room outside the opening on the pyramid for the both of them, and between them they also had Porter Bailey's lifeless body. The tiny steps that led down from the pyramid were too shallow, the angle too severe to try and carry him down. Felicity was stuck inside the tunnel, but she could see the bright sky overhead and feel the cool morning air on her face. She took deep breaths, trying to calm down, but she could hear the alarm from her platoon mates, and she wanted desperately to get away.

She couldn't see that several people had rushed to the

edge of the pyramid. When Staff Sergeant Dole pulled Bailey out of the tunnel to slowly lower him down to the outstretched hands of the troopers, she came out into the sunlight. Immediately she felt better, but when she toggled her com-link and called for Blake, there was still no reply.

"Lieutenant," she said. "Are you there?"

Nothing sounded in her earpiece, not even the clipped static that normally accompanied the release of the transmission key. She looked at Dole, who stood and stretched his back. His own earpiece was dangling from his collar. She pulled hers out.

"Fried," he said. "My guess is our weapons are toast, too."

"What happened in there, Staff Sergeant?" demanded a red-faced Captain Sullivan, who had scrambled up onto the ledge the pyramid was built on but kept a respectful distance from the structure.

"Something activated," Dole said as he began descending the narrow steps. "Bailey was hit by an electric discharge."

Felicity reached over and put her hand on the outside of the pyramid, which was covered with smooth, white stones. She could feel the electric hum. The entire building was priming with power.

"We need to get away from here," she said. "It's not safe."

She didn't have to convince anyone. The curiosity of the platoon ended the moment they saw Bailey's body. He had been popular with both the men and the women of the platoon—a friendly, easygoing man that everyone felt they could rely on. Seeing his blackened body made Felicity feel sick all over again. His face was blistered and blackened, the hair burned away, the skin taut from tensed muscles. His teeth stood out in contrast to the burned skin, a horrifying rictus that seemed to mock the solemnity of death.

Felicity quickly followed Staff Sergeant Dole. Everyone else had fled from the pyramid, and they both jogged away from the massive, white structure. After jumping down from the bedrock shelf, they hurried out to the camp. Felicity wasn't sure they were far enough away, but that was where the rest of the platoon had gathered.

"Explain yourself!" Captain Sullivan demanded.

"We went in and all was quiet," Dole said. "The interior is very much the same as the pyramid on Earth."

"And how in the world do you know that, Staff Sergeant?" Sullivan demanded.

"Lieutenant Cage explained it all," Felicity said, making a choice not to mention that it was done via com-link. "Everything he said about the pyramid on Earth was like what we found inside. Except for one thing."

Dole looked at her, realization dawning on him in that moment.

"What thing?" Sullivan demanded.

"The subterranean chamber," Dole said, more to himself than to the captain. "They didn't finish it."

"What?" Sullivan asked.

"The pyramid on Earth," Felicity said, taking a deep breath. "It has three chambers. The highest is called the king's chamber. The middle is the queen's chamber. And there's one underground, but it's unfinished—just an empty chamber and a tunnel that dead-ends in the bedrock."

"But it wasn't unfinished," Dole said. "We just didn't understand the design."

"What do you mean?" Sullivan asked.

"The chamber under this pyramid has a large, square pillar in the middle," Dole said. "At least we thought it was a pillar."

"But while we were in the room, something turned on," Felicity continued the story. "You could hear a hum, like some type of machinery powering up."

"I sent Corporal Mars down a small tunnel, and it also dead-ended in bedrock," Dole said.

"Only the rock is covered with soot," Felicity said, holding up her hands. "I was backing out when I felt the tunnel fill with static electricity."

"And when she got out, Private Bailey was looking in, and a bolt of lightning flashed through. It killed him and nearly killed us."

"Where'd it go to?" Sullivan asked.

"It's a grounding tunnel, a power outlet," Dole said. "Whatever that thing is, it draws in a lot of power, and as it builds up it has to let loose somewhere. That's what the tunnel is for. It's like a safety valve but for electrical current."

"Like a ground wire," Amber Case said.

"Exactly," Dole exclaimed.

"And what is it going to do now?" Sullivan asked.

"I don't know," Dole said. "There were no markings inside. No decorations or writing."

"It isn't a tomb," Felicity said. "The scientists back home are way off."

"Is it a weapon?" Sullivan asked.

"Maybe, but I don't think so," Dole said. "It's a communication device, maybe."

"You think there are aliens on this planet?" Sullivan demanded, as if the staff sergeant knew something he was keeping hidden.

"No, not on this planet," Dole said. "Maybe not even in this system."

"You're not making sense, man," the captain bellowed. "You're in shock."

"What? You think it's like a security system?" Lucinda Fuego asked.

Dole nodded, "Maybe."

"If so, we've tripped it," Miranda Dux said.

"Oh man, this is bad," Billy Oberton said as he looked around the clearing like he expected the aliens to suddenly appear, guns blazing.

"Or maybe it had nothing to do with you," Junior Knoxx said. "Maybe it's a solar charger, and you just happened to be inside when it needed to discharge."

"I don't believe in coincidences," Dole remarked.

"We should go," Jean Pierre said. "Leave this place."

"We aren't leaving anything," Sullivan declared. "I want around-the-clock surveillance of that structure. Mars, Oberton, Fuego, Dux, you are not to leave this valley without a direct order from me. Is that clear?"

"Are you serious?" Felicity said. "I don't even have a weapon."

"You don't need a weapon. You're a scout. Your job is to watch and report," he said, then turned to Amber Case. "Give me your sidearm!"

Amber looked at Captain Sullivan with an icy glare, but she drew her pistol and handed it to him. The captain, in turn, handed the gun to Felicity.

"That will do to scare off the wildlife. You stay here. We have a radio relay set up. If you see anything at all, you're to report to me directly. Is that absolutely clear?"

"Yes, Captain," the four specialists assigned to watch the pyramid said.

"The rest of you, prepare to move out," Sullivan said.

"What about Private Bailey's body, sir?" Dole asked.

The captain looked around. Then his eyes stopped on Felicity.

"This looks like the perfect place to bury him," Captain said. "The four of you can do that as well."

Felicity wanted to punch the condescending officer in the throat, but she had too much self-control. Instead, she backed away. The rest of the platoon seemed only too happy to be leaving. The pyramid had gone from a curiosity to a frightening structure, and they wanted nothing to do with it. Only Staff Sergeant Dole had any compassion for the remaining specialists. He pointed to his tent.

"You want me to leave that for you, Mars?"

"I wouldn't say no, Staff Sergeant."

"It's yours," he said. "Just leave it when you get the call back to base camp."

"Thank you, Staff Sergeant."

"Forget it," he said. "Just watch your six. That goes for all of you. No more losses. No more reckless decisions. Listen to Corporal Mars, and do not go back in that pyramid."

"You don't have to warn me," Fuego said. "That place is not for the living."

Felicity waited until the platoon was gone back down the valley. They had four tents, their supplies, and the radio receiver. But they were in the open, and she didn't like that. They needed some distance and some cover from whoever or whatever might turn up to answer the signal that the pyramid was sending.

"I don't know about the three of you," Felicity said. "But I'm moving back."

"I'm with you, Mars," Fuego said.

"How will we watch the pyramid if we fall back?" Dux asked.

Felicity held up the monoscope, but it was an electric device and the power surge had ruined it too. She tossed it on the ground.

"We could take turns," Billy Oberton said. "Whoever has the watch comes forward, and the rest of us stay back."

"If you think I'm going to sit out down here in the dark by myself, you're crazy," Fuego said.

"I'll do that," Mars said. "Lucinda and Miranda, take the day shift. Billy and I will cover the night, but you'll have to swap weapons with me when I'm on duty. I'll need your scope's night vision."

"Fine," Lucinda said.

"Agreed," Miranda said.

They moved their tents back by the thick bushes that ran along the stream as the valley narrowed. Miranda took the first watch and moved out near the radio relay dish that Amber Case had set up. Billy and Lucinda wanted to know everything that happened in the pyramid and what it all looked like.

"So, the stone block in the king's chamber was covered with something?" Billy asked.

"No, it was more like something was inside it," Felicity explained. "It was hot to the touch. And the surface shimmered like liquid."

"Man, this seriously gives me the creeps," Lucinda said.

"Lieutenant Cage told us yesterday that the one on Earth had been broken into, because it had been sealed up," Billy said. "What if they closed it up because it was dangerous?"

"Dangerous how?" Felicity asked.

"I don't know," Lucinda said. "Maybe the aliens lived in there or something."

"Or kept something in there that was dangerous," Billy said.

"I'm glad you made it out alive, Mars," Lucinda said. "But I'm starting to hate this planet. It's like we don't belong here and it's slowly taking us out, one by one."

"That's how it always happens in the movies," Billy said.

"This isn't a movie," Felicity said. "And we aren't going anywhere."

CHAPTER 36

BLAKE CAGE

Monitoring the heavy cargo drops took all day. The sun was nearly down by the time they finished. Fourteen cargo containers had been dropped, and they were all identified and recorded. The closest was only six kilometers from base camp, but the first priority was to get the platoon carriers, and the nearest one was half a day's march from the base camp.

"Let's get back up to the hilltop," Cage said. "We need to relieve Hugo and Pete."

"Sure," Devon said, stretching.

They had been sitting in the command post all day. It was tedious work, but they had completed it. In comparison, the idea of standing watch seemed like a relief. Cage was used to being indoors. On Earth he'd spent most of his time inside, but the air there was stale and tainted. Centuries of industry had pumped toxins into the air and forced the government to build huge machines to help clean the atmosphere, but it was a slow process. In some parts of the world, humans had to wear breathing masks anytime they went outdoors, and no animal survived in the wild—not even bugs.

But on Magnificus Prime, the air was sweet. Cage hated being cooped up in the tiny command post when he could be outside. The wide, open spaces were enthralling. But neither the boredom of dreary work nor the prospect of getting back outside could overshadow his fears for Felicity. He hadn't heard from her all day, nor had he heard from the platoon. He was getting worried, and in his mind he was already planning for what they would do if they didn't hear from the rest of recon platoon Bravo by morning. When Staff Sergeant Dole's voice came from the communication console, Cage and Devon both jumped. They had been about to walk out the door.

"Base camp, this is Staff Sergeant Dole, do you read?"

Cage snatched the mic from the surface of the table. "Staff Sergeant, we read you. What's your status?"

"We're on our way back to your location. We should be there shortly. We have one man wounded."

"What about the pyramid? What did you find?" Cage asked.

"Lieutenant, let's keep the radio clear," Captain Sullivan ordered angrily. "We will be at base camp soon. Tell me you have those heavy cargo locations mapped and ready for collection."

"Yes, Captain," Cage said. "Corporal Devon and I have them located and marked on the system. Fourteen heavy containers, all in the clear."

"It's about time we got some good news," Captain Sullivan said. "Clear out of the command post and help us with Private Laubin. Sullivan out."

The line went silent. The look on his face must have given

Cage away, but Devon put a hand on his shoulder and said, "I am sure she is well."

Cage shook his head. "What?"

"Corporal Mars. You are concerned for her safety, and Staff Sergeant Dole said they have one wounded."

"You're right," Cage said. "I've grown fond of Corporal Mars. Thanks for your reassurance and your discretion."

"Yes, of course," Devon Al'Farrah said with a slight bow of his head.

They left the command post and hurried to the tree line. It was deep twilight, and the platoon had turned on their head lamps. Cage counted only ten troopers, and he felt a lump form in his stomach. But he had to be professional. There was a reason the Magellan Corporation didn't allow married couples to join the militia. All Cage wanted was to ensure his wife was safe; nothing and no one else mattered. It was not the proper conduct of an officer, and he tried to hold himself in check—but if something happened to Felicity, Cage knew he would lose his mind.

The platoon came marching in. They were exhausted, that much was clear. It was hard to see faces in the dark. They were carrying Private Laubin. Cage moved along the line of troopers and felt his heart sink. Felicity was missing.

Captain Sullivan ordered Cage to set the watch for the night and see if there was anything that could be done for Laubin, then he went immediately into the command post.

"What the hell happened?" Cage asked as Laubin was moved into the light from the flood lamps mounted on the command post.

"He got infected with an animal venom," Staff Sergeant Dole said. "He's been paralyzed now for thirty-six hours, but I think it's starting to wear off."

"He can mumble some words," Sammy Jones said, "and drink a little if we let the water dribble right into his mouth. That's better than he's been for a full day and night."

"Where are the others?" Cage asked.

He tried to sound calm but failed. He couldn't hide the worry for his wife.

"We lost Private Bailey and Private Ficklestine," Dole explained. "I guess you heard about Ted?" When Cage nodded, Dole continued, "We went into the pyramid and everything was just like you said."

"Any markings?" Cage asked. He knew the answer already. If there had been inscriptions, Felicity would have mentioned them right away. But he needed to ask something other than what had happened to her.

"No, bare stone walls," Dole said. "The king's chamber was polished granite. It looked like it could have been from an actual king's palace. The entire place was spotless."

"And a sarcophagus?" Cage asked.

"No, not a sarcophagus—but there was a stone box. It was filled with shimmering metal. Something I've never seen before," Dole explained. "It was hot to the touch. We checked the queen's chamber—nothing, just an empty room. Then we went down to the lower level."

"The subterranean chamber," Cage said.

"It had some type of electric device down there. It was encased in stone, by the looks of it. I thought it was a support pillar. And there was a tunnel."

"Where did it lead?" Cage asked.

"Nowhere," Dole explained. "It just dead-ended in bedrock."

"That doesn't make sense," Cage said.

"That's what we thought," Dole said. "But that whole

building is one giant machine. The tunnel seems to be for excess power discharge—a grounding conduit. That's what killed Bailey and nearly took me and Corporal Mars with him."

"But you survived? Was Corporal Mars injured?"

The question was fraught with worry. Cage could feel sweat pouring out of him. His entire body was tense.

"No," Dole said. "She's fine. The captain left her, Fuego, Dux, and Oberton at the sight to keep an eye on the pyramid."

"What? Why?"

"Because," Dole said, "—and I've given this a lot of thought—I think we tripped something in that place. We activated it."

"Okay," Cage said, so relieved that his wife was okay that he nearly dropped to the ground in a trembling mass.

He managed to hold himself together and followed Staff Sergeant Dole to the mess pavilion. The older man poured himself a cup of water mixed with electrolytes and amino acids. It was fruit-flavored. He turned up the cup and drank it all down, then continued talking as he refilled the cup.

"Think about it," Dole said. "Say you're a spacefaring race, exploring the galaxy. Wouldn't you put your mark on any planet like this? It's perfect. Great atmosphere, just the right distance from the system star, and untouched by any other intelligent life."

"You're saying the pyramid is a marker?" Cage asked.

"Of sorts," Dole said. "I also think it's an alarm system. I think when we went inside, we activated it. And that thing sent a signal to someone."

"So they can come and get rid of the intruders," Cage said, his anxiety ratcheting back up.

"Exactly," Dole said. "We're in over our heads here, LT.

And the captain is starting to lose his shit. Don't you go and get squirrelly on me though—this platoon needs you."

"No, of course not," Cage said, still trying to process Dole's theory.

"And I've got another thought about the pyramid on Earth," Dole continued. "I seem to recall a lot of talk about grave robbers."

"Yes, the Egyptian tombs were almost all robbed. King Tut's tomb was a rare exception. Why?"

"Was the pyramid broken into?"

"Yes," Cage said. "The pyramid was sealed up. The robbers tunneled in and discovered the passageways that had been sealed. Most researchers believed a tenth century ruler opened the pyramid, but not everyone agrees."

"Why would they seal it up?" Dole said. "I'm thinking the builders didn't do that. I think people sealed it off because it's dangerous. Grave robbers didn't loot the Great Pyramid; they broke into it and did their best to destroy it. When they couldn't, they sealed it up."

"And we've just activated the one on this planet," Cage said.

"I could be wrong," Dole said. "And hell, if it's a signal, it could take ten thousand years to reach whoever might be listening. But I doubt it's going to take that long. I think whoever built it knows we are here, and they will show up, sooner or later."

"I'm hoping for later," Cage said.

"Yeah, me too," Dole said. "But I doubt we're that lucky, lieutenant. We've stumbled onto something here that might be the end of us all."

CHAPTER 37

FELICITY MARS

The change was noticeable even at dusk. As the skies faded and the shadows grew deeper, the pyramid didn't just reflect a ghostly glow from the starlight. The surface seemed to ripple and was lit by tiny pulses of light.

"What's it doing?" Felicity asked as she approached Lucinda, who had taken the afternoon watch.

"I don't know. I haven't seen or heard anything until it started getting dark."

Lucinda had her rifle propped on a rock. She was positioned near the communication receiver dish, which was set up on a boulder that was as high as Felicity's waist. The smaller rock with the weapon propped on it was the size of a human head and made a perfect bench for the assault rifle. It was a good spot near the edge of the clearing to watch the pyramid. There was some cover behind the rocks, and Lucinda was stretched out on her stomach in a sniper position, watching the structure through the scope she had mounted on her rifle.

"All right, why don't you head back?" Felicity said. "Try to get some rest."

"Okay," Lucinda said.

She got to her feet, and Felicity handed her the pistol that Captain Sullivan had given her.

"Keep it," Lucinda said. "I've got mine. And you better take my com-link too, just in case you see something."

She fished the com-link out of a tiny pocket in her fatigue shirt that was made for the device, pulled the cord that led to the earpiece out, and handed it all to Felicity.

"Have you heard anything from base camp?" Felicity asked as she took the com-link.

"Not a lot. The platoon just got back."

"Okay, I'll see you later," Felicity said.

Lucinda headed off toward the camp, and Felicity was alone. She felt fear, but not terror. Her mind told her that she shouldn't be there. The pyramid was dangerous. And yet it was her job—her duty—to stand guard. She wouldn't be much of a deterrent if something happened, but she could report it. The thought that she might be able to give the rest of the platoon a warning that might help them survive was enough to keep her there, even as night set in. She couldn't see much apart from the pyramid. The stars were out, and the ambient light filtering down into the valley made it a landscape of deep shadows. The pyramid itself was like a light fixture that had gone bad. It glowed softly, but occasionally sections flickered brighter.

An hour passed. Occasionally she looked at the pyramid up close through the scope on the rifle. There was nothing to see. Other than the lights, it didn't change. They had searched the interior, and unless there were hidden chambers, they saw no sign of anyone in the structure. There was no furniture—

nothing that might indicate an intelligent being would even want to be in the pyramid. It clearly wasn't a domicile or a fortress, as Staff Sergeant Dole had suggested. Why the captain had ordered them to stay behind and watch the structure was a mystery to her.

Her thoughts were broken by a familiar voice in the earpiece of her com-link.

"Corporal Mars, this is Lieutenant Cage. Do you read?"

In her excitement to respond, she knocked the rifle off the rock and didn't bother to pick it back up. She got the activation control for the com-link and replied to her husband.

"LT! I'm here...sir!"

"It's good to hear your voice, Corporal," Blake said. "Are you okay?"

"Fine," Felicity said. "We had a scare, but I'm fine."

"Staff Sergeant Dole told me all about the pyramid. Has anything changed?"

"Negative, it's quiet," Felicity said. "But the surface is lighting up—not brightly, but occasionally an area seems to glow or flicker."

"That is so strange," Blake said. "I wish I could see it."

"So do I," their conversation was getting overly friendly, but Felicity couldn't help it.

"We'll be monitoring comms at all hours," Blake said, sounding official. "If you see or hear anything at all, report it."

"Roger that," Felicity said, picking up the rifle and propping it back on the rock.

She noticed that the scope settings had been bumped from night vision to thermal. She leaned forward and looked through the scope.

"Lieutenant!" Felicity said. "The pyramid is hot."

"Repeat, Corporal. I didn't understand that."

"It's hot, sir. I just switched to thermal on my scope, and the pyramid is lit up like a fireworks display."

"Can you feel the heat?" Blake asked.

"I'm at least forty meters from the structure, but no, I don't feel it," Felicity explained. "But something is going on."

"All right, stay alert, Corporal Mars. I'm going to speak to Captain Sullivan. Stand by."

She could see the pyramid clearly through the scope. Even the passageway entrance, which was invisible in the regular spectrum of light, stood out in the thermal view. She was surprised that flames weren't shooting out of the cramped passageway.

A moment later, Captain Sullivan's voice came grumbling over the com-link.

"Corporal, what is happening?"

"I can't say for sure, sir, but the pyramid is glowing white-hot on thermal imaging."

"And?" Sullivan asked.

"And I'm awaiting orders, sir," Felicity said.

"So it's hot, that tells us nothing," he said angrily. "It could simply be residual heat from the sun. Stone often takes much longer to release heat than other substances."

"It isn't that," Felicity said. "The mountains around it are cool."

"Don't waste our time, Corporal," Sullivan demanded. "Keep this channel clear unless there is something of signifi-cance to report."

The line went dead. Felicity knew it was better not to transmit again, even though she desperately wanted to hear Blake's voice again. She needed time with him, and the chance to drop the formality of their positions. But there was no time. Something was happening with the pyramid, although she couldn't say what yet. She didn't want to alarm her squad unnecessarily, but her instincts told her it was time to act. She picked up the rifle and got to her feet. It didn't take long to reach the others.

"What's wrong?" Lucinda said as Felicity approached.

"Wake the others," Felicity said. "We need to take cover."

"Why?" Lucinda asked as she shook Miranda and Billy's tents. "Wake up. Something's going on."

"The pyramid is hot," Felicity said. "Take a look through thermal."

Their camp was nearly three hundred meters from the pyramid, but the huge structure dominated the valley. Felicity handed the rifle to Lucinda, who brought it up to her shoulder.

"Oh, man, what is going on?" she asked.

"I don't know," Felicity said.

"Is it going to blow?"

"If it does, we need some cover."

"What's going on?" Billy asked as he climbed out of his tent.

"Gear up," Felicity said. "We're moving."

CHAPTER 38

BLAKE CAGE

Fury burned through every cell in Cage's body. He knew that Captain Sullivan was opposed to anything happening that might rock the boat, but he had no control over the pyramid. Keeping Cage away from the site was lunacy.

"You aren't going to do anything?" Cage asked as Sullivan cut the connection with Felicity.

"There's nothing to be done," Sullivan said.

"Sir, I respectfully request that we send the platoon back to the pyramid. Something is certainly happening there. We can't turn our backs on it."

"We just came from that location," Sullivan thundered.

He didn't like being questioned, and Cage had expected the angry outburst. But he couldn't back down—not when the woman he loved was in danger.

"You should have sent me in the first place," Cage said. "Your petty jealousy is getting in the way of your duty."

"You upstart, insubordinate mutt!" Sullivan shouted.

"How dare you question my orders and my honor? You are completely out of line."

"No, sir," Cage shouted back. "You are. Our job is to investigate anything that might make this location unfavorable for the colony, and yet you're ignoring the pyramid which is obviously not of this world and certainly on the verge of doing something dangerous. Nothing else even comes close to the importance of that site. Have you even reported it to the *Bronx II*?"

"There's nothing to report, and you have no idea what it takes to launch a colony. You've never even been off Earth before."

"I know more about the pyramids than anyone in this platoon, yet for some reason you decided it was better if I stayed behind. You let your petty self-interest and overblown ego make your decisions for you. You're failing, Captain. I won't pretend anymore. If you don't send more troops back to the pyramid, I'm telling you we'll all regret it."

There was a knock on the door, and it swung open. Staff Sergeant Dole stepped in.

"You might want to take a step back," he said. "You're causing a scene out here."

Cage could see platoon members at the edge of the ring of light around the command post. They were lurking in the darkness, trying to see what was happening inside.

"Staff Sergeant," Captain Sullivan said. "Take Lieutenant Cage into custody for insubordination and failure to do his duty."

"You're out of your mind," Cage said. "You're the one failing to do anything at all. You sit on your ass all day and stuff your face with food."

"Do you hear that?" Sullivan snarled at Dole. "You heard what he said. You're my witness. He's out of control."

"The pyramid is white-hot on thermal," Cage said. "Something is about to happen, and a single four-man team is not enough. We can't just ignore what's happening in the mountains."

"He's right, sir," Dole said. "We should pull that squad back to a safe distance until we can reinforce their position."

"You see?" Sullivan screamed in Cage's face. "You see? Now you've got everyone questioning my orders."

"You're losing your composure, Captain," Cage replied calmly.

"Get out!" Sullivan screamed.

He tried to grab Cage, obviously intent on throwing him out of the command post. But living with Felicity meant plenty of self-defense practice. He slipped to the side and pushed the older man away. His first instinct was to hit the side of Sullivan's neck with an edge hand strike, just the way his wife had taught him. He raised his hand, but then stepped back, regaining control before he struck a superior officer.

The look on Staff Sergeant Dole's face was pure relief. Sullivan turned and screamed at Cage again.

"Get out!"

"Yes, Captain," Cage said through clenched teeth.

He moved to the door, and Dole stepped to the side. They were both looking into the command post. The communication system and tracking computer that had the locations of all the heavy cargo crates were in the command post. It was officially the entire platoon's building, but the captain had taken it as his personal lair.

"You are going to contact Corporal Mars?" Cage asked.

"Out!" Sullivan said.

He slammed the door so hard that the walls of the tempo-rary building shook. Cage felt a little ashamed; he had lost his cool, and while there was a reason for his pushback, Cage didn't think his actions were completely justified. He needed to rein in his emotions, but his love for Felicity had made that impossible.

"I'm sorry," Cage said quietly to Dole.

"Don't be, sir. Tensions are high," the staff sergeant replied. "All right, people, if you aren't on watch, you better be in your rack. Things are getting dicey, and sleep isn't guaranteed."

The platoon was down to eighteen people, and Grant Laubin was incapacitated. With a four-man team out of camp, they were down to thirteen people, and the captain was certainly not going to keep watch.

"We have to call the scout team back," Cage said. "What-ever is happening with that pyramid, they shouldn't be anywhere near it."

"Send them back to the ridge where we first saw it," Dole said. "We can reinforce them if something happens at the pyramid and relieve them tomorrow once the heavy cargo is brought in."

"All right," Cage said. "I'll give the order."

Cage didn't know how Sullivan would react when Cage made contact via the com-link, but he wasn't going to let fear or uncertainty over his own career keep him from doing what he thought was right. He toggled the activation key on his com-link and made the call.

"Corporal Mars, this is Lieutenant Cage. Do you read?"

There was a pause—longer than he liked—before the response came through.

"I read you, LT," Felicity said. Her voice sounded small

and far away. It made Cage want to run to her. He didn't like thinking that she was in danger and he couldn't help. She had always been able to look after herself, but they were on a foreign planet, and no one had any idea what was going on with the pyramid.

"We need you to pull back to the ridge where we first saw the pyramid," he ordered.

The was no response. He waited a few seconds longer than he felt comfortable and then gave the order again.

"Corporal Mars, you are ordered to fall back to the ridge where we first saw the pyramid. Please confirm."

Nothing. He felt a stone forming in his gut...then the lights on the command post went out. The sudden darkness made Cage blind. He dropped to one knee and raised his rifle, looking for trouble.

"What the hell is going on?" Dole shouted. "Webster, Ormond, check the battery connections."

Cage moved to the command post where Dole was at the door. He knocked firmly, then stepped back.

"Captain Sullivan, you okay in there, sir?" Dole called.

The laser blast burned through the metal door and hit the staff sergeant square in the chest. Cage didn't have time to think. He threw his shoulder into the door. It burst in, knocking Sullivan down. The captain's laser pistol went sliding across the floor. Cage jumped on his superior officer as Sullivan went crawling after the weapon. He landed on the larger man and got hold of his right arm that was reaching for the laser pistol. In the struggle, Cage didn't see Sullivan's left hand draw his knife. He only felt a nudge on the plate armor that protected Cage's abdomen, followed by a fiery pain across his hip. In the darkness Cage couldn't see what was happening, but he knew he was hurt.

The captain was losing control, and Cage was through showing the older man respect. He drove his elbow down in a violent strike against Sullivan's temple. The captain shuttered and lay still. Cage reached up and activated his helmet lights. Looking down, he saw the bloody knife and the wicked gash on his hip. He planted one hand on the wound and got to his feet. Devon Al'Farrah was in the doorway with Joelle Cotumba. They were staring at Cage and the captain wide-eyed.

"Get something and restrain him," Cage ordered, "before he hurts anyone else."

"Yes, Lieutenant," Al'Farrah and Cotumba said at the same time.

Devon stepped into the command post and picked up the laser pistol, then knelt down and pinned Sullivan's hands behind the captain's back. Joelle hurried off to find something to tie their CO up with. Cage moved outside, each step sending waves of pain across his side and down his left leg. He could feel the hot blood soaking his pants and welling up around his fingers, but his concern was for Staff Sergeant Dole.

"Is he okay?" Cage asked.

Amber Case and Sammy Jones were kneeling over Dole. His eyes were open, but he was struggling to catch his breath. Sammy was unfastening the velcro straps that held the staff sergeant's armor in place. She got the chest plate off just as Case powered on her helmet's lights. There was a tiny hole in the armor where the laser had penetrated.

"He's got a small burn, but nothing more," Case said, the relief evident in her voice.

"Penetrating the door and his armor must have stopped it from doing more damage," Sammy said.

"Why can't he breathe?" Cage asked.

"I think it knocked the wind out of him," Sammy said.

"I'm...I'm okay," Staff Sergeant Dole grunted. "Just...need a...second."

"LT," Devon called out.

Cage turned around, worried that Sullivan was waking up, but the older man was out cold. Devon had powered on his helmet lights and was shining them onto the computers.

"What?" Cage asked.

"Looks like the captain torched the computers," Corporal Al'Farrah said. "Everything is gone. Comms, data, tracking—it's all been fired on repeatedly. Probably with the laser pistol."

Rage filled Cage. He now understood why he had lost contact with Felicity. The bitter old fool had ruined their communications just to spite him. Their entire operation was in shambles. Two specialists were KIA, and four more were wounded, including Cage. All he wanted to do was go find Felicity, but he realized that the entire platoon was looking to him. He stood up as tall as he could and tried not to let his voice tremble as he spoke.

"Let's all just take a breath for a moment," Cage said. "Our priorities haven't changed. We still need to secure our heavy cargo, make sure our people in the field get back safely, and reestablish communications with the *Bronx II*. I'm taking command until Captain Sullivan is cleared for duty. I want Jones, Seine, Cunningham, and Knoxx on guard duty. Case, help the staff sergeant to the mess pavilion. Webster, Ormond, see if you can get the flood lights on the command post back online. At dawn, we will send a party to retrieve the heavy cargo. It should have supplies to get our communications back online. We'll also make sure our people in the field are okay.

Get what rest you can, people. I will be in the mess pavilion until change of watch."

Amber Case was helping Dole to the pavilion. He was leaning on her but walking well enough considering the fact that he'd just been shot. Cage limped after them, and Devon joined them in the pavilion with first aid supplies. He handed a tube of burn cream to Case, then took a bottle of numbing antiseptic and set it on the table.

"You're going to have to take your pants off, lieutenant," Devon said. "I'm sorry."

"Don't be," Cage said.

The pain was getting worse, and he knew he needed to stop the bleeding. Their fatigue pants were snug but stretchy. He had no trouble pulling the side of his pants away from his body and down to his thigh. Devon lifted the tail of his fatigue shirt and squirted the gash with antiseptic. Cage groaned in pain as the liquid hit the wound. It burned like liquid fire for a few seconds until the numbing action kicked in. Devon was liberal with the antiseptic, then squeezed a line of flesh glue into the wound.

"This is going to hurt," he said, pulling a staple gun from the first aid kit.

"Just do it," Cage ordered.

Devon squeezed the wound together and began stapling the gash closed.

"Looks like we both underestimated Captain Sullivan," Dole said as Amber applied a bandage to his chest. "I've never seen an officer melt down like that."

"I pushed him too hard," Cage said.

"No," Dole corrected him. "This was a bomb waiting to be triggered. Better that we got it out of the way. If he lost in combat, we'd probably all be dead."

"We've got to salvage things," Cage said, feeling shaky under the weight of responsibility for the platoon.

"You make the calls, and I'll see they're carried out," Dole said. "That's how this works, and I've got confidence in you, LT. We can turn this mess around."

Cage nodded. He didn't think he could talk without his voice cracking, so he kept his mouth shut. He was fighting back tears, both from stress over the incident with Sullivan and fear for Felicity. The pain of the staples was helping.

"How long until dawn?" Dole asked as he adjusted his shirt over the bandage.

"Six hours," Amber Case said, just as the lights on the command post flickered back to life.

"All right," Cage said. "Six hours."

"Everything will look better in the morning, LT. You can count on that," Dole said.

"Finished," Devon said. "I just need to put a bandage on it. The compression pants should help, but I'd keep this ice pack on there to keep the swelling down. Otherwise it will be painful to walk."

"Roger that," Cage said, just hoping they could actually make it through the night. It felt like they were walking on thin ice that was cracking beneath their feet. One wrong move, and the entire platoon would implode.

CHAPTER 39

FELICITY MARS

"Lieutenant? Lieutenant!" Felicity said, but she didn't raise her voice.

"What happened?" Lucinda asked.

"Base camp's not responding," Billy replied.

"They were suddenly cut off," Miranda said. "I've got a really bad feeling about this."

"But who got cut off, us or them?" Felicity asked. "It's possible the pyramid is blocking our signal."

"Man, we're in trouble," Billy said. "We need to get off this planet."

They were grouped by one of the rocky hillsides. Some fallen rocks were piled at the base and gave them cover. Felicity was just about to suggest they retreat back down the valley when they saw movement on the pyramid. They didn't need their scopes or night vision to make out three shadowy forms that appeared at the opening.

"Oh man," Billy whispered.

"Are those people?" Miranda whispered.

The figures seemed somewhat like humans. The details were hard to make out.

"No," Lucinda said, looking through the scope of her rifle. "Definitely not human."

"Where did they come from?" Miranda asked.

"They weren't inside earlier," Felicity said. "Nothing was in that place. It was empty."

"Maybe there were hidden passageways to other chambers?" Lucinda said.

"I don't know," Felicity said. "We'll watch and report."

"How do we report if we can't reach base camp on our comms?" Miranda asked.

"If we can't get the com-link working by morning, two of us will go back and two will stay," Felicity said.

"What do you think they're going to—"

Lucinda stopped mid-sentence as a disk came flying out of the pyramid. It was a thin object with a bulge in the middle.

"No way," Billy said. "No freaking way."

"Is that a flying saucer?" Miranda asked.

"It certainly looks like one," Felicity said.

The disk was bigger than the aliens—not large enough to be a manned craft, though, as the disk was too thin. But it was as wide as all three aliens. Felicity thought about the entrance to the pyramid. It was small enough that she could touch the sides with her arms stretched out to either side. The flying saucer must have flown diagonally to pass through the square corridor. It began to fly back and forth across the open area in front of the pyramid.

"What's it doing?" Lucinda asked.

"Searching for something?" Billy asked.

"Oh man, this is not happening," Miranda said.

"Everyone take a breath," Felicity said. "We don't know

who they are or what they want. We can't jump to the conclusion that they're hostile."

"Yes, we can," Miranda said.

"They're aliens," Billy pointed out.

"On this world, we're aliens," Felicity reminded them. "I want you to stay here and watch. Do not engage them under any circumstances. That's an order."

"You're not the captain," Miranda pointed out.

"But I'm a corporal," Felicity said.

"Wait, why are you saying that?" Lucinda asked. "What are you going to do?"

"Make contact," Felicity said. "We have to try."

"You're out of your mind," Billy said.

"I think we should just wait and report what we see," Miranda said.

"She's right," Lucinda added. "Those things are evil. I can tell."

"No, they're just different," Felicity said. "They're obviously intelligent beings. We need to make contact."

"No," Billy said, "don't do it. I've got a bad feeling."

"Me too," Lucinda said.

Miranda nodded. All Felicity could think about was what would happen if the aliens went back inside the pyramid and disappeared. Would anyone believe them? People on Earth had claimed to see aliens for hundreds of years. There were even ancient drawings of strange-looking people that some researchers theorized were extraterrestrial beings. She wondered what Blake would want her to do.

"All right," she conceded. "We stay put and watch."

Her companions all seemed to breathe a sigh of relief—but then the flying saucer stopped moving and hovered.

"What's it doing?" Miranda asked.

"It's right over the com-link receiver dish," Lucinda said.

She was looking through her scope using the night vision but had to look away when a bright light came on from the bottom of the saucer. It shone down on the rectangular dish. Felicity could see it clearly, and suddenly the dish was levitated up and hovered just centimeters away from the bottom of the flying saucer.

"Oh, damn, that's not good," Billy said.

"They'll know we were here for sure now," Miranda said.

"They must have already known," Felicity said. "Somehow when we went into the pyramid, we activated it."

"But now it's got our communication gear," Lucinda said. "They'll be listening to everything we say."

"That's only a problem if they're hostile," Felicity said.

"And they were probably listening already," Billy said.

"So where is it taking the receiver?" Miranda asked.

The flying saucer flew straight back to the pyramid, and one of the aliens went inside with it. It seemed clear to Felicity that the aliens were going to study the device. They wanted to know who had disturbed their pyramid, but she didn't know why. Felicity knew she needed to get back to the base camp. She needed to tell the others what they had seen and that the aliens had the comms relay. But she couldn't do anything while the aliens were watching. The pyramid glowed in the darkness, but the rest of the valley was completely dark. They would have to use the LEDs in their helmets if they were to try and get back to base camp before dawn. As long as the aliens were watching, that wasn't possible. She considered trying to find her way to base camp without any light, but then remembered the rock spiders eating Ted Ficklestine and rejected the idea.

Soon the flying saucer returned. They watched it in rapt

fascination. The object moved smoothly through the air, seemingly unaffected by gravity. Felicity thought back to the mapping drones they had sent out upon arrival. She wondered if the flying saucer was doing something similar. Was it checking to see what had changed in the valley since the aliens were last here? She rejected the idea that they had been in the pyramid all along. Perhaps there were hidden chambers, but if it were a domicile of some sort, why wouldn't they fully enclose it? Why leave the door open for anyone or anything to just walk right in? And how did the flying saucer move so smoothly through the air? It didn't wobble or drift. Even when it changed directions, it was precise.

It continued flying back and forth over the field, moving closer and closer to their location. Felicity didn't have to ask to know that her companions were thinking about what would happen when it got close to them.

"I think we should spread out," Felicity said.

"That thing will see us," Billy warned.

"We shouldn't be bunched up," Lucinda said, although she sounded worried.

"Look," Felicity said. "We've got some cover here, but if that thing gets here and isn't friendly, none of us have a hope of surviving."

"Oh God," Miranda said. "We should hit first. Don't wait on it to take us out."

She already had her auto-cannon strapped onto the harness. With a flick of a switch, the rotating barrels lowered into position and began to turn.

"We aren't starting a war with a species we know nothing about," Felicity said. "We do not fire unless you have no other choice. I'll go forward, the rest of you fall back. All we need to do is spread out so we aren't bunched together."

"Copy that," Billy said.

"Be careful," Lucinda said.

"We've got you covered, Corporal," Miranda said with a lopsided grin.

"Yeah, thanks," Felicity replied. "Let's hope I don't need it."

She moved without thinking too much about what might happen. Fear had a way of making her freeze up. Inaction always led to defeat in a sparring match, but it had much greater consequences in a real fight. She could hear her father's voice in her mind as she shimmied along the rocky hill. *Always keep moving,* he used to say. *A moving target is harder to hit.* She wished he were with her as she moved closer to the flying saucer. Better still, she wished she were with him, back on Earth, far away from the aliens and the disk that was moving straight across the field toward her position. She stood her ground but tried to blend into the shadows of the hill. Her hope was that it either wouldn't notice her or wouldn't be interested. She was just a living creature; it might assume she was an animal of some sort and pay her no heed.

One glance back toward the others gave her a boost of confidence. She couldn't see them at all, but that meant the aliens couldn't either—unless they were scanning with thermal or night vision. In fact, she realized, they might see in a completely different way than she did. There was no way to know.

Her fear shifted to terror as the flying saucer began approaching her. Her entire body trembled, caught in fear's icy grip. The saucer was big—at least a meter and half wide. It was hard to see clearly in the dark, but it appeared to be spinning. And then the light came on, blinding her. Behind her she heard someone curse, and then she was being lifted off the ground. It felt strange, almost like she was caught in a bubble of zero-gravity. She was floating, rising up toward the saucer. She couldn't really see it because of the light. It was dazzling and felt warm. Part of her wanted to just relax—the light and the weightlessness were almost hypnotic. But she hadn't given the disk permission to take her, and Felicity's father always said that anyone who tried to do something to her without her permission wasn't her friend.

She pulled her laser pistol from the holster on her thigh. Her thumb found the safety switch. She flicked it off and let her finger rest on the trigger as she raised the weapon toward the light. And then she squeezed, just the way Master Sergeant Eugene Davies had taught them in basic training: squeeze, don't jerk or pull. The weapon fired, and a single laser bolt shot up into the flying saucer. Immediately the light went out, and Felicity fell to the ground. Her feet hit first, but she was off-balance and leaning back too far. She let herself fall, throwing her feet up and rolling completely over one shoulder and using her free hand to give her support. Her toes found the grassy plain and she stood up, pointing her pistol, but the flying saucer was gone. It shot back to the pyramid faster than Felicity thought possible. There was no down draft, no buffeting force from the object. One second it was right above her, and the next it was gone.

She looked at the aliens. She was much closer to the pyramid, only twenty meters from the massive structure. The flying saucer had been carrying her toward it. She could see the aliens. They stood on two legs and had two arms, but that's where the similarities ended. The bodies were thinner than a human's, their hands had four thick fingers, and their heads looked like thin watermelons. They had faces with big, dark eyes, and their heads stretched back three or four times farther than a human's.

"Who are you?" Felicity shouted toward the alien.

They looked at each other. They had tiny little mouths, and she couldn't see them moving, but they seemed to be communicating. One even pointed at her.

"We come in peace," Felicity said. It felt silly to say, like she was quoting lines from a really bad movie.

And then her head filled with a strange feeling, or perhaps noise. It was hard to describe, almost like static. Something was interfering with her mind, as if a sinister presence was trying to get inside her head.

"No!" Felicity said. "Stop!"

She fell to her knees. Dozens of flying saucers, slightly smaller than the first, came racing out of the pyramid. And then the chaos started. Thunder sounded—the staccato of Miranda Dux's auto-cannon. Felicity saw the tracers flashing through the night. The bullets hit the pyramid first, chipping away at the polished surface. Then one of the flying saucers exploded. She felt a sense of anger and fear, then the static left her mind. More shots were being fired. In the space of a second, four more of the flying saucers erupted in flame. They fell onto the bedrock shelf, the flaming debris rolling down toward the grassy plain, too close to where Felicity knelt on the ground. She sprang to her feet and started running, just as the flying saucers fired back at her companions. Dark green bolts of light that seemed thick and powerful slammed into the hillsides and rained down dirt and rocks onto Billy Oberton and Miranda Dux. Their weapons fell silent.

Felicity looked over her shoulder. There were four flying saucers remaining. Two were headed straight for her. She didn't stop running, but she changed directions. The hillside was close and felt safe, but she turned away from it and raised her pistol, firing four quick shots as she ran. The laser bolts hit the nearest saucer. It didn't explode, but it lost control and slammed into the ground, burrowing through the turf and throwing up a hail of debris.

Felicity changed directions again, trying to keep the debris between herself and the approaching saucer. It worked. The flying disk slowed down and changed directions. The saucers were incredibly agile, but despite being taken out quickly by recon platoon gunfire, they didn't try to evade. The saucer was circling wide of the smoke billowing from the crashed saucer. Felicity had no trouble tracking it. She fired several shots. Most went wide, but a few hit. The reaction of the saucer reminded her of a spinning top that gets bumped. It spun around wildly, out of control, then clipped a hill and went careening into the mountains, where it exploded.

Light from the pyramid and the flames of the burning saucers lit up the valley. Felicity could see the charred impact points on the hillsides as well as the craters left as the rocks and soil were blown free. There were large mounds of rubble along the hills, and no sign of Billy Oberton or Miranda Dux. She spotted Lucinda Fuego peeking out from behind a big rock; she had run for cover, probably because she recognized the danger. Lucinda had taken out the last two saucers. One had fired a barrage at her, leaving a long, smoking ditch across the ground.

"You okay?" Lucinda called to Felicity.

"Yeah," Felicity answered. "What about Billy and Miranda?"

"Gone," Lucinda said. "What should we do?"

Felicity glanced back at the pyramid. The aliens were gone, but she didn't think the fight was over.

"We're leaving," Felicity said.

She was running away from the pyramid and toward her friend. Lucinda was a fighter, a survivor. She had grown up on the streets, doing whatever it took to avoid the gangs and scrape together enough food to live on. Her instincts in the fight had been right on. Movement and counterfire had won the first encounter, but if more of the saucers came, they would be hard-pressed to survive another.

The two girls met near the site of their camp. Felicity had moved Staff Sergeant Dole's tent, but she hadn't unpacked her small pack. It had food and water inside. She stopped long enough to snatch it up.

"We need more weapons," Lucinda said. "I'm down to just two batteries."

"You can use the plasma if they get close," Felicity said, taking a swig of water. She was extremely thirsty and breathing hard, more from fear than fatigue. "We can't stay here."

"Back to base camp?" Lucinda said.

"We have to warn the others," Felicity agreed.

They both fell silent as more saucers flew from the pyramid. They spread out and began a slow advance across the valley. Felicity didn't say anything—she didn't have to. She checked the power on her pistol. It was down to just a quarter of its charge. Their only hope was escape, and all they could do was start running.

CHAPTER 40

FELICITY MARS

They had run close to a hundred meters in the dark, following the shrubs that ran along the stream bed, when Felicity looked over her shoulder and saw one of the flying saucers rushing toward them.

"Look out!" Felicity screamed.

With her brain buzzing with fear, she leapt into the stream. It was only three quarters of a meter deep, but the banks of the river rose up another half meter above the surface of the water. Felicity hit the cold water with a splash. The water covered her head just as flashes of laser fire lit the valley. Even submerged in the water, Felicity could feel the ground shake as large sections were blasted up into the air.

Felicity lifted her head and saw the flying saucer racing past their position. She rose up, dripping cold water that had run off from the mountain snowpack. Lucinda wasn't far away, on the other side of an ugly gouge left in the ground by the laser fire—not that Felicity could make out a lot of details. She vaulted out of the stream and ran to her friend. Lucinda lay on her right side. Her left arm was smoking, and the material of her pant leg was mostly burned away. Felicity couldn't see the dark blisters from the laser burns, but she didn't need to. Lucinda was hurt, and they still had to get away.

The other flying saucers were searching the wide meadow in front of the pyramid, ensuring that no combatants had been missed. But the aircraft that had fired on them was coming back, moving slower, searching for survivors.

Felicity pulled her friend to an upright position and yanked the Magellan Infiltrator assault rifle over her head.

"We're getting out of here, Lucinda," Felicity said. "Do you hear me? We are not giving up, and we are not dying."

"Can't...walk," Lucinda said.

It was obvious; she was wounded and weak. But Felicity had a plan. She toggled the gun's controls to the plasma setting and dashed toward the approaching saucer. The ship jerked forward slightly, giving away the fact that it had picked up on her movement. Felicity couldn't wait any longer. She fired three plasma shells at the saucers. The fire bloomed to life, a flaming blue gas that propelled up toward the ship. The plasma hit the bottom of the saucer and two places on the spinning edges. It fed on whatever material the ship was made from like a spark landing on dry cedar. The entire ship burst into flames even before it exploded.

Felicity covered her face with both arms and felt something ping off her helmet then stab into her arm. Fiery pain spread through her, and Felicity screamed. She dropped to the ground and looked at her arm. A jagged piece of red-hot metal was stuck in the flesh of her tricep. She reached up and yanked it out, the pain forcing another scream from her clenched jaws, but there was no time to indulge the pain. Adrenaline kept her moving. She hung the rifle over her head, toggled the weapon back to laser, and fired at another saucer approaching from the direction of the pyramid. The aircrafts —or whoever controlled them—were learning to respect their weapon. Even though Felicity fired wildly from the hip, the saucer swung to the side to avoid being hit and crashed into the side of the mountain. The ship went spinning just like a top down the mountain's steep slope and across the valley.

"Here we go," Felicity said, jerking her friend up.

Lucinda sagged against her, but they weren't going far. She dragged her friend to the stream bed. Another saucer was racing toward them. She didn't have time to be gentle.

"Hold your breath," Felicity said, before flinging Lucinda and herself down into the water.

Her second time in the water, Felicity landed on her back. She saw the bright flashes as the saucer fired wildly across the valley. It felt like the world was being ripped apart, but somehow, the wild shots didn't find them in the stream. Felicity and Lucinda broke the surface as dirt and debris rained down. Something hard hit Felicity just below her eye. She flinched but didn't cry out. She had survived harder punches.

Lucinda was struggling to get out of the water.

"No," Felicity said. "Stay low. Let the water carry you."

Lucinda groaned but obeyed. They floated downstream. Felicity held tightly to Lucinda's wounded left side. They used their free arms to keep them from sinking too deep into the water. The stream bed was lined with stones, and the water wasn't deep, but it was deep enough to float them. Whenever a saucer approached, they dove down as deep as they could. The water shielded them from whatever sensors the flying saucers used. It was a lucky break, and not one that Felicity had counted on. She only wanted the cover of the riverbank and water to keep from getting hit by flying debris.

And the fact that they could float through the valley was a bonus with Lucinda's wounds.

But the cold water could only be endured for so long. Eventually, Lucinda was suffering too much from the freezing water, and they had to get out. The valley had narrowed considerably. Felicity couldn't be sure how far they had gone. It had taken half a day to hike from the slick rock to the meadow in front of the pyramid, and they had floated for about an hour. She hoped it had carried them faster than walking, but not past the familiar landmarks—not that she could see much. The towering mountains on one side and the rugged, rocky hills on the other didn't allow much starlight down into the narrow valley. At first, Felicity wasn't concerned with the land; all her attention was on the sky. She looked and listened for any sound of the flying saucers. She hadn't seen one in a while and hoped that they had either given up the search or that the stream had carried her and Lucinda beyond it.

"Time to get moving," Felicity said, pulling Lucinda up to sitting position.

"Can't," Lucinda said. "Too...cold."

"That's why we're walking the rest of the way," Felicity said.

She pushed her friend up onto the bank. Lucinda flopped onto the bushes. Felicity could only hope they wouldn't run into any of the local wildlife. They would be completely exposed and painfully slow with Lucinda's wounds. But they had to keep moving; they had to put as much distance between themselves and the pyramid as possible.

Felicity got out of the stream and onto her feet. Her clothes were waterlogged, and her body was shivering with cold. It was a bad combination for Lucinda, but it couldn't be helped. They were alive, and that was the good thing. If Billy and Miranda hadn't been killed when the laser blasts caused landslides to bury them, then Felicity would have to live with the knowledge that she had left them behind. It wasn't an option to try and save them—not when they were fighting for their own lives against a superior force. The fact that they had taken down so many of the flying saucers was a point of pride for her, but unless she was greatly mistaken, the saucers were unmanned. They were alien drones and taking them down was good, but it wasn't the same as losing a person. Felicity had lost three people to the aliens, and she felt those losses deeply.

She pulled Lucinda up onto her feet. They were friends, but not particularly close. Felicity moved to Lucinda's right side—her good, unwounded side. She wrapped one arm around her friend's waist and pulled Lucinda's good arm across her shoulders.

"All right, we're walking," Felicity said.

Walking was a generous term. They were shuffling, but they were moving. Their boots squished with water. The night air wind was soft but cold and felt like a winter gale to their soaked bodies.

"You sh-sh-should…l-leave me," Lucinda said through chattering teeth.

"No," Felicity said. "I won't leave you."

"I'm d-d-dy-dy-dying."

"Not if I have anything to say about it," Felicity said. "I'll tell you something to keep you alive."

"Wh-what?"

"You have to promise to keep the secret," Felicity insisted, trying to get Lucinda's mind off the pain and cold.

"I pr-prom-promise."

"You're not going to believe this," Felicity said. "Well, maybe you will, but it doesn't matter. Lieutenant Cage and I...we're married."

"Wh-wh-what?"

Felicity couldn't be certain, but she thought she heard a note of strength in Lucinda's voice.

"Yeah, almost two years now," Felicity said. "We lied on our application."

"Wh-wh-who d-did-didn't," Lucinda replied.

"You can't tell anyone."

"I d-don-don't think it ma-ma-matters any m-more."

Felicity wondered about that. The discovery of aliens did change things. The fact that they had fought was terribly frightening. But Felicity had tried to be diplomatic. They had made the first move, drawn first blood. Their pyramid had killed Porter Bailey. And they had tried to take her, using their technology to force her back into the pyramid. Aliens or not, that was the last place Felicity wanted to go. And then they had penetrated her mind. She wished she could open her head and scrub her brain with strong soap. It felt hostile to her, even though she couldn't really say what it was like, exactly.

"I hope you're right," Felicity said.

She was tired, cold, hurting, and sore, but they had to keep moving. The cold water had kept her eye from swelling shut, but it was puffy. The cut in her upper arm was deep and painful. She could only hope that nothing in the stream had infected her. Trudging on, they kept moving but had to stop frequently to rest.

Felicity could feel her strength leeching away. She needed rest and nourishment, but the power bar in her pack tasted like sawdust in her mouth. Drinking the water in her canteen helped. They moved from boulder to boulder. Felicity would prop Lucinda against the big rocks, refusing to let her go down on the ground. She was too afraid her friend wouldn't get up again. She could have moved much faster without Lucinda, but Felicity didn't want to lose anyone else.

Ted Ficklestine had been attacked and killed by the rock spiders. Porter Bailey had died in the subterranean chamber below the pyramid, struck by the power surge as the alien structure came online. Billy Oberton and Miranda Dux had been killed by the aliens. They were four people she thought of as friends. They were her platoon mates, their names forever branded to her memory. She couldn't help but think about the fact that she had been with each of them, or close by, when they died.

"Wh-what are y-y-you thinking?" Lucinda asked.

"You really want to know?"

Lucinda nodded. "T-ta-tal-talking helps."

"I was wondering if I'm cursed," she said. "I've been with every person we've lost so far."

"Th-that's b-bo-bol-bologna," she said.

"Maybe, but I can't seem to shake the feeling that it's more than a coincidence," Felicity said.

"You-you've been in the fr-fron-front lines," Lucinda said. "In the p-p-pryamid."

"Yeah, and when I see Captain Sullivan, I'll probably knock his teeth out."

Lucinda actually laughed. They stopped when they came to a big boulder. Felicity had taken to checking their surroundings with the rifle scope. The optics were the most fragile part of the assault rifle, yet somehow it had survived intact and with power. The lens was cracked, but she could still see through it. Nothing showed on thermal. But when she switched to night vision, she saw a large, balloon-shaped rock formation. It was smooth and unmarred by crumbling like most of the hillsides.

"Lucinda! We're almost there."

"What?" her companion asked.

"The smooth rock. I can see it. We're going to make it."

They weren't close to the smooth rock formation. It was nearly two hundred meters down the valley, but just the sight of it gave them strength. The two women trudged on, going from rock to rock, picking out the next resting point before moving on. It was excruciating and exhausting, but they were making progress.

The sky was turning pink when they reached the slick rock, and they hadn't seen a saucer since leaving the stream.

"We made it," Felicity said.

"But how," Lucinda said, struggling to work some moisture into her mouth, "do we get up...there?"

Felicity pulled the canteen out and let her friend drink. They would refill it before leaving the stream and struggling through the mountains. Felicity needed the time to come up with a plan, anyway. She wasn't even sure she could climb the slick rock. There were no hand- or footholds other than the single divot that was over two meters off the ground.

"We have to go around," Felicity said.

"But what about...the rock spiders?"

"We'll go the other way," Felicity said. "We'll take our time. Find a path we can work through. It won't be easy, but..."

"I know—we won't quit," Lucinda said. "I hate you."

"You can hate me when you're safe," Felicity said.

They left the slick rock and began looking for a way up through the rugged hills. The dawn brought light and hope.

They could finally see, and it didn't take long to find a game trail. It was steep, but Felicity knew they could make it work.

They went step by step. At times Felicity had to go first and pull her friend up. It took two hours just to reach the ledge. Felicity didn't want to see the pyramid. Even worse, she didn't want the aliens at the pyramid to see her. But she decided the intel might be useful. She used the scope and stayed close to the hillside. In the distance, she could see where the ground had been torn up by the laser fire, but nothing else. No ships, no flying saucers or even debris from the fight. The pyramid was spotless. It didn't seem fair. There was no proof.

She was just about to turn back. All she wanted was to get to her husband and the safety of basecamp. But when she turned, she was met by a group of men in battle armor.

"Hello, stranger," Blake said.

Tears flooded Felicity's eyes, and she threw her arms around him. To his credit, he didn't pull away. He held her tight.

"LT, we better get moving," Devon said.

"You see anything?" he asked.

"No, sir," Devon said.

Felicity pulled back. Blake had a look of grim determination on his face. She turned to Devon. "I'm so glad to see you."

She hugged him, and he stiffened but didn't resist.

"Albert, Junior, help Lucinda. We're heading back to base camp."

"Yes, sir," they both replied.

"What's happened?" Felicity asked as they all started back down the trail that led out of the hills.

"You would ask me that after all you've been though," Blake said.

"I survived," she said.

"Not unscathed," he pointed out.

"I lost Billy and Miranda," she said, the tears running down her dirty face.

"Yeah, Lucinda told us," Blake said. "But you survived, and you saved her. Tell us everything."

"Sure," Felicity said, even though her mind rejected the idea of going back over all the details. She knew she had to. And then they had to formulate a plan that would get them off Magnificus Prime and safely away from the aliens in the pyramid.

CHAPTER 41

BLAKE CAGE

By the time the sounds of the explosions rumbled through the mountains and reached base camp, Cage hadn't even tried to sleep. He'd spent the night on the hill, staring through the gap in the mountains and trying to see what was happening. His wounded hip kept him from getting to the summit in time to see the flash of laser fire, but he could see the flickering lights from the burning debris. Even with a monoscope, he couldn't make anything out. He did occasionally see objects passing back and forth across the gap. He knew something had happened, and at dawn he'd made his choice.

"I came up here because I needed to know what happened," he said. "Hugo Webster and Peter Ormond are leading the rest of the platoon out to try to find the heavy cargo."

"Can't you find it pretty easily?" Felicity asked. "You have the trackers that will take them right to it."

"*Had* the trackers," Devon corrected. "Captain Sullivan slagged the entire computer system."

"What?" Felicity asked.

"He had a mental breakdown," Cage told her. "We had a shouting match, and then he locked himself in the command center and blasted all the equipment with a laser pistol."

"Before turning it on Staff Sergeant Dole," Devon added.

"No," Felicity said.

"Dole's okay. Just a small laser burn," Cage said. "We broke into the command post and subdued the captain."

"Is that what's wrong with your hip?" Felicity asked.

"He was stabbed," Devon replied.

"I wasn't stabbed," Cage said. "It's a scratch, that's all."

Devon shook his head, and Felicity looked at Cage but didn't press the matter. Back home it would have been an entirely different matter, but since her emotional response seeing him on the ridge, she had respected the nature of their current relationship.

They were all heading together back to base camp and had to stop regularly to let the girls rest. Cage knew that if his wife was tired, things were bad. She could run for miles and hardly even be breathing hard. He had seen her spar with men twice her size and come out on top. She was, in his mind, indestructible, and yet she seemed exhausted. It terrified him almost as much as the thought of losing her.

"So we don't have the trackers?" Felicity said.

"No," Cage replied. "We have the coordinates for each heavy cargo container."

"Because the LT made me write them all down," Devon said. "He was wise to do this."

"But we don't have the equipment to assess our coordinates,"

Cage continued. "Staff Sergeant Dole did some navigational computations, but they're based on Earth's size and relation to the sun. We could be way off. And we don't even have communications with the team that's out there looking for the cargo drops."

"So we can't signal the *Bronx II*?" Felicity said as they started back toward base camp again.

"No," Cage said, "and the captain refused to tell them anything. I think I must have filled his head with delusions of grandeur about the pyramid. He didn't want anything to steal the spotlight."

"And he nearly got us all killed," Felicity said bitterly. "This is a disaster."

"I take responsibility for that," Cage said.

"Oh, no way you're doing that. You don't get to throw yourself on your sword, Lieutenant Cage. You're the only one with the knowledge and strength to get us out of this fix. So start figuring things out."

"She is right," Devon said. "We need you."

Cage nodded but felt helpless. Who was he, really? Just a history geek. He had been through officer training but never a real crisis. How was he supposed to lead them out of the mess they had fallen into? He had no idea, but the weight of the responsibility was firmly on his shoulders.

"Okay, so let's talk about what those people at the pyramid were," Cage said.

"Not people," Felicity said. "Aliens."

"How did the aliens get there?" he asked.

"I don't know. They weren't in the pyramid when we searched it."

"And everything was just the way I described?"

"Yes," Felicity said.

"Well, many researchers believe there are other chambers inside the Great Pyramid," Cage said.

"You should have told us that," Felicity said.

"It's not proven fact," he countered, "just theory. And most researchers believe the cavities are either to relieve weight or part of the building process. Internal ramps, that sort of thing."

"I don't buy it," Felicity said. "That place was like a cave. It was completely empty. No sign of life anywhere."

"Maybe the aliens were in cryogenic sleep," Devon said. "When the pyramid's systems were activated, they were awakened."

"Okay," Cage said. "But why would they attack us? If they were just waiting for people to discover them, why start out being hostile?"

"It doesn't make sense," Felicity said. "I think they came to the pyramid in response to a signal."

"But you didn't see any spacecraft," Cage said.

"No, they didn't fly here like we did," Felicity said. "I think that pyramid is a portal. They can come through it."

"Is that even possible?" Devon asked.

"I would have said no yesterday," Cage said. "Today, I'm thinking anything is possible."

"There were only three of them," Felicity said.

"Three that you saw," Cage pointed out.

"I think they came through some portal inside the pyramid. Think about it. Why are there empty chambers? Because it isn't a storage building or a domicile—it's a transporter of some kind. Maybe interdimensional travel or something."

"We tripped it going inside," Cage said, trying to reason it all out.

"And they sent a team to investigate," Felicity said.

"The staff sergeant has a similar theory. He thinks it's an alarm system—that whoever built the pyramid was marking this world as their own and leaving it to send them word if anyone else comes around."

"That makes sense," Felicity said. "We've discovered hundreds of worlds but only a handful that were fit for habitation, and nothing as perfect as this planet."

"The way Earth might have been before modern man," Devon said.

"Yeah," Cage said. "That's what bothers me about this. Let's say the aliens arrived on Earth and found it similar to this world. They build their pyramid and leave it on Earth, but eventually we find it. What happened then?"

"You said there are crackpots who believe that aliens influenced early human development," Felicity said.

"When did the lieutenant tell you this?" Devon asked.

Felicity started to reply, then abruptly shut her mouth. Cage had to do some quick thinking.

"We talked about it the night before the expedition to the pyramid," Cage said. "That's how she knew I was upset about not going."

"And you contacted only her on the com-link?" Devon asked.

Cage could see that Devon Al'Farrah was no fool. But Cage wasn't going to spill the beans on his marriage right then. It would only cause trouble with the platoon, and they were in enough of that already.

"Yes," Cage said, before picking up the thread of conversation again.

They were within sight of base camp now. Junior Knoxx and Albert Malone were practically carrying Lucinda. She was barely even conscious, but from the looks of the burns, Cage guessed that was probably a good thing.

"There's a ton of popular theories," Cage said. "From ancient civilizations that were highly advanced to tales of Atlantis. What we know for certain is that the pyramid was closed up sometime before the bronze age. Whatever was inside—which I'm guessing since you said the one on this planet has the same basic layout as the one on Earth—was removed before the pyramid was sealed off. It makes me think that people revolted against the aliens. Shutting down their pyramid was part of that fight.

"They sealed it and removed the casing stones," Felicity said. "Maybe they had a reason."

"It's something to think about," Cage said.

They got to camp and settled Felicity and Lucinda in the mess pavilion where Amber Case, who had become the de facto medic, could see to their wounds. Cage filled Staff Sergeant Dole in on what had happened at the pyramid.

"So they're here already," Dole said. "It won't take them long to find us."

"I agree," Cage said. We're too close and exposed right here."

"You thinking of moving to the forest?"

"It makes sense strategically," Cage said.

"Damn straight it does," Dole replied. "I'd suggest we make the move now."

"All right, but you want to tell me why?" Cage asked.

"You said there was nothing left from the fight last night, correct?" Dole asked. "No wreckage in front of the pyramid?"

"None," Cage said. "Corporal Mars confirmed it."

"Sounds like they might be nocturnal," Dole said. "My guess is, they come looking for us tonight."

CHAPTER 42

BLAKE CAGE

They emptied some of the cargo crates the platoon had brought along on the drop ship. They were just big enough for Lucinda and Grant to sit in, making them workable gurneys for the journey across the savannah. They were just about to head out when the rest of the platoon returned. They had mounds of supplies in their packs, mostly computer equipment.

"We found one of the heavy cargo containers," Hugo Webster explained. "It had computer systems inside. I think we've got enough to track the other containers and get comms up and running."

"Outstanding work," Cage said, although in reality he wished they had found one of the platoon's vehicles. "How long will it take to set up?"

"An hour, maybe two," Peter Ormond said.

"If we can contact the *Bronx II*, we could get an evac down here," Felicity said.

"It's worth a shot," Staff Sergeant Dole agreed. "If they

can't get us out, then we hightail it to the woods."

"Agreed," Cage said. "Let's keep an eye on the time, though. I don't want to get caught out in the open once night falls."

"Roger that, LT."

"Lieutenant," Sammy Jones said. "We also got some weapons."

"Two tripod-mounted, computer-controlled rail guns," Lori Cunningham said. "And two cases of ammo."

"Along with a case of explosives," Sammy added.

"Excellent. If we have to fight, we'll be ready."

The news of the fight at the pyramid was all anyone talked about. The entire platoon had heard the explosions, and they wanted details. Cage kept Webster, Ormond, and Amber Case, their radio operator, busy reconstructing their computer systems.

The day seemed to speed by. It was just past midday when they got the communications back online. Unfortunately, the *Bronx II* wasn't reachable.

"They aren't there?" Cage asked.

"They must be on the far side of the planet," Amber replied. "The *Bronx II* is orbiting the planet."

"Don't we have satellites to relay the signals?" Cage asked.

"We do have satellites, but they may not be online," Amber replied. "We haven't calibrated for them yet, either. That process takes time, hours probably."

"The *Bronx II* will be back around sooner than that," Cage said. "You did good, Private."

"Thank you, sir," Amber said.

"I want those tracking devices locked on the signals from the heavy cargo containers," Cage told Hugo. "We can't afford to lose track of them again."

Hugo Webster spent the next hour with Staff Sergeant Dole making a map of the savannah and marking down the location of each of the cargo containers relative to their base camp. Cage had the rest of the platoon packing up their supplies. The buildings would stay, but the weapons and anything that might be construed as intelligence had to go."

"How long?" Felicity asked.

"I have no idea," Cage said. "We haven't even contacted the ship yet."

"But they'll send drop ships, right?" Felicity asked. "It shouldn't take too long."

"Hope for the best and plan for the worst," Cage said. "That's what they taught us in OTS. We have no idea what's going on in the ship. They may not be able to fly down and get us right away."

She nodded. He knew she understood, but no one could envision what the aliens might be capable of better than Felicity. Added to that, she was clearly exhausted. He had urged her to rest, but she wouldn't hear of it. He loved her tenacity and tireless work ethic. It was killing him not to be able to tell her what she meant to him at that moment.

"Lieutenant, I've got the *Bronx II*," Amber Case said from the doorway of the command post.

Cage hurried forward, right past Captain Sullivan who was tied up between the command post and the mess pavilion. Grant and Lucinda were asleep in the shade of the mess pavilion. Everyone else was either on watch or packing up the last of the platoon's gear.

"What have you told them?" Cage asked.

"I just made contact," Amber replied, handing Cage the mic.

He held it to his mouth and pressed the transmit button.

"*Bronx II*, this is recon platoon Bravo, we have come under attack from an intelligent species that we do not believe to be indigenous to this planet...Over!"

There was no reply. Cage looked at Amber, and she shrugged her shoulders before making a few minor adjustments to the communications equipment.

He tried again. "*Bronx II*, this is recon platoon Bravo. Do you read? Over."

There was another pause, and Cage felt a sick feeling descending over him. It wasn't fair. They had been through so much, and their help wasn't responding. He sighed and lifted the mic to give it one last try when a voice crackled through the speakers.

"We read you, Bravo platoon. Please stand by. Over."

Cage felt a sense of relief. His muscles relaxed, and he felt the stress of the last twenty-four hours melting away. They were going to be okay. He understood the order from the ship in orbit above them, but he was too excited to wait. "*Bronx II*, we have casualties down here. We request immediate evac. Over."

Another pause, then a frightened voice said. "Be advised, Bravo Platoon, we have another ship in system. We are attempting to ascertain—"

The communication officer's voice was cut short by an alarm. Cage heard another voice shout, "They just fired on us!"

Then the transmission ended.

"Should we try to get them back, sir?" Amber Case said.

"They aren't there to get," Cage said. "Like it or not, we're on our own. Pack this up as quickly as you can, Private Case. We have to be gone from this place when night falls, or we'll be next."

She stood up and immediately began unplugging the communication system. Cage walked outside and found Hugo and Peter waiting.

"Do we have more solar power equipment?" Cage asked.

"In the heavy cargo, sir," Hugo said.

"We can't risk it," Cage said. "There's no time to get those cargo containers off the savannah before nightfall. Get the solar cells off the command post. We are leaving in fifteen minutes, with or without you."

"Roger that, Lieutenant," Hugo said.

Peter Ormond gave Cage a dirty look but followed his partner. Cage knew he was pushing his people hard, but they didn't have a choice.

"Staff Sergeant," Cage said once he found Dole in the mess pavilion. "How long until the next ship from Earth arrives?"

"It was scheduled for three weeks, sir," Dole replied.

Cage waited while Junior Knoxx and Lori Cunningham carried out the last case of MREs that were in the pavilion. Once they were gone, he continued.

"There's an alien ship in the system."

"That's impossible," Dole said. "They couldn't have gotten here that quickly."

"You know that's not true," Cage said. "For all we know, they've been in the system all this time."

"What happened?"

"I don't know. But I heard an alarm. Someone shouted about the other ship firing at them, and then nothing."

Dole shook his head. "This entire project is going to hell in a hand basket. We can't even contact Alpha platoon and warn them of the danger."

"No," Cage said. "For now, all we can do is survive. I want

you to take the platoon to the woods. Get deep and lay low. We stand watch through the night."

"You want me to take them?" Dole said, following Cage out of the pavilion.

"You can leave that," Cage told Albert Malone as he pulled a case marked "Explosives" toward the rest of the cargo that had been packed up.

"Sir!" Dole said. "What are you planning?"

"The aliens are going to find us tonight," Cage said. "When they do, I'm going to be waiting for them."

"No sir, we can't afford to lose you."

"I don't plan on getting lost, Staff Sergeant."

"Let me do it," Dole pleaded.

"Under the circumstances, you have the most skills and experience to keep us alive," Cage said. "I'm just a junior lieutenant."

"A damn fine one," Dole said. "Don't be a hero."

"I'm not planning to be a hero. I want to live. But we've got one shot at hitting the aliens where it counts. It may not be much, but we need to prove we're not just going to run away."

"Fine, but I don't like it," Dole said. "We should stay together."

"If they don't find us here, they may spread out and find our heavy cargo containers. We need to stop them. One more day may make the difference."

Dole nodded. "Okay, sir. But don't do anything stupid."

"I'll do my best, Staff Sergeant."

They shook hands. It felt good. In the midst of the fear and chaos, having a man like Wyatt Dole look Cage in the eyes and shake his hand made him feel really good. He watched the staff sergeant start barking orders. The platoon was about to head out. Hugo and Pete came from behind the command post with the solar panels. They weren't in a good position, but they had several hours before nightfall, and hopefully it would be enough to get everyone across the plain and into the forest.

"What are you doing?" Felicity asked quietly.

"Taking care of things."

"You aren't leaving with the platoon?" she asked.

"I'm following after," Cage said. "I have some things to get done first, but I'll be along."

"I think maybe splitting up isn't a good idea," Felicity said. "We should stay together."

"Not this time," Cage said.

"You're going to fight them," she said, "all by yourself?"

"We have to keep them from finding the heavy cargo containers or searching the woods for us."

"They don't know we're here," Felicity said. "For all they know, they killed us all in the valley."

"I don't think so," Cage said. "Don't worry, I don't plan on taking chances."

"Good, because I'm staying."

"No," Cage said. "That's an order. Go with the platoon."

The platoon was already heading out. A few of them cast glances back at the base camp. Leaving it was hard. It was the closest thing they had to civilization on the planet.

"Don't pull that on me, Blake," she said softly. "If you force me to go, I'll tell everyone we're married."

"You think I care?" Cage said.

"I know you do," she said. "You're a rule follower and I love that about you, but from now on, we stay together."

"Fine," Cage said. "I've got a plan. You want to hear it?"

Felicity smiled, and he felt his heart melt a little. "I thought you'd never ask," she said.

CHAPTER 43

BLAKE CAGE

Alone at last, Cage realized that it had been nearly twenty years since he was last completely alone with his wife.

"So, what's this plan of yours?" Felicity asked.

"You said they tried to take you, right?" Cage asked.

Felicity nodded. Cage could tell the memories were painful. He didn't like bringing them up. And he didn't like putting her in more danger, but they couldn't just run away.

"Then we'll let them take this place," Cage said, "along with a few surprises."

He pointed to the last crate left in the base camp, and Felicity smiled.

"I like the way you think," she said.

Their preparations took them the rest of the day. As dusk set in, they moved to the river. It was much wider than the stream that flowed through the valley in front of the pyramid. Its banks were gentle slopes, but enough to give Cage and Felicity some cover.

They settled in to wait. Both were armed with assault rifles and were surrounded by extra ammunition. There was no fire, and neither slept, despite being tired.

"You think they'll come?" Felicity said.

"Don't you?"

"I guess so," she replied. "I keep thinking about that ship."

"What about it?"

"Well, if the pyramid really is a transporter, why send a ship at all?"

"Greater firepower," Cage said. "The ability to strike at us from multiple fronts."

She moved closer to him, leaning against him. His hip was aching, and he knew her wounded arm must be equally painful. She had a black eye from the debris that struck her the night before.

"You could get some sleep," he told her. "I'll keep watch."

"I can't sleep," she said.

"Me neither," he replied. "This place seemed like paradise at first."

"It was too good to be true," Felicity pointed out.

"I should have known we wouldn't be able to stay."

"You think Magellan Corporation will just walk away from a perfect planet?"

"I don't know that they'll have a choice," Cage said. "If the alien ship fired on the *Bronx II*, odds are they'll fire on anything coming into the system. The Magellan ships are built for war."

"So if they're all destroyed, what happens to us?"

The question hung between them. Cage wanted to say they would live out their days on the planet, but he wasn't sure how much living they could do with hordes of aliens tracking them down.

"I don't know," Cage said.

They spent the first few hours of darkness staring up at the stars and wondering what the future held. They had so little control. Earth was their only glimmer of hope, not just because it felt safer than Magnificus Prime but because humanity had found a way to end the threat of their pyramid. If humans had done it once, though, surely they could do it again.

"You hear that?" Felicity asked.

"All I hear is the river," Cage replied.

The river was flowing briskly behind them, making a gentle murmur. He cocked his head and concentrated but couldn't hear anything.

"I thought I heard something," she said.

"Like what?"

"A mechanical sound," she explained. "A kind of whirring."

"Like a drone? Did the flying saucers make a noise like that?"

"No," Felicity said. "I mean, there was a lot going on last night, but I don't remember hearing them. They were silent."

The night dragged on. Cage took energy tablets from their supplies to stay awake. His eyes felt dry, and his body ached. They were stretched out on their stomachs just below the riverbank. Cage had a good view of the base camp. There were even some tents between the river and the command post. It wouldn't take much investigation to realize that the camp had been abandoned, but Cage was hoping that wouldn't stop the aliens from taking what his platoon had left behind.

Eventually he was in a daze, almost convinced the aliens weren't coming at all. His careful planning and work had been for nothing. They had set an ambush, but the aliens had failed to show up...until they did, just a few hours before dawn. Spotting the first of the saucers was difficult since they had no running lights. If not for the night vision on his monoscope, he might have missed them.

"They're here," he said to Felicity, as a spike in his adrenaline burned through his drowsiness and fatigue. "My God, there's so many."

"They aren't messing around," Felicity said.

Cage counted twenty-eight small flying saucers. Some moved back and forth, scanning for signs of the humans—at least Cage guessed that was what they were doing. The rest stayed back, surrounding two larger flying saucers.

"This is surreal," Cage said, as the scout ships hovered over the camp.

"I told you," Felicity said, but there was an edge to her voice.

"You okay?"

"Terrified," she replied. "But I owe these bastards."

"Let's hope they take the bait," Cage said.

He tucked the monoscope into a waterproof case and slid it neatly into one of the ammo loops on his armor. Then he picked up the assault rifle and brought it to bear on the alien aircraft.

"There they go," Felicity pointed out.

The scout ships had formed a line just beyond the camp, and several of the others moved over the hills and hovered over recon Bravo's base camp. Lights came on, shining down from the flying saucers, and the structures began to rise up. Cage felt a thrill—his plan was working. He watched in almost breathless excitement, his hand taking hold of the detonator.

The flying saucers had the command post, the mess pavilion, the tents, and several large crates. Eight of the thirty alien ships had taken the bait and were slowly moving back toward the mountains. Cage waited until they were close to the other ships, then he pressed the button on the detonator.

Eight explosions rocked the night. Fire filled the sky. The flying saucers were torn apart, knocking several of the other flying saucers down as well. The scout ships went crazy, zigging and zagging all around.

Beside him, Felicity began firing her rifle, targeting the bigger saucers. Her first shot was good but didn't bring the bigger craft down, and immediately the other ships moved to block her shots. Several started toward them. Fear tightened in Cage's stomach, but he stuck to the plan. The detonator was useless once the explosives had been set off, but beside it was the activator for the rail guns that Bravo platoon had brought back from their heavy cargo run. The two guns were equipped with auto-targeting software. Once they were activated, they would fire at anything that moved in their zone. Cage and Felicity had hidden them in the trees on the far side of camp.

"Rail guns going hot," Cage said.

"Go!" Felicity said urgently.

Cage hit the button on the activator, and the rail guns boomed instantly. They fired large-caliber explosive rounds. Two of the scout ships exploded instantly, and the flying saucers turned toward the new threat. The rail guns fired every four seconds, and because the scout ships were moving the most, the guns targeted them. One of the other saucers fired back, and a pulsing blaze of bright green light blasted through the trees, taking out one of the rail guns. But the other kept firing. The scout ships were down to two, and half of the alien armada was gone, but there was still plenty left to kill Cage and his wife.

"I'll take the one on the right," Cage said, returning his attention to the rifle.

"I've got a shot," Felicity said.

Cage looked through his scope and spotted the larger alien ship that was on the right.

"Fire," Cage said.

Their laser rifles shot tiny streaks of light. They seemed like children's toys compared to the rail guns and the lasers on the flying saucers, but they were effective. Their fire was masked by several of the alien ships taking out the last rail gun along with the entire grove of trees in a blinding display of power.

Cage's shot didn't disable the big saucer he was shooting at, but Felicity's shot caused the large craft to the left of the other to suddenly lose control. It slammed into the ship on the right, then careened forward, taking out three more flying saucers. Cage tracked his target, which was wobbling like a spinning top that's winding down. He fired again, and the ship dropped straight down.

Then Felicity's target exploded in a ball of flaming light. The husband and wife team were prepared to dash to the river and throw themselves in, hoping the water would mask them the way it had in the valley, but the remaining saucers, one scout ship, and eight of the other aircraft sailed back over the hills and into the mountains.

Cage couldn't believe it. He lay there, moving his rifle from one target to the next before scanning the skies for signs of more alien ships.

"I have to admit," Felicity said. "That worked out far better than I expected."

"You didn't have faith in me?"

"Let's just say you're untested," she giggled.

Cage wanted to leap to his feet and dance for joy. He wanted to grab his wife and kiss her like she had never been kissed before—but the threat of the alien ships returning hung over them like a dark cloud. They spent the two hours remaining before dawn searching the skies for any sign of the aliens. The flames of the wreckage had died down. The last hour before dawn was quiet and dark. They used their monoscopes, searching every direction just to make sure the aliens didn't flank them. But the battle was over—and the humans had won.

CHAPTER 44

FELICITY MARS

They didn't leave their spot on the riverbank until dawn. When the sun came up, they got up and glassed the mountains again. There was still no sign of the aliens.

"Did we really win?" Felicity asked.

"They underestimated us," Cage said. "They won't do that again."

"You think they'll come back?"

"I can't imagine they wouldn't," Cage said. "Let's search the wreckage and then get to the forest."

They climbed over the bank and walked through the ruins of Bravo platoon's base camp. The lush grass was burned and blackened. There were shards of metal scattered on the ground. Cage picked up several pieces and put them in a small pouch on his belt.

One of the bigger flying saucers—the one that Felicity had fired on—was gone. It had exploded during the fight, but the other lay on the ground. It was cracked in half. The spinning ring around what they discovered was the cockpit was broken loose and lay at an angle to the central compartment of the ship.

"Maybe we shouldn't touch it," Felicity said.

"Why not?" Cage asked.

"I don't know, radiation or something. Maybe there are diseases in there."

"Maybe, but you saw the aliens outside the pyramid, and they weren't wearing suits, right?"

"Yeah," Felicity acknowledged.

"Then they must think the atmosphere here is safe," Cage said. "I doubt there's anything to worry about here."

He stepped onto the ring and climbed over it to the bulbous part of the ship. It was cracked open like an eggshell. He grabbed hold of the ship and wrenched the metal apart. Seeing Cage tearing the alien vessel open with his bare hands sent a shiver through Felicity. She had spent her life around macho fighters and knew the difference between real strength and bravado. There was no doubt in her mind that Cage was strong, but seeing it in action made her feel a little weak in the knees.

"I can't believe it," Cage said.

"What?" Felicity asked, moving around the saucer so she could get a better view.

Inside the flying saucer was one of the aliens she had seen at the pyramid. She couldn't say for certain that it was the same one, but it looked like the others. Its thin body and elongated head were unmistakable. Fortunately, the large eyes were nearly closed, and its head hung at an impossible angle. She knew it was dead but had to ask.

"Is it dead?"

"Must be," Cage said, pulling out his monoscope and starting to film. "The head—it's just like the old crystal skulls.

I mean, not exactly like them, but close enough. They must have been patterned after these beings."

"Doesn't it give you the creeps to think that aliens were on Earth?" Felicity asked, scanning the mountains and hills for any signs of the aliens.

"Should it?" Cage asked.

"I don't know. How many of our beliefs were influenced by them?" Felicity asked. "What role did they play in our development of civilization?"

"Good questions," Cage said. "Right now I'm more interested in how we kill them."

"That's good too," Felicity replied.

Cage didn't touch the alien body. Felicity was grateful for that. The entire camp was giving her the creeps. They moved to another of the ships that was mostly intact, but inside they found only machinery.

"Drones, just like you suspected," Cage told her.

He was still filming when she caught sight of something in the sky. It was too high up to make out—just a small dark spot against the bright green firmament. She lifted her monoscope and focused on the dot. What she saw dashed her hopes.

"Cage," she said. "Look!"

She was pointing up, still looking through the monoscope. The dot was a ship, but no one of their own. It was glossy black and seemed to float rather than fly. It was a perfect pyramid, but all one color.

"I can't believe it," Cage said.

They were both still looking up at the aircraft when parts of it separated and began to descend.

"They're coming down here," Cage said.

"Here?"

"That's my bet," Cage said. "Just like at the pyramid, they're going to collect their fallen. We have to move."

They ran back to the river. All their gear was packed up in heavy packs. Felicity was used to carrying a smaller pack, but she didn't mind the extra weight. She knew what they carried were the only supplies they had.

Cage picked up as much ammo as he could, and Felicity checked down river using her monoscope's thermal imaging. There was no sign of wildlife.

"Looks clear," she told him.

"All right, let's move out. We need to find the rest of Bravo platoon."

"And then what?" Felicity asked.

"Then we stay alive," Cage said. "Fight when we can. Sabotage their efforts. Wait for reinforcements."

"What if no one else ever comes?" Felicity asked.

"Humanity beat these aliens once," Cage said. "I'm betting that we can do it again."

Felicity loved his confidence, but she wasn't so sure. There was something different about the ship coming down from the sky. It made her nervous. There was so much they didn't know. And for the time being, they were on their own.

They walked for an hour, following the river, hoping the sloping riverbank would give them some cover. They turned back and watched their old base camp. Just as Cage had predicted, the smaller ships searched the area and collected the remains of the spacecrafts. They couldn't make out a lot of details even with their scopes, but they saw the big saucer being carried away.

"They aren't going to the pyramid in the mountains," Felicity pointed out as the ships moved back toward the larger spacecraft that was still in the sky.

"No," Cage said. "I get the feeling that what we saw at the pyramid and the saucers we fought last night were just the advance party."

"Their recon platoon?"

"Something like that," Cage said. "These new ships are completely different. Much slower, less agile."

"You think they're another race?" Felicity asked. "Different aliens?"

"I suppose that's possible," Cage said. "I really have no idea."

"But what about the theories on Earth? There was evidence of something on Earth, right?"

"Sure, cave drawings and ancient sculptures," Cage said. "They looked strange, but then so did the paintings and sculptures that were clearly humans. Researchers believed the other, stranger depictions were just exaggerated humans."

"But if they weren't," Felicity said. "If they were depictions of aliens, we could learn something. Like the fact that they weren't all the same."

"It's possible that more than one race of advanced beings visited Earth," Cage said.

"Maybe, but we've been a spacefaring species for nearly two hundred years. We have several colonies and drones in hundreds of systems, and we've seen no sign of intelligent life in the universe until now. It's kind of hard to believe that Earth could have been visited by multiple alien species."

"You're thinking just one race, with different types of intelligent beings?"

"Why not?" Felicity said. "And I don't think they ever left. Not completely."

"What do you mean?"

"I mean all the stories of UFOs, alien abductions—maybe it isn't just bunk. Maybe they've been watching us all along."

"If that's true, then wouldn't they have been more prepared?" Cage said. "They would have known our weapons technology. The aliens you saw in the mountains and that we fought last night, they seem curious."

"I guess you're right," she said.

"It's a good theory, though," Cage said. "In fact, it may be right, at least partially."

"What do you mean?"

"The stories could be true," Cage explained. "Maybe we were being watched or studied. Who knows? But whoever's been watching isn't who we've stumbled upon here."

They watched the ships that left the pyramid in the sky return, but the floating structure didn't leave. The monoscope registered the structure at somewhere around five thousand meters in altitude.

After a few hours, they stopped to rest. Felicity leaned into her husband, and he wrapped an arm around her. They forced themselves to eat, but their bodies were running on fumes and energy pills.

"Think we'll find the others?" Felicity asked.

"Sure," Cage said. "They're probably looking for us."

"I never imagined anything like this," Felicity said.

"Me either," Cage replied. "Do you regret leaving Earth?"

"Yes and no. I don't want to die out here. We didn't come all this way to get killed."

The images of Ted Ficklestine, Porter Bailey, Billy Oberton, and Miranda Dux flashed in her mind and made unwelcome tears sting her eyes.

She cleared her throat and went on. "But we're doing

something important, not just surviving. We have knowledge now that the human race needs."

"We'll find a way to get it to them," Cage said.

"And to live our lives," Felicity said. "The two of us, together."

"Always," Cage said, stroking her cheek. "How did I get so lucky?"

"You are out of your mind," she said.

"I'd fight a thousand aliens to be with you, Felicity Mars."

"And I'd fight them with you, Lieutenant Cage."

They kissed. It was tender and full of hope.

CHAPTER 45

BLAKE CAGE

They walked for two more hours before they saw the platoon carrier. It was gliding slowly along the riverbank.

"They're searching for us," Cage said.

"For our bodies," Felicity added.

"I guess we're going to surprise them."

It didn't take long for the couple to be spotted. A few minutes later, the carrier settled less than twenty meters from Cage and Felicity. Staff Sergeant Dole and Corporal Al'Farrah jumped off the carrier and hurried over to them.

"You're alive," Dole said with a grin.

"What'd you expect?" Cage said.

"After the battle last night, we weren't hopeful," Dole said.

"It is good to see you both alive," Devon said.

"And good to be seen," Felicity said. "A ride would be great. I'm exhausted."

"I'll bet you are," Staff Sergeant Dole said. "Come on, let's get back to the forest. Being out in the open with that thing in the sky makes me nervous."

"Me too," Cage said. "It's a good bet they're watching us right now. When night falls, they may come pay us a visit."

"Let them come," Dole said. "We've been busy. While you were fighting, we collected the heavy cargo."

"All of it?" Cage asked.

"Damn straight. We got to the first carrier yesterday afternoon and got it running," Dole explained. "I figured your distraction would keep the LGMs busy while we got some work done."

"LGMs?" Felicity asked.

"Little Green Men," Devon said with a chuckle.

"That's what my grandfather called them," Dole said. "He was a believer. I wish I could tell him he was right."

"You have comms established?" Cage asked.

"We do," the staff sergeant said, but the look on his face was grim.

"Any word from the *Bronx II*?"

"No, sir. It's gone."

"So we're on our own," Cage said.

"Not entirely," Dole said. "We got word from recon platoon Alpha. They're mad as hell and ready to join the fight."

"We're outnumbered and probably way behind in technology," Cage said.

"But we make up for that in sheer ferocity," Dole said. "You and Corporal Mars showed them sons-a-bitches that last night. And when they come for another fight, we'll give them one to remember."

Cage looked at his wife. She smiled. He thought it was crazy that she'd smile at the prospect of a good fight—and then he realized he was smiling too. They were near the carrier and he could see the rest of the platoon members watching him, waiting to see how he would respond.

"All right," Cage said. "Let them come. This is our planet now. We're making it our home, and one human fighting for his home is worth a hundred aliens. If they think they know us, they're sadly mistaken. We're recon platoon Bravo, and we're just getting started!"

The platoon cheered. Cage felt a sense of hope as he climbed aboard the platoon carrier. The enthusiasm of his platoon mates buoyed his exhausted body. And as the vehicle lifted on its repulsors and turned toward the forest, Cage looked up at the dot in the sky. If they were watching, he would watch back. If it was a fight they wanted, he would give them one they would never forget.

"Got something on your mind, Lieutenant Cage?" Felicity asked.

"Just the future, Corporal Mars. I'm just thinking about what's coming next."

COMING SOON

Thank you so much for reading Magnificus Prime. I hope you loved it and will consider leaving an honest review on Amazon and Goodreads.

Ready for more action with Recon Platoon Bravo? Don't worry, the second book in the Mars & Cage series is coming in November 2020!

Incursio - Cage & Mars #2 - Coming Soon

www.ingramcontent.com/pod-product-compliance
Lightning Source LLC
Chambersburg PA
CBHW051953240626
47153CB00005B/1736